ADVERSE REACTIONS

A NOVEL OF THE PARANORMAL

OTHER NOVELS BY DEBORAH J. LIGHTFOOT

Waterspell Book 1: The Warlock
Waterspell Book 2: The Wysard
Waterspell Book 3: The Wisewoman
Waterspell Book 4: The Witch
The Karenina Chronicles: A Waterspell Novel
The Fires of Farsinchia: A Waterspell Novel

ADVERSE REACTIONS

A NOVEL OF THE PARANORMAL

DEBORAH J. LIGHTFOOT

Seven Rivers
Publishing

Seven Rivers Publishing
P.O. Box 682
Crowley, Texas 76036
sevenriverspublishing.com

Cover by Damonza
Purity and the Ranch map by Deborah J. Lightfoot

Adverse Reactions: A Novel of the Paranormal / Deborah J. Lightfoot
First paperback edition: March 2026
First electronic edition: March 2026

Summary: Gifted individuals in Purity face a stark choice between immediate death or the horrors of the Peaceful Hills sanatorium. Devin Perridin, the "One Who Got Away," seeks to reclaim her psychokinetic powers and bring retribution, with the aid of a denim-clad desperado and a generous helping of Old Magic. *Fantasy/Paranormal*

ISBN 978-1-7377173-9-3 (Paperback)
ISBN 979-8-9943901-0-8 (Ebook)

This book, dreamed up in 2005 & fully fleshed out in 2025, was written by a human.

Dedicated to every antifascist who joined the fight, from 2025 on, to defend American democracy against would-be dictators.

This book was written by a living, thinking, freedom-loving human being.

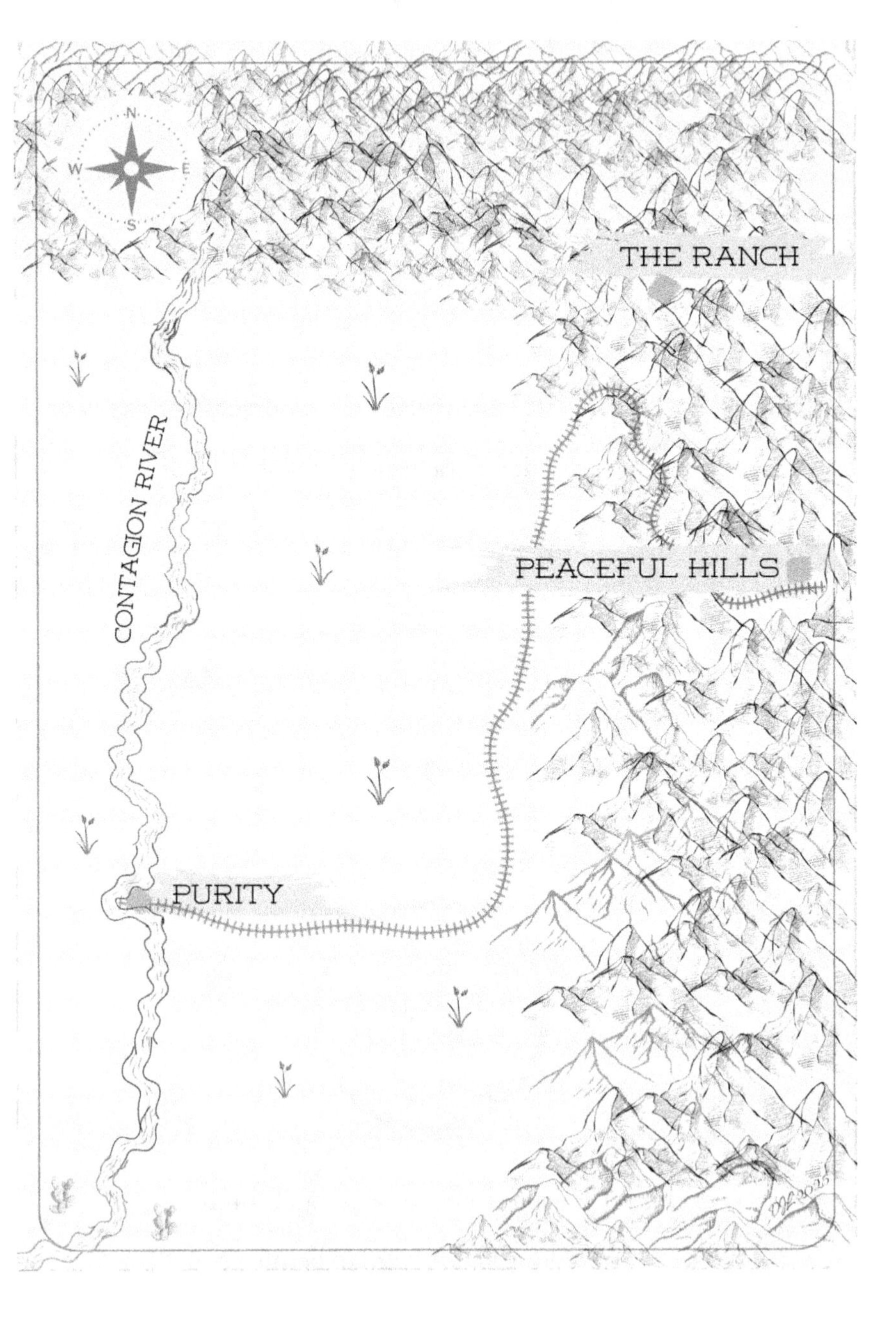

N
W
E
S
THE RANCH
CONTAGION RIVER
PEACEFUL HILLS
PURITY

Contents

ADVERSE REACTIONS: A Novel of the Paranormal 1

Epilogue 309

Note on the Origins of the Town of Purity 313

Note on the Lineage of the Three Wise Women 315

Note on the Origins of the Great Contagion 316

About the Author 319

"Your absence of mind we have borne,

till your presence of body

came to be called in question by it."

Charles Lamb

(1775–1834)

English essayist and poet

☙ 1 ❧

VAPORS BILLOWED INTO the chamber in thick masses of orange. Devin choked on the sickly sweet odor.

"Don't fight it, child," came the voice—equally cloying—from the darkness beyond the floodlit, glass-walled chamber. "Give yourself up to it."

The gas surged into Devin's face, blinding, gagging her. She made it go away. By force of will, a moment's mental reflex, she flung it back.

Fresh air flooded her nostrils and drove out the syrupy stink. She sucked in a cool, clean breath.

"No!" snapped the voice, crackling with amplified static. "You must not."

The therapist dropped her with two thousand volts. Devin collapsed to the chamber's floor, her body jerking, her nerves on fire. The pain was beyond enduring. A pain this intense must be lethal. But she did not die. As she convulsed, her muscles knotted in spasms, she could not scream. No part of her, not even her voice, was under her voluntary control.

"Try it again, child." Smooth and saccharine once more, her unseen therapist spoke from the concealing shadows as the shock ended and Devin's pain faded. "Stand up," the torturer ordered. "And this time, *do not fight it.* Or your punishment will be the same: swift, sure, and severe."

Devin struggled upright. She had to brace against the curved glass wall of the gas chamber to keep on her feet. Her muscles had melted from knots into jelly.

An orange cloud flooded the chamber and filled her nose with the stink of rotting fruit.

"Breathe it," her therapist instructed. "You must."

But again, Devin reacted by instinct alone. No conscious thought interposed between stimulus and response. The cloud approached; she pushed it away. Pure reflex, action of mind: act of self-preservation. The gas held back, suspended in midair, blocked by the power of her impulse.

On the instant, thousands of volts knocked her to the floor. Pain engulfed Devin, such a pain as must be lethal but wouldn't do her the service of killing her. She writhed, silent and barely conscious.

Her therapist withdrew the punishment. Devin remained on the floor of the isolation chamber, curled in the fetal position, her long brown hair covering her face. Her body was hers to command once more, but her muscles had no strength to obey.

"You give new meaning to the word *persistent,* don't you, girl?" muttered the disembodied voice. Then, more forcefully: "The first step toward healing is to admit you are diseased, Miss Perridin. You have an illness. A mental disorder. I am offering you the cure—in a pleasant aerosol spray that you need only breathe. Once inhaled, the drug acts quickly, and its effects are lasting. But you must take the first step and acknowledge that you *want* to be cured."

The voice grew soft, sugary. "Child, for as long as you hold to the notion—the mistaken notion—that your disorder is in some way a strength or a benefit to you, you will continue to fail. And you will suffer the consequences of that failure. We can't have that, can we?"

Devin gathered the remnants of her strength and rolled onto her back. To stand was impossible; she could barely shape a word.

"No," she whispered.

She wasn't speaking to her tormentor.

But: "That's the spirit!" the therapist responded, sounding genuinely enthused. "Now we try again. Take your medicine like a good girl."

The orange stink flowed in at the top of the chamber. Devin, lying face up, watched through the curtain of her hair as the cloud descended. She had time to ward it off, to make it go away. But in the soul of her being, nothing sparked. Her reflexes, her instincts, failed to respond. What had been a spontaneous force of mind over matter could offer no resistance.

Devin's mouth filled with the sickening taste of defeat. The orange cloud enveloped her, a sticky weight, and she choked down lungfuls.

"Wonderful!" her therapist exclaimed. "My dear, I couldn't be more pleased. This is the tipping point. Your recovery will be much easier from now on, I promise."

Devin breathed the sickly sweet drug and felt the core of her mind go dead.

Then came the retching. Her body contorted in gut-shredding paroxysms as the drug made her vomit—or attempt to vomit. Her keepers had starved her for so long, her stomach had nothing to bring up. The dry heaves racked her with such violence that she could not breathe. After long moments, unconsciousness brought relief.

* * *

The therapist had lied, of course. Under the influence of the pollution that she had both inhaled and swallowed, Devin's "recovery" was an even worse torture than the treatments she had endured.

Two broad-shouldered orderlies held her head under water and she was drowning. In her drug-induced torpor, she had no urge to free herself from their grip, no impulse to will the water away, as she would once have done. Enough remained of her instinct for self-preservation, however, that she felt a moment's fear. One moment only, but it was sufficient to trigger an "adverse reaction to her medication," as the therapist termed it. Adrenaline mixing with the absorbed poison was the sure way to start her belly heaving. Devin choked on puke and water, and blacked out. Had her keepers not pulled her up and forced the liquids from her lungs, she would have strangled.

"Easy does it," the therapist chirped, wavering into her view, looming over her when Devin regained partial consciousness. "Remember our Peaceful Hills motto: *'Serenity, Tranquility, Quiescence.'* Keep your heart and mind perfectly still, child, and you'll avoid the side effects. Let's try again."

The orderlies threw Devin in with an eight-foot rattlesnake. She sat quietly and let the creature strike. Nothing came from the depths of her existence to force it aside. She felt no mental impulse to ward off the serpent's bite. The pain, sharp at first, became a burning sensation. Her arm purpled and swelled. As the venom spread, her lips and face grew numb, and her toes and fingertips tingled. Her mouth began to twitch. She felt no alarm, only a faint, far-off sense of relief at the absence of nausea. Her belly muscles were sore and her throat raw from her previous hours of retching.

"Better! Much better, child," her therapist gushed. "You're a fast learner when you're properly motivated."

Her keepers pinned the snake in a corner and gave Devin the antivenin.

Through more trials, she passed. They locked her in an airless, pitch-dark box no bigger than a coffin and waited for her to panic and choke on her own vomit. But she outwaited them, as passive and indifferent as the walls of her tomb.

They subjected her to plagues of biting insects, of a species Devin didn't recognize. A type of fly, the creatures seemed, but equipped with razor-sharp mouthparts that slashed her skin. In a black, crawling mass they encased her from her brow to her bare feet, and with their needlelike suckers the flies lapped up her blood. Limply, Devin put her hands over her face to keep the swarms out of her nose and eyes. Otherwise she sat unmoving, giving herself up to the ebony horde's insatiable thirst. From her wounds, blood first dripped, then streamed, puddling red on the gray concrete floor under her. Her breathing grew rapid and shallow.

When at last she slumped to the floor, too weak to sit up, her keepers released a foul-smelling mist that drove away the engorged flies. They put Devin on a stretcher and carted her off to the infirmary. A physician of vacant expression stopped the head-to-toe bleeding and gave her a transfusion.

When she had recovered somewhat—how much later, Devin couldn't say, for there were no windows anywhere, and no hours when the overhead lights did not glare—her therapist had the orderlies stand her on a narrow plank above a field of iron spikes. For hours—possibly all through the day, or possibly through the night into the next unseen dawn—she balanced upon the plank. A fit of retching would have sent her tumbling, to die impaled on the spikes below. In Devin, the danger provoked no response: no adrenaline rush to trigger the punitive sickness, no defiance, not even boredom. Where she had once had emotions, she now embodied only apathy.

"You are making fine progress, child," purred the therapist, emerging once again into Devin's view. "The medication is most effective when the patient remains calm. You'll want to remember that." The therapist paused, then went on brightly: "Let me rephrase. You *will* remember that. Of course you will. I personally guarantee it. Our programs here at Peaceful Hills are dedicated to the goal of ensuring our patients' successful attainment of lifelong serenity."

As a final test, her keepers locked Devin in a fire-filled room. She had been through that particular exercise early in her stay at the sanatorium. The therapist had called it "diagnostic." The first time they tested her, Devin had psyched the fire out. The flames had died as she thought them away.

No, *thought* had little to do with it. The mental reflex arose far deeper than the level of cognition. Never in her sixteen years had Devin needed to consider her responses. She had simply reacted. In much the same way that a person jerks back from a hot stove without conscious intent, she extinguished flames—or any perceived danger or discomfort—with a flash of her will. Her mind controlled matter and made it obey.

As a young child, she had defied parental attempts at discipline. Any hand that threatened to clout her, she flung back with force enough to cow her elders. Guildmaster Perridin and his wife Mariah had struggled to keep their daughter under control and guard the secret of her affliction. Long before she reached adolescence, Devin had recognized that her parents—her father, particularly—saw her as diseased. She had tried—she'd really tried—to control her impulses. But she never reached the level achieved by the abstainers: those rare ones her mother had told her about, who could refrain from using the powers of the mind that instinct summoned within them, and thus remain concealed, avoiding death or captivity.

"Heaven help me, my daughter is a persistent Syke." Her mother whispered the terrible truth when she thought Devin couldn't hear.

The Perridins never entertained, had no social life beyond the minimum required by her father's position as Guildmaster for the town of Purity. Only in such seclusion could Devin hope to escape detection. Her reflexes were too keen to permit any interaction with others. When provoked by a stimulus, however petty, she reacted. Simple as that: simple, direct, unstoppable.

And impossible to hide forever. At just shy of sixteen she was discovered, her illness made public. The outcry bordered on hysteria.

"Euthanize her!" some demanded. "You'd shoot a rattler, wouldn't you?"

"Off to the loony bin," urged others. "She can maybe be treated, maybe mended. She's young yet. Give the girl a chance at life. If they can't cure her at the nuthouse, they'll kill her trying, thank the medicos, and that'll be an end to it."

So the doctors put Devin into a coma—the only way to safely transport her by cross-plains train, over the western prairie and into the remote mountains, and thence to the Peaceful Hills Sanatorium and Rehabilitation Center for the Treatment of Persistent Mental Disorders. Had she been conscious during the journey, Devin could have broken the heads of her attendants. With a fleeting urge, the most short-lived impulse, she could have killed everyone around her, and without lifting a finger to do it. So the people warned each other as the train rolled out of town, muttering darkly amongst themselves about the monster who had hidden in their midst all these years.

At Peaceful Hills, the medicos knew how to deal with the likes of Devin Perridin. An untold number of Sykes had suffered as lab rats in the sanatorium's search for the perfect program of conditioning. *"So the psychos respond by reflex, their actions not planned or thought out aforehand? Then we'll grind 'em down until they have no reflexes."*

The treatment had killed many persistent Sykes. The ones who survived did not emerge from it whole.

At her final test within the asylum's blind walls, Devin stood in the midst of flames, the heat beating at her, a singed odor rising from her clothes and hair. In the smoke and the scorched air, she couldn't breathe. It didn't matter. She was inert, uncaring. The witnesses to her concluding test at Peaceful Hills might have been hard put to know when she passed from indifference into unconsciousness. But apparently they saw enough to be convinced that her instincts were dead, her fight-or-flight reflex permanently annihilated. They ended the test before she burned past all healing.

Devin came to her senses reeking of smoke and in savage pain, but only vaguely aware of it, for she was gone from herself, lost in a mind and body she no longer recognized. The sweet, mind-killing drug had done its damage. The shell she inhabited was a stranger to her now, her wits murky and far distant.

"I am elated," said the one who had done this to her. "They told me you were a particularly hard case. Most likely incurable. But we showed them, didn't we, girl?"

A cold hand patted Devin's burned arm. She did not flinch from the horror of that touch. Nor did she open her eyes to see again the face of her tormentor, seared permanently into her memory.

"Rest now, child. After your blisters have healed—they'll leave scars, but who cares for that?—you'll be heading home on the train. This time, you'll be awake to enjoy the trip. Guildmaster Perridin will certainly know he's gotten his money's worth when he sees the wonders I've worked in you."

* * *

Devin was indeed conscious as the train clicked down the tracks, making its slow, winding descent from the forested mountains that hid the sanatorium. The healthy population of Purity, out on the treeless plains some two hundred miles to the southwest, wanted a wide buffer between themselves and the nuthouse at Peaceful Hills. The sanatorium was reachable only by the narrow-gauge train that threaded its way through a long, tapering gorge. The train kept no set schedule, but ran when required to deliver patients and—only very occasionally—collect the cured.

As the latest, lonely discharge from Peaceful Hills, Devin had the train much to herself. She should go exploring, from caboose to locomotive. After the sixteen cloistered years of her childhood, she ought to begin satisfying a pent-up curiosity about the world. She *could* roam and explore, now. She didn't have to hide. People would not fear and hate her now. A normal life was hers for the making. No time like the present to begin discovering the possibilities.

But the urge to act—to take any action at all—had drained from her the moment she allowed the orange gas into her lungs. Thus, Devin only sat in the sleeping car, vacantly watching the mountain scenery crawl past her window as the train switchbacked down from the pine-clad heights, still some distance above the gorge. She thought of nothing: not her parents, not the isolated life she had known or the promise of a full new life to come; not the ordeal she had endured in these mountains. She did not mourn her lost mental powers, nor wonder if they were gone for good. She only sat and stared, her mind empty.

Even when the train lurched to a stop, so abruptly that Devin was thrown from her seat, she couldn't be bothered to grab for support. She hit the floor, indifferent to the jolt, and sprawled on the none-too-clean carpeting. The attendant who brought her meals would find her eventually, and get her back into her seat if it mattered. If it mattered at all.

The train did not resume its motion. Nobody within earshot spoke. In the absence of wheels clacking on rails, the silence was profound.

For the first time in this journey, Devin heard birdsong, lilting from the trees that lined the tracks. Involuntarily, she straightened a little, still on the floor, and cocked her head to listen. The songs conveyed such a feeling of freedom, of unrestrained primitive energy, they almost roused her from her lethargy.

Almost. She was sinking back into lassitude, her eyes glazing over, when footsteps sounded along the corridor outside her compartment. A door slid open nearby. Perhaps the sleeping-car attendant was checking on other passengers, if the train did indeed carry any. Whether the neighboring compartments were empty or occupied, Devin had neither looked nor asked. It did not matter. Very little mattered now.

The footsteps came to her own door, and with a scraping sound, it opened. The man who appeared in the doorway was not the attendant who brought Devin's meals. He was no one she'd encountered at Peaceful Hills. She had never seen anyone who looked like him, except in books. Her education, from six to sixteen, had consisted largely of books. Her mother had encouraged her reading, as a way of diverting her mind from its syketic impulses. Devin knew the world mainly through the words and pictures printed in books.

The man who now stood in her doorway looked like a figure from an historical photograph, like he'd stepped out of a book about the former times, those yesteryears before the Great Contagion. In spite of herself, Devin's gaze sharpened, taking in the man's cowboy boots, denim trousers, tooled leather belt, and the shoulder-hung bandolier bag over a shirt of rustically coarse fabric. *Homespun?* she wondered, recalling a word from her reading and surprised into a momentary flash of curiosity.

Around his neck, adding to the novelty of his appearance, the man wore a fivesome of wolves' teeth knotted on a leather lace. A band of dried snakeskin encircled the crown of his broad-brimmed hat. He'd pushed the hat back on his head, revealing tawny hair of a length to curl past his shirt collar. The sweat-dampened strands framed the face of a man who might be about forty, although his age was difficult to guess, his skin weathered and darkened by exposure to wind and sun.

The man was looking at her with the frankest sort of interest. Such was the intensity of his dark-eyed gaze, something akin to self-consciousness stirred within Devin. Perhaps it *did* matter whether she stayed on the floor or got to her feet.

Hesitantly, she gripped the edge of the seat that she'd left when the train jolted to a halt. Not taking her eyes off of her visitor, she started to push herself up.

"Here." The man flashed a roguish grin as he extended his hand. "Let me help you, gal."

The man's voice was light, a little amused, and friendly sounding. Devin had no cause to trust the sound of a friendly voice, and so she paused in her effort to rise.

But a flutter of cautious interest had twitched within her, the sort of interest that she had not felt—in anything or anyone—since the orange gas killed her mind. The proffered hand beckoned, and the flutter urged her to take it.

When she did, the man pulled her to her feet.

"My apologies for dumping you on the floor," he said when she was standing. His voice had a confident ring, and its affable, drawling tones bore no resemblance to the cloying excess of Devin's psych-ward tormentor. "I've never stopped anything as heavy as a train before." The man laughed, seeming pleased with himself. "Maybe I channeled a tad too much focus. The crew went flying. Out of commission but not dead, so far as I can tell. Maybe I'll be wanted only for kidnapping, not murder. That'll ease my path, I'm sure." His grin widened.

Devin gave a faint shake of her head—hard to do beneath the apathy that weighed her down, its weight so relentlessly crushing that she could neither move freely nor think clearly. But the hand that still held hers seemed to momentarily lift her out of the heaviness, even as it had raised her from the floor. The sensation of lightness, of freedom, lasted less than a heartbeat, but long enough to permit Devin another flicker of wary curiosity:

Who was this stranger who stood smiling at her, speaking casually of kidnapping and murder? And what did he want with a brain-damaged psycho like her?

"Get your gear, friend, and come on." The man released Devin's hand and jerked his head toward the passageway of the sleeping car. "If you want your stuff, grab it and let's get going. We've got a fair ride to make by dark, and the day's not getting any younger." He turned from her and moved into the corridor.

Devin did not move. She didn't look around for her belongings. Had she any? She couldn't think why she should. Owning things or lacking them; going off with this man or staying here on the train; taking action or keeping still; living or dying: they were all the same to her. The apathy had reasserted itself, entombing her once more in the orange-cloud cure.

"Gal, I need you to get a move on." The man had turned back to face her. His gaze shifted upward to the luggage rack over Devin's berth. "That your kit?" He reached above her head and pulled down a rucksack. Devin looked at it without recognition.

The man slung the bag over his shoulder, carrying it along with his own as he stepped again into the passageway. "Now come on. I don't want to tote you, too."

Stay or go: it made no difference.

So Devin went, trailing her kidnapper down the corridor and outside by way of the sleeping car's vestibule door. As she stepped down onto the packed gravel of the trackbed, the sharp, clean scent of sun-warmed pinesap filled her nostrils. She breathed it in, and the memory of a syrupy stink faded by a whiff.

As her kidnapper led her alongside the train, Devin glanced up at its dark, smudgy windows, incuriously looking for the crew. It made no difference whether she saw them, or they saw her. Still, she looked. No one came into view.

Before they reached the rear of the train, the man stopped and turned to contemplate the sleeping car they had exited. "It's a soldier's duty," he said, "to hinder and harass the enemy every chance he gets. I believe I can do a mite more hindering before we ride out of here. Watch and learn, friend. Watch and learn."

Devin stood facing him. She had not turned when he did. The man gazed over her head—he stood a foot taller than she—and squinted slightly, as if the better to see.

From behind Devin came the squeal of metal deforming under stress. It didn't seem to matter, but nonetheless she looked toward the noise, turning languidly, but in time to see the sleeping car buckle as though struck by an invisible wrecking ball. The car toppled sideways off the tracks and crashed downhill into the pines that lined the slightly elevated roadbed. Against their trunks it settled, with a groan that could have come either from the trees or from the contorted metal. The sleeper had crumpled through its middle like a tin can. Cars behind and ahead of it remained upright, but two of them were half off the rails.

Devin stared for a long moment, then turned back to her kidnapper. Her voice was flat and emotionless, rusty from disuse, and sounding distant in her own ears as she said:

"You're a Syke."

"As are you, friend." The grin on the man's face was one of sheer delight. "As are you."

☙ 2 ❧

FROM THE SITE OF the train crash, they rode north on horseback, a party of four: Devin, her kidnapper, and his two accomplices who had waited in the trees with their horses. Those men were younger than their leader. One appeared to be in his early thirties, the other not more than nineteen or twenty. Devin registered nothing else about them, though they surveyed her with open curiosity.

As they pressed on, deep into the mountains, the riders kept to the ridges and long rock ledges that took them across the slopes without much climbing, but no descending. The train would have taken Devin on down to the city on the plains where her parents lived. But her kidnapper seemed intent on remaining high in these mountains.

Devin had never been on a horse before, knew little of horses except what she'd read of them in books. She took an instant liking to her mount, however, and the feeling stirred a faint sense of surprise.

The mind-deadening effects of the orange gas had made sentiments such as *like* or *dislike* largely irrelevant to her.

But now, riding through a pine forest in the company of three talkative men, she could almost believe she was enjoying the experience. The freshness of springtime filled the crisp mountain air. Birds sang in the trees or flitted past in colorful streaks. The chestnut horse under her didn't seem to mind his rider's ignorance.

"Give Diego his head and let him pick his way along behind me," her kidnapper had instructed. "He'll take care of you. That horse is as sure-footed as any mule."

So Devin sat in the unfamiliar saddle, holding on with both hands, swaying with the animal's steps as Diego followed placidly behind the lead rider. She looked at nothing in particular, and her formless thoughts were as dust motes landing nowhere. But her ears caught the banter among her companions.

"Hey, Sutter," called the thirty-something rider behind her. "Why didn't you pick up that whole damn train and chuck it on over to HQ? We could've used the supplies, and that metal was salvageable. Waste not, want not."

The lead rider laughed. "Orlando, I appreciate your faith in me. And though I do admit to being an outstanding specimen of a Syke, lobbing a locomotive a two-days' ride away is maybe—just *maybe*—beyond the capacity of one person."

"Nah," Orlando scoffed. "You're just lazy. You don't like to break a sweat."

"You know me too well, friend," said the man called Sutter. "There's no fooling you." In the ridgeline they were following, a roughly U-shaped bend brought her kidnapper briefly parallel with Devin. He looked across at her. "But like they say, two heads are best. When I've got my junior partner trained up, together we'll be wrecking trains—or leveling jailhouses—without doing a hand's turn."

"You think this girl is the one?" asked the youngest man, from his fourth-place spot at the rear. "Sutter, I'll give you one thing: you don't discourage easy."

Sutter laughed again. He urged his horse to a brisker pace as the ridgetop flattened toward a lightly wooded summit. "You've got the right of it there, Jack. I'm all optimism about this gal. If I can glue her mind back together—and if she lives up to her reputation—she could be the strongest Syke since yours truly to come out of Purity. But if she's too broken to fix, at least we've scared the shit out of those butchers at that hellhole. They won't be sleeping too peaceful tonight, when they find out we stole one of their hatchet jobs out from under their noses."

The foursome rode until dusk, then pitched camp beside a mountain brook with a stony streambed so pale, it cut through the dark pines like a white scar. Devin ate what she was handed—dried meat, a biscuit, a piece of hard cheese. Everything tasted salty, but no one seemed to mind, least of all Devin. She'd lost the power to mind, back in the glass-walled gas chamber with its poisonous orange cloud.

After the meal, she was left alone to do what had most occupied her since her stay at the sanatorium: she sat and stared into space. This evening, however, her mind was not a total blank. The day's events drifted through, vague but present, and claiming some small part of her consciousness. Before today, she had not cared what the future held. It didn't matter, one way or the other. But now, a faint uneasiness crept upon Devin as she sat in the woods by a crackling campfire, its dry heat fretting her skin. Not since her final, weak flash of fear had been extinguished at the asylum had she known any such feeling as this.

It was not enough, this sense of disquiet, to provoke her to any action. Mercifully, the feeling proved insufficient to induce the retching that accompanied any release of adrenaline into her bloodstream. But a trace of wariness rose in her like a speck of wood-ash that swirled aloft on scorched air.

The fire hissed, and someone moved near her. Despite the soft prodding of her unease—and her hazy memory of being burned in a fire—Devin did not look around. Her attention, wispy as it was, could not engage with the hint of movement, and so she remained staring into space, even when a burning brand came at her from out of the dark night. But she flinched. Ever so slightly, she flinched.

"An unconditioned reflex, as I live and breathe!" Sutter exclaimed.

He was crouched beside her, the flaming piece of wood in his hand but held out to the side. He had not touched it to her skin, but he'd brought it close enough that tongues of its heat licked her arm. To those approaching flames, Devin should not have reacted. The whole point of Peaceful Hills was that she *not* react. But the barely sensed threat of renewed burning had tugged a thread tight inside her, a thread badly frayed but not wholly broken despite all that had been done to rip it out of her.

With his unencumbered hand, Sutter clapped her on the shoulder. "Those butchers didn't take every last instinct you've got, girl. There's hope for you. The last Syke I peeled out of the bastards' clutches was an empty husk. They might as well have done a lobotomy on him. He had nothing left."

The man stood and tossed the brand into the campfire. "In you, my friend, there's still a spark. Those bastards may think they got it all, but you just proved them wrong." Sutter stepped into the darkness and returned with a blanket that he draped around Devin's shoulders. "Get some sleep. It's another long day in the saddle tomorrow. Once we're back at the ranch, your deconditioning begins in earnest."

Devin curled up in the blanket, far from the fire. She spent her last moments of wakefulness that night trying to put a name to an alien sensation, something new that had settled in her stomach. It was, she dimly supposed, a feeling akin to anticipation. It vied in her gut with her faintly stirring wariness.

* * *

The ranch, as Sutter called his headquarters, looked more like a combination fortress and commune. Behind a timber stockade wall, the stronghold housed an impressive number of people. When the four riders appeared at its gates, late in the evening of Devin's second day on horseback, armed guards admitted them into a bustling stable yard. Grooms took charge of the horses, and Jack took charge of the grooms, issuing instructions in a low, calm voice. Orlando did not linger there, but headed for the noise and the bright lights of what might be a dining hall—or maybe a saloon, to judge by the lively groups of patrons who came and went through paired, swinging doors.

"This way, friend," Sutter said. With his hand on Devin's shoulder, he steered her in the opposite direction. "I'm putting you up in the old house. We don't have the comforts of town here. But after that godforsaken so-called sanatorium—chamber of horrors, more like—maybe you won't mind the simple pleasures of country living. I took to it like a flea to a dog. Came here more than twenty years ago, and not a day passes that I don't know how lucky I was to get out of Purity with a whole hide and a working brain."

They climbed the steps of a three-story frame house that occupied the compound's quietest corner. Sutter ushered Devin through the front door into a softly gaslit parlor, and closing the door behind them, shut out the noise from the saloon.

She surveyed the parlor with a glimmer of genuine interest. It was nowhere near as grand as her parents' mansion in Purity. This place was older, the furniture worn and faded, the rose-patterned rug on the dark oak floor frayed at its edges. But the room had a comfortable feel, and its slight mustiness was that of old books. The familiar smell, evoking Devin's own library at home, invited her to choose a book from the shelves between the lace-curtained windows, and—had there been light enough to see by—to curl up among the sofa cushions and read.

Without a word—she spoke little these days—Devin went to the shelves and took a volume at random. She did not glance at the title, merely carried the book back to where Sutter stood watching her. Only then did she notice that the man had her rucksack slung over his shoulder. The bag had traveled with her from the train; Sutter had tied it onto the saddle behind her. But in the two days of their journey here, Devin had never once opened it.

Sutter gestured at the book in her hands. "You're welcome to the whole collection, friend. Just don't sit up reading all night. We've got work to do, starting at first light tomorrow." He inclined his head toward a staircase that hugged the wall opposite the front entrance. "Let's find Angelina. She'll have a room ready for you upstairs."

The stairs creaked loudly in the silence of the old house. As Devin followed behind Sutter, ascending to the second-floor landing, a door opened down a hallway. Through it stepped a tall woman immaculately dressed in a close-fitting white blouse and a slim dark skirt that fell long enough to have brushed the tops of her boots, had she been wearing any. She looked like a woman who would own multiple pairs of boots, and would cut a striking figure on the back of a horse. But this evening she wore soft slippers, embroidered all over with intricate designs. The woman's hair, jet black with silver streaks, tumbled past her shoulders in loose waves. Her olive skin was more leathery than Sutter's; she appeared to be at least twenty years his senior. But those years had not bowed her. She carried herself like royalty.

"*Buenas tardes,* Miguel," the woman said, gliding toward them. "Welcome home." She looked Devin up and down. "I see that you have had success."

"More than in my wildest dreams, I'm starting to think," Sutter replied. "Angelina Rojas, meet Devin Perridin."

The sound of her own name came close to startling Devin. No one had called her by name for a long time. Her keepers at the sanatorium had addressed her as "child" or "girl," and to Sutter she was "friend." An odd thought, since Devin had no friends.

She looked at him. "How do you know my name?"

Sutter broke into the roguish grin that seemed to be his default expression. "Wake snakes! My latest find speaks."

He looked past Devin to Angelina. "That's only about the third word out of her mouth since I got her off the train, and she's asking a question! Doña, did you ever hear the other one question anything or anybody? He was about as curious as sawdust. The cretin didn't give a shit about anything, least of all living."

"Mind your tongue, Miguel," snapped Angelina. "It is not right that you should use such language, not in front of the young lady, nor in my presence. You forget yourself." The woman placed her hand on Devin's shoulder, her touch warm and comforting. "Señorita Perridin has asked you a question. Will you answer it?"

The reproof seemed lost on Sutter. He only grinned wider. But he looked again at Devin, straight into her eyes, and replied.

"Friend, you're *famous*. Everybody in Purity and any who ply the Contagion River know your name." He chuckled. "Blowing out the back wall of the family mansion, in a fit of pique over not getting your way, tends to attract a deal of official attention. When your jumped-up polite-society pappy had to admit, right out in public, how you'd done it: what an uproar!" Sutter leaned slightly toward her, one finger raised and pointing at her forehead. "Pure mental power, a simple act of will—and teenage willfulness at that. For sixteen years—pardon me if I've not got the number quite right, but that's what I'm told—for all the years, in any case, since you were a baby, Guildmaster and Missus Perridin harbored a persistent Syke, smack dab in the best part of town. A deadly danger to the whole place, you were. And a high-society scandal, to boot."

Sutter clapped her on the shoulder that was unprotected by Angelina's gentle touch. "News like that spreads fast and far. It reached all the way up here. We also heard you were being sent to that hellhole, that butcher shop they call 'rehab.'" He gave her shoulder a squeeze before releasing her. "If your parents weren't rich and powerful, friend, the good sheriff of Purity would have shot you dead. Sykes from the part of town where I grew up don't get sent to 'rehab.' We peasants are exterminated like rats."

His face lost its cheerfulness. For the first time since Devin had laid eyes on her kidnapper, Sutter looked and sounded serious. "All I wanted, when I was your age, was to get out alive. Well, I did that, twenty years ago and more. Now I'm bringing out others, rescuing Sykes from the shanty side of town when I can. We've been living like outlaws all these years, hiding up here in the heights."

Sutter's voice grew cold, taking on an edge that Devin had not heard in it before. "Now I've got new ambitions, friend. Now, I'm thinking that the best defense is a strong offense. I'm thinking that maybe the ordinaries of Purity have been right to be scared of the Sykes all along. Get a bunch of us together, with a couple of the best in the lead, and we could be an army. We could march down out of these mountains and take that town without firing a shot. Just *thinking* about it, we'd take it and own it. ... And then who'd be doing the exterminating?"

❦ 3 ❦

"MIGUEL."

Angelina's voice was soft, but it carried an undertone of warning. "It is time to say good-night. You are tired, or you would not be so free with your words. And I am sure that Señorita Perridin must wish to rest and refresh herself. Both of you are covered with the dust of the trail." She tsk-tsked them. "Come with me, chica, *por favor,* and I will get you settled for the night. Have you no *valijas*—no bags?"

"This is hers."

Sutter unslung Devin's knapsack from his shoulder and put it into her limp, nearly unfeeling hands. "I'm right glad to be done hauling this thing around. You keep up with it now, friend."

To Angelina, he added, "Let me know if you see anything interesting in there. She had it with her on the train, but she doesn't exactly treat it like a prized possession, so I'm thinking those bas—er, butchers at 'Peaceful Hills' packed it for her. Just a change of clothes probably, but who knows what those devils might try to send home with her." He arched his shoulders and stretched. "Good night to you both. I'm turning in." Tapping a finger to the brim of his hat, he saluted them cowboy style, then swiveled on one boot-heel and strode off down the hallway beyond the stair landing.

With her hand still on Devin's shoulder, Angelina steered her in the other direction. "I have made up the tower room for you, chica. It is like a fairy tale, no, to sleep in a tower? Señor Sutter's house is *muy grande*, with room for many guests. But you are more than a guest. This is to be your home, if you so wish it."

They reached the end of the upper-floor hallway, and together entered a front corner room that was, as Angelina had said, straight from a fairy tale. The far corner curved outward in a semicircle, creating much the effect of a castle tower. Three tall windows wrapped the curve, the center one square-topped with latticework, but those at either side rising to spearpoints. Light filtering through the windows from the compound below, the illumination coming from some little distance, revealed a sitting area with a table, two chairs, and a small sofa. Tucked into a roomy alcove away from the windows was a bed draped with embroidery and lace.

Angelina turned up the flame in the gaslight beside the door, then crossed to the windows to close the curtains. "I hope you will be comfortable here, chica. Tomorrow, we will heat enough water that you may bathe properly. If you permit me then, I will help to wash your hair. But for tonight, there is a pitcher on the washstand, with soap and towels. Clean sheets are best enjoyed with clean skin, is it not so?"

Devin stood under the gaslight and looked at the woman, then at the washstand in the alcove, and then at the lace-covered bed. For some time now, she had not cared whether she was clean or filthy. Her keepers at the sanatorium had scrubbed her down occasionally, mostly after the messier sorts of "therapies" had left her blood- or vomit-stained. Keeping herself clean, however, had become a matter of indifference to her. Did it matter?

Angelina Rojas, standing before the curtained windows in the curve of the tower, looking regal in her fitted blouse and slim skirt, gazed back at her with an expression that suggested it mattered quite a lot. When Devin did not move, the woman glided to her and reached for the knapsack that Sutter had handed off to its impassive owner.

"Let me help you unpack, chica." She gently pulled the bag from Devin's nerveless fingers. "Perhaps you have a nightdress in here? I will lay out your things on the *sofá* and we will see, yes? And if you wish, you may set your book on the table."

The mention of the book that Devin had taken from the downstairs parlor was enough to move her, slowly, toward the table between the paired chairs. She put the book down—she'd forgotten she held it under the knapsack—then stood and watched as Angelina pulled a scant few items of clothing from the bag. Her keepers had packed the simple skirt and tunic that Devin had worn when she arrived at Peaceful Hills. They'd returned the hairband with which she had once tamed her long brown hair. The band was no longer needed, since her keepers had cut her hair short. They'd put in a comb, nevertheless, along with a toothbrush and paste, and three changes of underwear.

The knapsack yielded nothing else, except a sealed envelope with the Peaceful Hills' logotype, addressed to Guildmaster and Mistress Perridin; and under the envelope a smock-style hospital gown of the sort Devin had worn to bed every night of her stay at the sanatorium

… except for when she'd been in the infirmary, recovering from the burns of her asylum discharge test. Then, she'd worn only bandages.

At the sight of the smock, Devin flinched. Her motion was slight, barely perceptible, but Angelina caught it. The woman straightened, holding the garment in one hand, and looked intently at her.

"The *camisón de noche* displeases you, chica?"

Devin made no response.

Angelina crushed the fabric in her slender, strong fingers. "I will take the rag to the kitchen, and *mañana* the maid will scrub the floor with it. For nothing else is it fit. No woman can be expected to wear clothes that she dislikes." Angelina glanced at the plain skirt and tunic, and shook her head. "Tomorrow, señorita, we will find you something pretty to wear. For tonight, sleep in your skin. *¿Por qué no?* The house is private; in your room you are private. Bare skin against clean sheets is *muy agradable,* yes?"

She picked up the envelope that was addressed to Devin's parents. "If you permit me, I will give this to Señor Sutter. He may find it of great interest. Since it bears the emblem of that place you have escaped, I think it will not interest you so much."

Devin managed to nod.

"*Buenas noches,* then." Angelina made to go, the smock and the envelope in her hands. "Sleep well, chica. If I know Miguel Sutter … he is not a man *fácil de comprender*—easy to comprehend," she translated, "but I do sometimes understand him, and I suspect he will set you a busy day tomorrow."

After the door had closed behind the woman, Devin slipped out of the green cotton pants and T-shirt that had encountered the grimy floor of a train car and the sweaty hide of a horse. With slow and clumsy movements, she filled the washstand basin and attempted the half-forgotten ritual of cleaning herself.

Naked and still damp, she padded across to the table in the sitting area and reclaimed the book. Again not looking at its title, she took it to bed unopened and cuddled it as though it were a teddy bear. Wrapped in soft sheets, she became aware that her body ached, her thighs and backside hurting from two days astride a horse. It was a good hurting, a good feeling, and a dim reminder that she'd known other good feelings before the orange gas claimed the part of her that *could* feel.

* * *

Wearing her only clean clothes, the skirt and tunic, Devin came downstairs early in the new day. The distant sound of voices guided her through the parlor to a kitchen at the rear of the house, where Angelina and a hatless Sutter were at breakfast. He sat at the head of a long, mostly empty table, with Angelina at his right hand.

"*Buenos días,* chica," the woman greeted her, gesturing to the place across from her own. "Sit, and I will fill your plate. Did you sleep well?"

Devin gave a half nod. Without a word she began shoveling down a mound of scrambled eggs, fried potatoes and onions, sliced fresh tomatoes, and refried beans. She had not realized she was hungry. To meals, as to most everything, she was largely indifferent. At the sanatorium, her meals had been routinely withheld. So Devin ate whenever food was before her. When it was not, she had little capacity to miss it.

"I'm glad to see you've got an appetite, friend," said Sutter, watching her as he spread fruit preserves on his toast. "From the looks of you, you haven't been eating regular. I've seen scarecrows less skinny." He swallowed a last bite of bread, then pushed his empty plate aside. After a silent moment while he sipped his coffee, he drew a few folded sheets of paper to him, from where they lay farther along the table. Slowly he opened the papers along their folds, flattening the creases with his thumb.

"The report they made on you at rehab is a corker," he said, still looking at Devin. "I couldn't put it down. It's some of the best reading I've gotten my hands on in ages." He riffled the pages, then moved the top sheet to the bottom. "That place doesn't come cheap. Do you know how much your parents paid to send you there?"

Devin shook her head, and kept eating.

"Well, if you get curious, the first page lists everything they did to you and how much it all cost. I wouldn't blame you if you don't want to be reminded of the ... particulars." Sutter cleared his throat, then took another sip of coffee.

Angelina refilled his cup. When she set the coffeepot down, it made a loud *thunk*, and the table shook with the force of the impact. Devin's incurious glance, as she looked up briefly from her plate, caught a scowl of anger on the woman's face. Angelina was glaring, not at Sutter, but at the papers he held.

Sutter studied the woman, then turned his attention back to Devin.

"The list of tortures they used on you explains ... uh, a lot," he went on, his words punctuated by barely noticeable pauses. "But it's page two that really cleared up the mystery for me. You haven't read any of this, have you, friend?"

Devin shook her head, and helped herself to more eggs.

"I won't spoil your breakfast, then, with the, um ... details." Sutter paused again, then swore with unhesitating vehemence. "*Hell.* You were there. You *lived* the goddam details."

"Miguel," Angelina snapped.

"Sorry. But I know what *you* think of that hellhole, Angie, and I think the same, or worse. It'll have me cussin' a blue streak anytime the name gets mentioned. And here I am, not a week's ride from the place, reading this crap about 'Therapeutic Rationale and Strategies' that was actually written by one of those butchers, firsthand. It's all I can do to sit here and not head out right now to blast that rotten pit off the mountain."

"Shh. Control yourself, Miguel," Angelina admonished him. "You would not be wise to go off—how do you say?—half-baked."

Sutter smiled, some of the tension leaving his face. "'Half-cocked' is the word you're after, I think." He shifted to look at the woman more directly. "Or maybe you've got it right, if by half-baked you mean stupid."

"I would not say such a thing, Miguel. You are *el gran maestro*—the grand master." Angelina tapped the empty envelope that lay on the table. With her blunt but neatly manicured fingernail, she pointed at the Peaceful Hills logotype. "You have told me that you dare not attack this terrible place with you alone in the lead. You have said that two *maestros* are necessary—one to destroy *el infierno,* and the other to be sure the first is not, himself, destroyed."

Sutter nodded. "Yeah, you're right. I'd be a fool to try to take that place, with just the people we've got now." He turned an appraising eye upon Devin. She, over her second piece of toast slathered with plum preserves, had been following this exchange with her usual vacant attention.

"No, I'll stick to the plan," Sutter continued. "First things first. Still, I'm mighty glad to get this account of what really goes on inside those walls. The details. There's been a question in my mind for years: How do they make it stick? Sure, you can get anybody to do—or not do—almost anything, if you torture them long and hard enough. But how come the Sykes who leave that place alive don't go back to using their brains the minute they're free? What keeps them half dead?"

Through narrowed eyes, he scanned the papers he still held. "It's making more sense, now that I've had a peek inside that chamber of horrors. The poor buggers come out of there with their minds poisoned. Listen to this."

Sutter read from the sheet in his hand: "'Before employing drug therapies, which carry with them an increased risk of *permanent* impairments to mental and emotional health ...'"

Once more he paused to study Devin. Over the rim of her cup, she met his gaze, but only indifferently, and only because he was sitting right beside her while she washed down the last bite of her prodigious breakfast.

Sutter cleared his throat again, and went on. "'Before employing drug therapies, this facility exhausted all standard methods of behavior modification through aversion therapy. Among the techniques employed were sleep deprivation, solitary confinement, stress positions, disorientation, sensory overload, reduced diet, and reductions in typical levels of personal and environmental hygiene.'"

Sutter thwacked the papers with quick snaps of his fingers. "Let me see if I can translate that into plain words." He spoke now in a harsh staccato. "They starved and beat you. They strung you up by your thumbs. They locked you in a cell no bigger than a grave and left you to lie in your own vomit and filth. They blinded you with light for days at a time, then shut you in the pitch-black for a week. They blasted you with noise and made you stay awake for so long that your mind turned to mush. *Therapy,* they call it. Sounds like torture to me. Does that about sum it up?"

Devin swallowed her coffee, and managed no response except a small shrug.

"Those bastards!" Sutter growled. Angelina had her eyes closed, her lips tight. She let Sutter's swearing pass without comment.

"But they couldn't break you that way, could they, friend?" He looked at Devin with an expression that she might have taken for admiration, if such things had mattered to her. "It says right here." Sutter continued reading aloud: "'Miss Perridin exhibited remarkably high levels of resistance to, and toleration of, these techniques—thus rendering necessary the administering of impulse-blocking drugs.'"

Sutter thumped the papers again. "That's the explanation I've been looking for. Drugs. Now I know why that last Syke I tried to save wasn't even a shadow of a human being. They'd killed his mind with poisons."

He skimmed to the end of the papers, and gave a short, mirthless laugh. *"It is with great pleasure,"* he read aloud in a voice dripping sarcasm, *"that this facility reports the successful completion of the aforementioned therapies, with Miss Perridin incurring no undue harm."*

Sutter ended the reading with a pithy "Shit!" and tossed the papers from him, landing them on the unoccupied end of the breakfast table. With a firm shove of his chair across the floorboards, he pushed back and stood, and beckoned to Devin. "Let's get started, friend. I think you've still got a brain. They did you harm, but they didn't destroy you. The first thing we do, is we sweat those poisons out of you."

"¿Qué?" Angelina interjected, getting to her feet also. "What do you propose, Miguel?"

"Work! That's what I propose." He took his hat from a peg beside the back door and settled it on his head. "If she's going to eat like a horse, then she'll do her share of the work around here to earn her meals. And while she's breaking a good honest sweat, the crap they shot her full of oughta come oozing out of her pores."

"They didn't give me a shot."

As one, Sutter and Angelina whirled to stare at Devin. She hardly knew who was more surprised to hear her whisper those words—the two of them, or she herself. Words did not come to her readily these days.

When she did not elaborate, Angelina rounded the table and took Devin's hand. "*Por favor,* chica. Tell us what you mean. The bad people who hurt you—they did not give you drugs?"

Devin gazed at the hand holding hers, and then into the woman's high-cheekboned face. "I breathed it," she murmured. "No shots. They put it in the air." In her mind's eye loomed the electric torture chamber and its swirls of orange gas. "They made me breathe it. It stank."

"No joke!" Sutter took a step forward and slapped the table. "Whew!" he whistled in consternation. "That stinks to high heaven, if they're *gassing* people. What if they released a big cloud of the stuff near the ranch? They might turn us all into zombies." He shifted his glance to Angelina, frowning.

She regarded him with dismay.

"We could not protect ourselves from this poison, Miguel?"

He shrugged as he shook his head. "I don't see how, short of conjuring up an airtight dome big enough to fit over the whole ranch, and keeping it over us twenty-four hours a day. I'm pretty sure I don't have the fortitude for that, not on my own." He gazed at Devin, who had risen to her feet and stood now with Angelina opposite him. "All the more reason to get this gal detoxed and deprogrammed. We may need her worse than I thought."

Devin looked from one worried face to the other. Her stomach clenched. Her gut threatened to explode. With a suddenness that brought a gasp from Angelina, she bolted from the table and sprinted out the back door into the kitchen garden. Between rows of wax beans, she went to her knees in the dirt and threw up her huge breakfast.

ଓ 4 ଛ

ANGELINA MATERIALIZED at her side. "*¡Pobrecita!* You poor child. It is my fault. I should never have allowed you to eat so much." With a damp cloth, she cleaned Devin's face. "You come to us half starved, and I am such a fool that I let you gorge on rich food when you should have only *sopa y verduras*—soup and vegetables."

She pulled the hem of Devin's skirt out of the puddled vomit and wiped at the soiled fabric. Over her shoulder, Angelina called to Sutter. "Miguel, this *joven* will not work today. She needs a hot bath, and then a little broth and to rest. Help me get her up to her room."

Sutter mumbled something unintelligible as he strode into the garden and scooped Devin into his arms. Handling her thin frame as though she weighed nothing, he carried her upstairs to the tower room and deposited her on the sofa.

Angelina dismissed him. "Go and find Raquel. Send her to me. There is a bath to prepare, and clothes to wash. We will need much hot water. Have one of the men see that the woodbox is full."

"Yes, Doña." Sutter tipped his hat to the woman. On his way out the bedroom door, he looked back at Devin. "Friend, I'm sorry you're feeling poorly. Do us all a favor, yourself included, and get back on your feet quick as you can. You're needed here."

Angelina shooed him from the room, and for Devin the next several hours passed in a haze. She was vaguely aware of rapid conversations in Spanish that passed over her head. Angelina, joined by a dark-haired young woman named Raquel, stripped her of the vomit-splattered skirt and tunic, and led her down the hall to a bathroom. They settled her in a claw-foot tub and scrubbed her from scalp to toes. Devin soaked in the hot water in passive lassitude and nearly fell asleep, soothed by the women's hands and the ceaseless soft sounds of their language.

After her bath, they put her to bed, and Devin slept more soundly than in the night just past, or for any night that she could really remember. She slept, woke, swallowed a cup of warm broth, and slept again.

Late in the afternoon, the women got her up and dressed her in a bright red circle-skirt and a lacy, embroidered blouse supplied by Raquel, who was near to her own slim size. The young woman gave her a hug as she left, as though the two were close friends. Raquel went out waving, and was still speaking rapid-fire Spanish as she descended the stairs.

"You look better, chica. There is more life in your eyes," Angelina commented as she fed Devin a small bowl of fresh vegetable soup, lightly seasoned to sit easily on the stomach. After waiting a few minutes to be sure the soup would stay down, the woman ran a comb through Devin's cropped hair, dry now from her morning bath but mussed from her day in bed.

Together then, they went down to the parlor, and Angelina installed her charge in a comfortable chair under a sunlit window. As she plumped the chair's cushions, she brushed against the scarred skin from the mostly healed burns on Devin's arm. Reflexively, Devin twitched her arm aside. Angelina uttered a soft, *"Lo siento,"* stood looking down at her for a moment, and then left Devin to read while she went to prepare the evening meal for herself and Sutter.

It took only a few paragraphs for Devin to descend deep into a racy novel about a frontier schoolmarm who swoons, repeatedly, as she's carried off by desperadoes. Caught up in the woman's overwrought woes, she paid no mind to the distant sound of the back door opening. But the creak of the door was followed, presently, by Sutter entering the parlor from the direction of the kitchen. He took a seat facing her.

"Angelina tells me you're feeling better," he said as he settled himself in the cushions. "I'm glad to hear it."

Devin only looked at him blankly, her splintered mind struggling to leave the storybook world. For the here and now, she could frame no appropriate response.

"I see you've gone mute again." Sutter rubbed the back of his neck, and sighed. "But I guess that's better than running off at the mouth when you've got nothing to say." In the waning daylight that turned the room golden, he thumbed through a loose clutch of paper. Devin recognized the papers from Peaceful Hills. "There's more of this shit I want you to hear. Listen." He slanted the top sheet to get the best light on it, and read:

"'Miss Perridin may experience occasional, brief episodes of nausea. These occurrences, while temporarily unpleasant, should be welcomed as positive indicators of the medication's continuing effectiveness. Nausea will be experienced only in conjunction with the emotional outbursts—or the threat thereof—which were a deleterious factor and consequence of your daughter's mental illness. Transient episodes of drug-induced stomach-upset need occasion no concern. They are simply your guarantee that you may have confidence in the lasting efficacy of the treatment administered by this facility.'"

Sutter lowered the paper and scratched his head. "That hokum is hard to follow, but I think I get the gist. You start throwing up your toenails anytime you get emotional. If you get mad or excited, or scared, or the like"—his fingers made small circles in the air as if to encompass every possible emotion—"or if you even *start* to feel much of anything at all, it hits you in the gut. The drug you breathed makes you sick to your stomach. Is that right?"

Devin thought about it, as well as her nebulous powers of concentration would allow her to think, and slowly nodded agreement.

"Is that ...?" Sutter paused, seeming to weigh his words. "Is that what's keeping you so quiet? I mean, do you *work* at staying tight-lipped and hollowed out, so you won't get sick?"

She fingered the book in her hands, wishing he would leave her alone so she could return to reading it. Talking was difficult under any circumstances, but when the subject was her own mental breakdown, she found it nearly impossible to form thoughts and give them voice. But Sutter kept looking at her, his expression half hopeful, half ... desperate?

Devin put her book aside. She closed her eyes. To marshal what was left of her faculties cost her an effort, one she would not have been able to deliver except for the day of rest and pampering that Angelina had given her. Making the required effort, however, Devin was rewarded with a sharp, though fleeting, glimpse of the wreckage inside her brain.

The vision disgusted her. She opened her eyes and shook her head. "It's not that simple." Swallowing was painful in her suddenly dry throat. "May I have a glass of water, please?"

Sutter jumped up. "Sure. I'll be right back." He returned in half a minute, carrying a wooden tray loaded with a crystal decanter and water goblets for them both.

As he handed her a glass, Devin noted his expression. He had brightened. He looked less worried. If she could return the grin to his face with just a few words, how happy Sutter would be if she managed to say all that she knew of her condition. She sipped the cool water, and gave it a try.

"It's a good thing, when I get sick ... It means I'm not totally dead inside." She spoke slowly, pausing between sentences. Sutter listened and did not rush her. "Most of the time, I'm numb ... I don't feel anything ... I don't think about anything. Nothing matters. It's like I'm an empty bottle."

Devin's quiet sigh rose from the depths of that emptiness. For a long moment, she was silent. Sutter refilled her water glass, then sat back, waiting.

She pulled more words together, and pushed on. "But once in a while, the bottle fills up ... just partway. Not even half full. But something will get in, and it'll touch me. I'll have a feeling. A reaction. Not often ... but sometimes I *care*. Then I'm not empty."

Devin pressed the cool goblet to her forehead. It felt good. When she lowered the glass, beads of moisture remained on her skin. Through the lace-curtained window, the breezes of early evening kissed the wetness and deepened the welcome chill on her brow. She sat silent for another moment, daring to savor the sensation.

"The gas they made me breathe," she went on then, in a whisper, "... it keeps me empty. I'm not supposed to feel. The drug killed parts of my mind ... so that I don't get mad ... or scared ... about anything."

Devin looked directly at Sutter as she added, more forcefully: "Except ... sometimes I'm *not* empty. And when that happens—when I get partway filled up—the drug makes me puke. After I puke, I'll be empty again ... too empty to do things with my mind. They're afraid of my mind." She leaned slightly toward Sutter, who was listening intently. "You see? It's good when I get sick. It means ... it means the bottle isn't closed so tight that nothing can get in. Or out."

Sutter studied her. Then he drained his water glass and got to his feet.

"In that case, friend, I don't care if you're upchucking your liver and lights tomorrow. You're going to work, and work hard. We'll sweat that poison out of you." He grinned as he reached a hand to help her out of the overstuffed chair's deep cushions. "Angelina will be happy to hear that it wasn't her cooking made you sick."

* * *

He was a man of his word. By first light the next day, Sutter had hustled her out to the kitchen garden and set Devin to weeding. He disappeared then, to his own affairs or those of the ranch. But as the morning sun rose higher, peeking over the shoulder of the mountain that shadowed the ranch, Angelina brought her a straw hat and better instructions.

"*¡Ay!* Why should Miguel think a girl from the *delicado* side of town would know the difference between velvetweed and summer squash? Let me show you."

Angelina demonstrated, and Devin caught on. The need to distinguish between a wanted plant and a similar-looking weed brought her mind into focus with a clarity she had been unable to sustain since the earliest days of her "therapy." And if her attention did fade, Angelina snapped her back with a sharp: "*¡Ay, no, chica!*"

After a couple of hours, they were interrupted by a passing rider. It was Orlando, the middle member of the party that had brought Devin to the ranch.

"'Morning, Doña," Orlando said. "How are you getting along with Sutter's latest victim?"

Angelina glared at him. "Do not say such things. Señorita Perridin is no one's 'victim'." She paused, as if weighing the possible untruth of her statement. But she did not amend or qualify it to acknowledge what had befallen Devin at the sanatorium. "*La joven* is one of us now. Here is her home. You should make her feel welcome."

Orlando snorted. "Yeah, sure. I'll do that. For as long as she lasts." The mocking smile he gave Devin suggested an amused sort of pity. Then he reined his horse around and rode off in the direction of the compound's main gate.

Angelina stared after him, frowning. "*¡Idiota!*" she muttered under her breath. With a renewed vengeance, she returned to ripping up weeds.

At midday they went indoors, joined by a late-arriving Sutter for a meal of chicken and dumplings.

"Doña Angelina," he said after a few bites, "far be it from me to criticize your cooking, but I think you left something out. Salt and pepper, maybe? This has about as much flavor as glue."

Angelina bridled. "If you do not like it, Señor Sutter, then find your dinner elsewhere. You know the *comidas pesadas*—the rich foods—are very bad for this young woman."

Sutter shook his head. "I'm telling you, Angie, the girl doesn't have a weak stomach. It's the poison she breathed that makes her sick." He looked at Devin. "You can eat anything, can't you, friend?"

Devin gave a half nod, her mouth too full of tender, juicy chicken to attempt speech.

"Even so," Angelina insisted, "I give her no *chiles* or salsas. What she needs are the *hierbas* for the stomach—*menta* and parsley in a little sweet persimmon ... with a pinch of *lo sobrenatural.*" The woman spread an orangish, green-flecked mixture on a small flatbread and handed it to Devin. "Chew this slowly, chica. Eat it all."

She obeyed willingly enough, for the mint-parsley-persimmon concoction was delicious—easily the best medicine Devin had downed in a long time.

After lunch, Sutter took her to the stables and showed her how to curry and brush the horses' coats. She began with Diego, the easy-going chestnut she'd ridden from the train. The horse nickered a greeting, and he stood quietly as she worked her way carefully from his head to his tail, and down his legs on both sides.

For hours through the afternoon, she dawdled in the stables in companionable silence with the horses, relieved to be among beings that didn't talk and who wanted nothing from her but strokes and ear-scratching. The fragrance of the hay in the stalls and the warm smell of the horses helped to subdue the remembered stench of poison and pain, those odors of fear that remained etched in her memories of the asylum.

"Hello, there!"

A man's voice from the stable door brought Devin's head around with disconcerting speed. She typically moved slowly, sluggishly, her reactions dulled by drugs and "behavior modification." But at the sound of the voice, she jumped. Her stomach tightened—a sensation that generally preceded puking.

"It's me, Jack," the man said, approaching. "Remember? I rode with you from the train. How's it going? You settling in okay?"

Devin stepped into the corridor between the stalls, the better to see who was speaking. Her attention, however, was less on her visitor than on her stomach. A moment's startlement was generally more than enough, in her experience, to trigger her violent retching. But for this moment, despite a distinct feeling of queasiness, she was not losing her lunch.

"Say," came the voice. "You feeling all right?" Jack pushed his hat back on his head as he walked up to her. "You look a mite wobbly." He grasped her shoulders and eased her back against the bars of the nearest stall. "Grab ahold and steady yourself."

Devin locked one hand on a wooden rail, and with the other she clutched Jack's arm. For long moments her eyes refused to focus. A loud buzzing filled her ears. A sharp pain shot low through her belly.

She swallowed hard and shut her mind to all things, emptying it of thought and sensation. Mental blankness was the surest way to make the illness pass.

It worked. Her symptoms eased, and she released Jack's arm.

He stepped back, putting a little space between them.

"Maybe you better go on up to the house and have Angelina take a look at you," he said. His voice was a pleasing tenor, and in it, Devin heard genuine concern. "I'm kinda surprised to see you out here on your own, you being just released from the ... er, hospital." He pulled a sprig of hay from the only bale within reach and chewed it.

After a pause, during which Devin did nothing but look at him, he spoke again. "I'm glad Sutter's not hounding you, like he did—"

Jack broke off, but then continued quickly as if to gloss over what he'd started to say:

"—like I've seen him do people. He can be a real bully ... er, bulldog, when he gets an idea in his head. So I'd take this as a good sign, if I were you ... him leaving you alone on your own for a while, I mean. That's a good thing." Jack looked searchingly at her.

Devin found herself meeting his gaze with vision that no longer blurred. Clarity came also to her thoughts, to a degree she couldn't typically muster after a sick spell. She noticed Jack's light brown hair and his dark blue eyes. She saw, beneath his sun-bronzed skin, a young face, well-favored. He appeared to be only a few years older than Devin. Still, she couldn't find anything to say to him.

Jack smiled. "You're not a big talker, are you? Well, that's fine. I've never cared for chatterboxes." He inclined his head toward the stable door through which he had entered. "Let me walk you back to the house. It's getting on towards suppertime."

Together they strolled through the lingering warmth of the early evening. Springtime had not yet given way to summer in these mountains, but even so, the scent of sun-warmed pinesap hung heavy in the air. The compound was unusually quiet, as though suspended between its occupations of the daylit hours and the amusements that came with nightfall. Jack said nothing more until they reached the front steps of the old house. Then he turned to her, and spoke in a voice too low for anyone else to hear, had there been anyone around.

"Listen," he muttered. "Even if you're not much of a talker, I don't think there's a lot wrong with your hearing—or your gumption either, I hope. So let me give you some advice." He glanced over his shoulder, as though checking for eavesdroppers. "You'll make Mike Sutter a very happy man, but more than that, you'll do yourself a world of good if you can find a way back into your right mind."

Jack's blue eyes seemed to darken as he looked into Devin's. But maybe it was only a trick of the dusk that was falling around them.

He went on. "You know what I'm talking about, right?" He tapped his temple. "Try to get there on your own. Don't leave it to Sutter to drive you so hard that you're hurt. He's got ... peculiar ways about him." Jack paused. "Let's just say he's been known to push people down dangerous paths."

Devin stood on the porch steps transfixed, unable to look away. Silently she cursed the inertia that robbed her of the power to react or to question. At intervals today, her wits had sharpened unexpectedly, only to relapse into numbness. Right now, she felt exceedingly dull.

Jack looked disappointed with her dullness as he touched his finger to the brim of his hat. "Well then, I'll say good night." He nodded toward the door of the house behind her.

Devin heard the latch click open, and a loose panel in the door rattled softly between the stiles. But no sound of footsteps reached her, from either the wood floor indoors or the veranda at her back.

Feeling as though the opening of the door had broken an ensorcellment upon her, she turned to look, seeking confirmation that she and Jack were still alone. It was as she had thought: No one was there. No human hand had touched that door. It had opened under the power of a thought: the action of a mental intention.

She looked back at the young man, and this time she found words.

"You're a Syke, too, aren't you?"

Jack's eyebrows lifted. "Sure. Of course." He raised his hands in a questioning gesture. "Didn't you know? We all are. Everybody at the ranch is a Syke." Jack nodded again at the house, this time without producing paranormal effects. "Not one of us can hold a candle to Mike Sutter, though. ... Not unless there's truth, that is, to the rumors about Miss Devin Perridin."

He gave her a nod, and left her standing in the doorway that he had syketically opened. As Jack walked away, Devin's gaze followed him until he rounded a distant building, perhaps a bunkhouse, and he disappeared from her view.

◌ 5 ◌

WITH EACH NEW DAY, Sutter ratcheted up his program for sweating the poison out of Devin. He moved her from weeding the garden and grooming the horses to more intensive labor. For a week she toiled as a planter. In earth turned by a horse-drawn plow, she poked holes with a stick, dropped in corn kernels, and trod on the soil to firm it around the seeds.

As she grew more familiar with her new home, Devin realized she had misjudged the place, thinking it was more fortress-commune than working ranch. This community of fugitive Sykes did indeed raise cattle in alpine pastures plentifully watered by lakes of snow-melt, and on the lower, gentler slopes they grew crops to feed both the animals and themselves. There were hayfields as well as corn-fields, and throughout the compound vegetable gardens flourished. There was even a makeshift greenhouse, upslope from a well-tended orchard where fruit trees grew in neat rows.

The orchard was an oasis of cool shade, in stark contrast to the treeless, slanting cornfield where the sun beat on Devin's back, and the work was numbingly monotonous. Or so Devin gathered from the groaning of her fellow planters. She herself could make no complaint about the monotony. Her dulled wits wanted nothing more.

When the planting was done, Sutter assigned her to the construction work going on within the ever-expanding compound. Devin moved stacks of lumber and armloads of tools to the various building sites. She hoisted heavy timbers over her head. She hauled sand and water in buckets that seemed to weigh a ton. When the construction foreman, a swarthy man named Nicolas, discovered she had no fear of heights—being essentially incapable, in her mindless "serenity," of fearing even a high-wire act—he put a hammer in Devin's hand and sent her scrambling up to nail rafters to ridgepoles.

Sweat, she did. The labor built muscle on Devin's light frame and gave her stamina that was nearly equal to her brawniest coworkers. In this community of outlaws, she found a niche as a slow but steady worker. Though she seldom spoke with others in her crew, she got on through a sort of sign language. They needed to show her only once what to do. Where manual labor was concerned, she proved a quick study.

Mentally, however, progress was glacial. The work that came increasingly easily to her hands did little to enliven her brain. Most hours of most days, Devin existed in a state of profound indifference. Only three things would reliably lift her lassitude: a hot meal in Angelina's kitchen at the end of a hard day; an evening curled up with a book from the parlor library; and a few words exchanged with Jack when he came in from riding herd on the cattle and goats that were pastured high above the compound's walls.

Devin took to sitting on the front porch most evenings, with one eye on her book and the other watching for Jack's arrival through the main gates. As he approached the house, he would dismount and walk to greet her, always stopping at the foot of the steps, never setting a boot on them. Nobody, so it appeared, would enter Mike Sutter's house or even step up on the veranda except by Sutter's express invitation.

"'Evening, Miss Devin," Jack would say on each occasion of their twilit meeting. "You getting along okay?"

Devin would nod, lower her book, and struggle for words. Sometimes she would manage a halting conversation about the work she'd done that day, or the prospects for moving to a new task tomorrow, or how badly the fields and pastures were already starting to need rain. Other times, she could produce nothing intelligible from her mushy brain and seemingly paralyzed vocal cords.

Either way, Jack never stayed long. Bidding her good-night, he'd lead his horse to the stable, and Devin would go indoors to bathe and fall into bed, physically and mindlessly exhausted.

* * *

Sutter allowed this state of affairs to continue for weeks before he tested her, or tested his theory about sweating away her Peaceful Hills poisons. One evening as he met Devin climbing the stairs while he descended, he touched a finger to his hat brim, making his usual courteous salute. Then he took her by the shoulders and shoved her backward.

Without thinking, Devin grabbed the handrail, saving herself a fall down the steep stairs.

"Miguel!" shouted Angelina, witnessing it all from the hallway above Sutter. "*¡Qué diablo!* Have you lost your mind?"

Sutter laughed. "That's a funny question to be asking me, Doña, when I'm obviously not the one who has. Lost his mind, I mean." He gestured at Devin, who still hung onto the handrail, catching her balance two steps below him. "Don't get worked up. I'm just checking her reflexes. That's the quickest I've seen her move since I got her off the train."

He stepped aside and motioned for Devin to continue up the stairs. "Go get rested, friend. You've shown me I'm on the right track. We've worked enough of the zombie-dope out of your system that your instincts for self-preservation are coming back." He grinned broadly. "Tomorrow, we'll start digging other reactions out of that drug-curdled psyche of yours. Get your sleep. You'll need it."

Devin went to her room and threw up in the chamber pot. Long afterward into the night, she lay awake, the smell of vomit strong in her nostrils.

* * *

With Sutter leading the way horseback, Devin hiked on foot behind him, up a trail into the forested mountains directly overlooking the ranch headquarters. In the shape she'd been in at their first meeting, after her discharge from the asylum, she could not have made the climb. Weeks of labor had hardened her, though. With one foot in front of the other, attentive to nothing, she trudged upward at a steady pace, and when they reached a grassy meadow at the foot of a towering bluff, she wasn't even breathing hard.

"This'll do." Sutter reined to a halt. "Nobody's likely to trouble us up here." He dismounted, flipped open his saddlebag, and drew out a sack. "Here's lunch. Come get yours before I eat it all."

Devin hung back, shaking her head. "I'm not hungry," she managed to mutter.

"What's the matter? Afraid you'll chuck it up?" Sutter took a sandwich from the sack. He sat on a tree-shaded rock to eat. "Angelina tells me that herbal mess she's been feeding you has helped with the puking. She claims to put her ancestors' 'old magic' in it. *La magia antigua.*" He chuckled. "Could be she's done you more good than all the sweating in the world. I might be as wrong as tits on a boar to think that hard work can counteract poison."

He chewed and swallowed. "But at least you've earned your keep these past weeks, and you've lost that hospital pallor. You look to be as fit as a fiddle on the outside. What's going on in here, though?" Sutter lifted his hat and tapped his skull. "That's what I'm aiming to know."

Devin looked around the meadow to which he had brought her. Grass and wildflowers carpeted a level shelf of rock, the mountain rising steeply on one side and dropping sheer on the other. The only way in or out was along the trail they had climbed. Was it the "dangerous path" that Jack had warned her about?

She glanced back at Sutter and found him observing her.

"It's pretty up here, isn't it?" he said around a bite of sandwich. "I come here for the peace and quiet, and to be alone for a while. The ranch is getting crowded. Back when we first started rescuing Sykes from Purity"—he waved a hand in a generally southwestward direction—"we never thought we'd find so many. A Syke in the city has to stay out of sight to stay alive. Most of them who still hide in town think they're alone. They think there's no one else like them in the world." Sutter chuckled. "Imagine their surprise when we bring them up here and they find a whole mob of us."

He gestured at a rock in the shade near the one he occupied. "Come sit down. If you won't eat, keep me company while I do." He gave Devin a searching look. "You're acting a mite odd—odder than usual. What's the matter? People been telling tales about me?"

Devin shrugged, a noncommittal gesture. With hesitant steps, she walked to the indicated rock and sat. Sutter fished in the lunch sack, took out two apples, and tossed one to her. Her hands raised of their own accord, and she caught it. A simple act, but a response that would have been unthinkable a few weeks ago. Had anyone at the sanatorium thrown her an apple—a hot coal would have been more likely in that place—she would not have reacted. Sutter was right: her instincts were awakening.

"Come on—talk." He grinned his roguish grin. "I know you can when you want to. What's the scuttlebutt about me? Why are you acting spooked?"

Devin shook her head. "I'm just tired." After a pause, she went on in her faltering way. "The work is hard here ... not like at home."

"Your mama didn't give you chores to do?" Sutter answered his own question: "No, I guess she wouldn't—a rich kid like you, and a bratty persistent Syke to boot, who'd be more likely to pull the house down around mama's ears than clean it." He leaned forward and spat an apple seed into the grass at his feet. "You know why they call us 'Sykes,' don't you?"

"It's short for 'psycho'—insane." Devin spoke without inflection. She toyed with the apple in her hand, still not inclined to bite into it. "That's what the books say."

"You're reading the wrong books! Back at the house, I've got one that tells the real story. I'll find it for you when we get home."

Sutter took a swig from his canteen, then tossed the bottle to her. Again she caught it without thinking. She uncapped it and had a long drink.

"'Syke' is short for *psychokinesis,*" Sutter said. "Ever hear that word?"

Devin shook her head.

"I'm not surprised you don't know it. It's a word most ordinaries won't say. It means 'motion by the mind'." He tapped his temple. "For generations now in Purity, the common people have been dead set on the idea that psychokinetic power is the most dangerous kind of lunacy, not a mental gift. If they talk about it at all, they whisper behind closed doors." His lip curled in a sneer. "Ignorant fools. They don't know their own history. The Sykes were the saving of the human race during the Great Contagion. It was the Sykes who buried the dead and kept the infection from spreading all the way to the last island in the farthest ocean."

Sutter stretched a hand toward the western plateau, though the flatlands were invisible from this mountain flank. "Hell, the Sykes buried whole cities of rotting corpses. Just with the power of their minds, they opened the earth and caused it to swallow the dead places. That's what the stories say, anyhow."

He let his hand drop. For a moment his gaze was unfocused, his thoughts seeming to wander.

Then he returned his attention to Devin. "You do know about the Great Contagion? Maybe they don't teach it in school anymore."

Devin shrugged. "I didn't have school. My parents were afraid ..."

"Yeah, I suppose they would have been terrified," Sutter resumed as she trailed off. "Who knew what damage you'd do, out among people? If some kid pulled your pigtail or a teacher pissed you off, like as not you'd think a dark thought, squint their way, and send the poor bugger crashing through the nearest wall." He chuckled. "Believe me, I know the feeling. I was tempted more than once to let loose during my schoolboy days."

His expression sobered. "But if I wanted to live, I had to control my urges. Anyone in my part of town who showed a trace of syketic power got blown away by the sheriff or his sharpshooters."

Sutter took a last bite from his apple and tossed the core into the pine trees that fringed the meadow. "You didn't answer my question. Ever hear of the Great Contagion?"

Devin nodded. "I read the history. People died ... some kind of infection ... spread fast."

"Real fast. No place was safe. You couldn't escape it." Sutter gazed into the middle distance as though glimpsing a bygone era. "The world was a big bloody mess of people dead or dying. It was a bleeding disease, you know? Yeah. The poor buggers bled into their guts, and they bled from every opening in their bodies." He made a face. "Imagine cities with blood running in the gutters, blood in the drains and the drinking water. And the bodies piling up, putrefying. Get near that cesspool, and you're infected. No help for it."

Devin placed her uneaten apple on the rock beside her. Food interested her less and less. The history book she'd read had been short on detail. It had said only that countless numbers died, vastly reducing the world's population.

"How did the contagion end?" she asked. "How did anybody survive?"

Sutter smiled as he shifted his gaze back to her. "That's where the Sykes come in, friend. In the last years of the epidemic, a family came down out of the mountains—maybe these mountains here." He tossed a glance over his shoulder at the slopes rising above. "The stories don't say for sure where they came from, but this could be the place. Down at the ranch, the old house was standing empty when I got here, and I've always wondered if they might have abandoned it because they went down to the prairie to save the world." He shook his head, and Devin got the impression that Sutter might have chosen—if he'd been around back then—to stay in this mountain refuge instead, and let the world fend for itself.

"Anyway," he went on, "wherever they came from, they were a big family. I guess you'd call them a clan. And all of them, every single one, had syketic powers. They could move things—boulders, water, even the air—just by thinking about it, focusing their minds." Sutter leaned toward Devin for emphasis. "And that wasn't all. Those Sykes had a natural immunity to the contagion. They didn't get sick. Even better, they could heal other people by giving them a little of their blood. It took only a few drops transfused directly from a Syke's arm into a sick person's vein."

He straightened and drew back. "Probably the two things were connected—the syketic abilities and the natural immunity, I mean. Whatever gave a Syke his powers also kept him healthy." Sutter laid a long look on Devin. "Nobody really knows what makes a Syke tick. It's a mystery." He sighed, as if with regret. "If we knew where syketic ability came from, it'd make it easier to get yours back, I expect."

Sutter's words had a curious effect on Devin. She felt her mind opening to them, to the strangeness of them. *Syke* and *healthy* had never before been used together in the same sentence—not within her hearing, anyway. Equally novel was the idea of a lost time in history, as Sutter described it, when Sykes had been a force for good. People with abilities such as she had formerly displayed were diseased, deranged, unnatural monsters: so Devin had been taught since she was old enough to listen.

A sensation arose, a mental tension at odds with her chronic lethargy. Devin realized with a tingle of surprise that she felt a deep interest in the story Mike Sutter was telling. Nothing had held her attention for this long, had filled her concentration so completely, since she'd breathed the orange cloud and lost the better part of her mind.

Sutter reached for the lunch sack and started to tie the neck closed. He held it up to Devin's view, his eyebrows raised in a question. "You sure you don't want your sandwich? It's roast beef with tomato and Angelina's special dressing. She'll have put in those magic herbs of hers, for your stomach."

Devin shook her head. "The Sykes," she murmured, prodding him to continue his story. "They gave their blood freely ... to save ordinary people?"

He nodded. "They did, and that wasn't all. They used their powers to wall off the survivors behind a sort of mental curtain, down on the Contagion River." He pointed west with his thumb. "Though I think the river had a different name back then. Anyway, they picked a spot with nothing around but the river and the prairie. Whoever had lived there before had cleared out by then—on the run from the disease, I suppose—and it was just about the only place this side of the Arrowrocks that was clean of the sickness. From there, the Sykes went looking for people they could save, folks who weren't too near dead for a transfusion of Syke blood to work a cure. They brought the survivors to that spot on the river, and they made their stand there."

Sutter finished tying up the lunch sack. He crooked his hand at Devin; she passed him his canteen. He drank, then recapped the neck.

"With the Sykes keeping the sickness away," he went on, needing no further prompting to continue his story, "that section on the river outlasted the Great Contagion. The day came when the disease had run its course worldwide. Everyone who could have spread the plague was dead. With no one to pass it on, finally the contagion died out, too."

Sutter's face had an almost dreamy look now. Repeatedly, he ran the shoulder strap of his canteen through his fingers, an absent-minded gesture. He kept talking.

"When they were sure the danger had passed, the Sykes let go of the curtain they'd held in place with their thoughts. For years, they'd taken it in turn to keep up the protection all around the town. It *was* a town by then, with the survivors marrying into the clan of Sykes and having mixed-blood kids."

He frowned, shaking his head. "I don't suppose anyone could have predicted what would happen. The syketic trait didn't breed true. More children were born without, than with. It skipped generations, and in many lines it died out entirely. After maybe a hundred years, maybe even less, the Sykes were in the minority. The common people started to treat them like freaks. And then somebody decided they were *dangerous* freaks."

Sutter shrugged, still frowning, and his next words came out through gritted teeth. "It doesn't take a lot of imagination to know what probably happened. Some asshole pushed a Syke too far, and without moving a muscle, the Syke broke the fool's neck. And from that day to this, the ordinaries have been terrified of us. We save their lives and give them a city, and look how they repay us."

His attention snapped back to Devin, so suddenly that his eyes meeting hers came like a physical blow. "Nowadays, the kids in town who are like I was, they try to exterminate. But if an accident of birth gives you rich, powerful parents, they send you off to be tortured into mindlessness. Eh, friend?"

Like a camera jolted from its tripod, Devin's mind lost its focus: sharp and clear one moment; unable the next to fix upon what Sutter was saying. At his mention of torture, her thoughts blurred and fell away as if in a dark fog. Out of the murk, she could frame only one coherent question: "The city the Sykes made ... Purity?"

Sutter looked at her through narrowed eyes. "Of course. It's obvious, right? Since Purity is the only town this side of the Contagion River, and the only sizable outpost of humanity for five hundred miles past the Arrowrocks." He spat on the ground beside the boulder where he sat. "To call it a 'city,' though, is stretching things. You and I will never see a real city, but there's pictures in books of what they called a 'metropolis' back in the day. Purity sure as hell isn't one of those."

He got to his feet, ambled off a few steps, and arched his back in a tension-relieving stretch. "How'd we get onto that subject?" he demanded half-accusingly, looking over at her. "I didn't bring you up the mountain to tell you the history of the world. We're here to hone your reflexes." Sutter motioned for her to stand. "Get up. Let's get at it."

Devin rose unsteadily, teetering on the edge of torpor. The damage she had sustained at Peaceful Hills was always present, gnawing at her, working in its poisonous ways to shrivel her mind into an empty, arid waste. Each time she had roused lately, whether for a few minutes or for an hour, whenever the bottled-up space inside her hollowed-out shell was filled with a spark of curiosity, an emotion, a sustained effort of concentration: she paid for those moments of awareness with a subsequent descent into nothingness. That's where her mind headed now, and nothing Sutter could do to her would change that.

"Here, catch!" he called. He threw the half-full canteen at her.

It hit Devin at the top of her breastbone, hard enough to stagger her back a step. But her hands hung limp at her sides. Not one of her muscles had twitched to raise them to her defense.

"Damn!" Sutter swore. "That's not good." He made a noise of displeasure, sharply sucking a lip against his teeth. "What's with you? You've gone zombie again, when a minute ago you were all ears and acting almost normal." From the ground at his feet, he scooped up a stone the size of his fist. "Duck, friend, or I'm likely to brain you."

The rock came sailing toward her head. Devin did not move. The stone clipped her left temple and ear. Vaguely she knew pain and the sting of blood welling from broken skin. She didn't care ... it didn't matter.

Sutter stalked toward her, his hand raised as if to strike her. Then he halted and visibly gathered himself.

"Listen, friend." He snarled the words. "I know you're getting your reflexes back, because I've seen them. What are you trying to prove here? You showing me how brave and self-controlled you are?" He sneered at her. "It's not your self-control I'm interested in, girl. Persistent Sykes like you—they're nothing but instincts wrapped in skin. I want to see those instincts come busting out."

He stepped close and jabbed a finger in her face. Devin didn't flinch.

"That's why you got caught and ended up in that hellhole of a 'sanatorium.' You know that, don't you?" Sutter demanded. "I lived in Purity until I was seventeen, and I didn't have anybody covering my ass the way your parents covered for you. I *had* to control my impulses." He dropped his hand but remained looming over her. "If I'd let myself get riled enough to break someone in two by willing it to happen, the law would have come down on me with everything it had." He smiled, grimly. "Oh, sure, I'd have cracked a few skulls and snapped some spines. They wouldn't have got me without a fight. But one Syke can't singlehandedly take out a platoon of ordinaries packing carbines. Nobody can concentrate in every direction at once. I'd have caught a bullet in the back before I'd killed 'em all."

His imagined battle with the peace officers of Purity seemed to improve Sutter's mood. He suddenly grinned at Devin with his usual devil-may-care ease. "A persistent Syke like you, though—your sort hardly needs to concentrate, the way I understand it. You act before you think. Or maybe it is that you *never* think."

He pushed his hat back on his head. The pines that fringed the meadow's western rim had the sun behind them now; they cast dappled shadows over Devin and her kidnapper.

"When I came to the ranch in my teens"—Sutter gestured down the mountain toward the compound below—"I met an old man living up here. He was a persistent sort—one of the few to ever get out of Purity alive." Sutter gave a slight nod which included Devin in that select group. "His name was Santiago. The way he told it, you persistent Sykes can't help yourselves. Same way a person blinks when he gets the sun in his eyes, your type reacts without thinking." Sutter tapped his right temple. "It's automatic. Something catches you by surprise or gets your dander up, and you cut loose."

His grin broadened. "What I wouldn't have given to be in the room when you blew out the back wall of the Perridin family mansion. What set you off? Your mama nag you to eat your vegetables?"

Devin didn't answer. Her sluggish mind could not summon the memory of that morning when her pent-up frustration had found release, and the town of Purity had had to face the truth about the Guildmaster's daughter. She didn't think about the episode often, even when her mind possessed the capacity for thought. At this moment, such reflection was beyond her.

Sutter's anger returned in a rush. "Oh, right," he snapped. "You're playing possum again, aren't you."

His hands came up, as if to give Devin a shove. He didn't touch her physically. But the pressure of his willpower lashed out at her.

A quality in herself that was deeper than thought, deeper than sentience, recognized the power that pressed against her. It invited her to respond, to meet the force of his mind with the potency of her own.

But Devin's faculties remained dormant. From her drained state, she could not rouse. She was an empty bottle, tightly corked, sealed off.

"Defend yourself, damn it!" Sutter yelled. "If you've got anything to show me, friend, now's the time."

If he had bent the full force of his psychokinetic strength upon her, Devin would have ended as crumpled and ruined as the train car Sutter had derailed. But even this obviously restrained attack caused her spectacular pain. An invisible blow slugged her in the stomach, slammed her off her feet, and arced her through the air. At the meadow's rim, Devin crashed into the high branches of a pine tree. And there she hung, gasping for breath that would not come. Her lungs burned.

Below her, the mountain fell away in a sheer drop of a thousand feet. She was one broken branch away from plunging to her death.

Sutter walked to the brink and stood for a moment looking down into the chasm below. Then he backed away to safer ground, and gazed up at Devin.

"I've already lost one potential partner down there." He nodded to the abyss. "If you don't want to go the same way, friend, then I suggest you find it in yourself to stop me from killing you."

☙ 6 ❧

DEVIN BARELY HELD ON to consciousness. Her chest hurt from the effort to draw in air. Sutter's blow had doubled her over. She'd sailed into the tree bent at the waist, leading with her backside, her arms and legs trailing like feathers on a shuttlecock. She'd landed in a vee shape, wedged between the branches so that she could not straighten her back. A limb pinned her shoulders, pressing her chest against her thighs.

Her position was intolerable. Bent in half, she couldn't breathe. Her head pounded and her ears felt stopped up, full of liquid. Worse than anything was the pressure on her belly. Her folded midsection began to convulse with the dry heaves.

Then the branch snapped under her, giving way with a loud *crack*.

Devin fell, and time stalled. She crashed downward on a zigzag course, slow-motion through the tree's lower limbs. Knocked to and fro, she had time to note the scraping and tearing of skin against bark, the pricking of pine needles, the jabs from the tree's innumerable woody points and knobs. Then she was in the clear, falling, falling through open sky, dropping past the meadow-carpeted ledge and plummeting toward heaped boulders far below.

Before she hit the boulders, Devin tumbled into an invisible net. It closed around her, a palpable force but as unseeable as air, a net woven from the mental powers of a Syke. It arrested her fall, then yanked her upward hard and fast, high up to the meadow where Sutter stood.

At his feet, Devin spilled from the net that he'd thrown her. She lay on the grass panting for breath and clutching her belly. Her eyes would not focus, not until Sutter leaned over her and locked his gaze onto hers.

"Well, friend," he drawled, settling his snake-banded hat firmly on his head. "We don't seem to be making a lot of progress." He scratched his chin. "I thought sure that falling off a mountain would spook you into action. I expected some fancy Syke fireworks from you." He shook his head dolefully. "What is it going to take to stir you to life?"

With one hand, Sutter hauled her up out of the grass. When Devin's legs refused to support her, he lifted her in his arms and carried her to his horse.

On the ride down to the ranch, Sutter spoke into his captive's ear. "You know what my dad used to tell me, friend? It's nothing original, but he'd always say: 'Mike, son, what doesn't kill you makes you stronger.' That's good to remember when things get rough."

* * *

As a new sunrise spread its light over the ranch, Devin awoke in her tower room, bandaged, wrapped, and poulticed. Angelina had washed and dressed each of her wounds, from her temple where Sutter's thrown rock had clipped her, to every abrasion collected in her ricocheting fall through the trees. None of the wounds was serious, but so many together were remarkably uncomfortable. It took Devin two tries to get out of bed, and half an hour to pull on her clothes.

She groped her way downstairs. Long before she reached the kitchen, the loud sounds of an argument wafted up to her.

"*¡No más,* Miguel!" Angelina was exclaiming. "Stop trying to 'cure' her. You will fail, as you failed before."

"Not with this one," Sutter shot back. "She's different. Deep down, she's got fire. The other one was a cold, dead cinder. He wouldn't even look at me when I—"

Sutter broke off as Devin entered the kitchen. He stared at her, then turned back to Angelina. "For chrissakes, Doña! You've got her wrapped like a mummy. Give me a break, would you? She ain't beat up that bad."

Angelina ignored him. "You poor child," she greeted Devin, her voice gentling from the tones she had used on Sutter. "Come sit. Eat."

Woodenly, Devin obeyed, with no word to either of them.

While she lingered over a heaped plate of eggs and potatoes, picking at the food, Sutter talked past her. "You see, Angie? Do you remember that other one coming to the table on his own? Not even once." Sutter's spoon clinked as he stirred his coffee. "Hell, that sod wouldn't eat unless you put the fork in his hand and started him making the motion. He was one brain cell above a vegetable. I didn't have much to work with, in that first specimen. You gotta admit the raw material is more promising this time."

Angelina sniffed. "All the more reason to stop before you've done harm *permanente*. The girl could live happily here. She works hard, she gives no trouble. In time, she may heal on her own—if she is not made to suffer further injury. Let her be, Miguel. *¡Por Dios!* What you are doing is no better than the things those terrible people did to her in that place over the mountains."

Sutter's face darkened. He shoved back his chair and stood, visibly angry.

"Those are the wrong words to say to me, Doña," he snapped. He grabbed his hat off the peg by the door and jammed it on his head. "What I'm trying to do is the exact opposite of what those bastards put her through."

When Sutter had left them, banging the kitchen door on his way out, Devin let her fork sink to her plate. Abandoning her eggs, she chewed slowly on a slice of bread topped with Angelina's mint-parsley-persimmon blend. Whatever its properties of *magia antigua,* the taste appealed. It was the only thing that appealed, though Angelina suggested she go back to bed.

"Rest, chica. Yesterday is best forgotten, *¿sí?* Sleep, and think of it no more."

Devin could not sleep, but for some time now, she had ceased thinking. Her mental shutdown stretched on through the day. Hours passed unnoticed. No one put her to work. Sutter did not reappear, nor send anyone to collect her. She sat on the sofa in the parlor, unmoving, a book open on her lap but unread. Conversations flowed around her as Angelina and a few helpers tended to the work of the household. Devin sat indifferent, through the lunch hour and through the long, sun-bright afternoon, devoid of emotion, empty of thought.

In the late evening, Sutter came in and found her thus. He hesitated as he passed by, as though he would speak to her. But he said nothing, only climbed the stairs and disappeared for his night's rest.

Devin stared into space a while longer, until Angelina turned down the flame in the gaslight and quietly sent her to her tower room.

* * *

The pattern repeated the next morning, with little variation other than Angelina removing most of Devin's bandages. To some of the deeper wounds, she applied fresh dressings. Then she left her patient sitting alone in the parlor again, surrounded by books but heedless of them.

Sutter came through just before lunch, and this time he stopped. He tossed his hat onto one of the faded armchairs across from Devin, and seated himself in the other.

"Friend, it appears I have miscalculated." He wiped sweat from his brow; he had not been as idle as she this morning. "You look to be in worse shape now than when I got you off that train. Then, you were the walking wounded, at least. Now you just sit and stare." He shook his head. "I don't know if you're even hearing me. I've never seen a blanker expression on any living face."

A fragment of Angelina's commanding voice reached them from upstairs, too muffled for her words to be distinct. Sutter paused, listening, until he seemed satisfied that the woman was not heading their way.

He jerked his head toward the sound. "*She* tells me I screwed up. She says I rushed you, that I should have given her 'old magic' a chance to work. She claims it was making you better. But I undid all the good when I tried to scare you into defending yourself the way any self-respecting Syke would." Sutter shrugged. "I don't know about that *bruja* stuff. The woman comes from a long line of shamans, so maybe she's onto something."

He fingered his chin, pensive for a moment. Then, sharply, he continued. "Me—I'm more the practical sort. Tomorrow, you'll be getting off that sofa and going back to work. You're not the cripple Angelina likes to pretend. She's trying to make me feel guilty." He snorted. "Anyhow, I've got a notion that we might wring the zombie out of you, yet. But if it's hopeless, at least you'll make yourself useful around here."

He stood. As he started to reach for his hat, his gaze found a shelf of books beside the paired armchairs. Sutter let the hat lie and instead pulled out a thick volume.

"This reminds me." He hefted the book. "The last time I knew you were listening to anything I said, I told you about the Sykes who saved civilization. Here's the whole story." He laid the book on the end table at Devin's right hand. "Maybe this will get your attention. I'm done with sitting here being ignored."

He scooped up his hat and then made as if to swat her with it, stopping just shy of her face. When this provoked no response, not even an eyeblink from her, he sighed and drew back. "It'll be too hot this afternoon to do much outdoors," he grumbled, sounding resigned. "Summer's well and truly here. So sit and read if you want to. Or just look blank, if that suits you. God knows, gal, you've got a talent for it." As Sutter headed for the kitchen and his midday meal, he called over his shoulder: "Enjoy your last day of loafing, friend. Come morning, you'll be sweating with the rest of us."

An hour or so after he had left her, Devin extended her hand, and moving by slow degrees, she took the book from the end table. To bring her eyes into focus upon the cover was a difficult and drawn-out exercise. But at last she managed to read and comprehend the gilt-stamped title: *Mind Over Malady—The True Story of the Psychokinetic Pioneers of Early-Day Purity and Their Triumph Over the Great Contagion.*

The book smelled of age. Its cherry-red leather covers, rubbed and worn, opened to pages that were brown-stained and spotted. The type, however, lay clear and readable. Devin found herself scanning the table of contents, her brain engaged as it had not been for the last forty-eight hours.

"Contributions of the Beskil Family of Sykes," read one chapter title.

Beskil. That was the family name of Devin's mother. Mariah Beskil Perridin came from an Old Family of Purity.

Years ago, before her mother grew afraid of Devin, she had sat her daughter down and shown her a crumbling and yellowed scrapbook. An antique, the book had wooden boards for covers, the boards painted front and back with faded scenes of people long dead, people dressed in the styles of a bygone era. The paintings showed them at their ease, picnicking on the banks of the Contagion River, or looking out over Purity from the front verandas of stately homes.

Bradded to the scrapbook's front cover, an engraved brass plate bore the title: "Notable Names and Achievements of the Honorable Lineage of Beskil." The brittle pages inside told a history going back generations. Successive owners had filled the album with certificates of birth, naming, marriage, and death; pen-and-ink portraits and locks of hair; ribbons and medals for winning at every sort of competition, from quilt making to horse racing to target shooting; children's artwork and pressed flowers; and handwritten accounts in elegant penmanship of people's lives, their loves, their losses and triumphs.

"These are your people, Devin," her mother had whispered. When she had shut and fastened the album's board covers, Mariah put the treasure away in the bottom of a chest and never showed it to Devin again. But from time to time, she would remind her daughter of it. "Take pride in your ancestors, my darling, going right back to the beginning of Purity. They started with nothing but what they had here"—Mariah tapped Devin's forehead—"and here." She put her hand over the girl's heart. "You have everything they could give you. You are just as smart and brave and talented as any of them."

Devin remembered her mother's smile. "Someday," Mariah had said, "you'll add your own pages to the Beskil family book. Whatever you do with your life, my girl, I'll be proud of you."

But then Devin had started doing things she didn't want to do, and causing trouble she didn't intend to cause. The least upset, any fleeting emotion or fit of pique, would trigger a Syke reflex. Before she knew what she'd done, something in the house would be broken.

Or worse: someone would be hurt. Guildmaster and Mistress Perridin could not keep household help. One brush with Devin's unruly impulses, and gardeners fled, cooks resigned.

To quiet the rumors, the Perridins withdrew behind the walls of the family mansion and bade no one enter. They lived in a few rooms of the big house and gave the rest to dust and spiders.

That was the state of life for Devin and her mother, anyway. The two of them were seen no more outside the walls of their home, and when people inquired after them, the Guildmaster spoke vaguely of "a nervous condition ... poor child ... must have her rest. Her mother is devoted ... won't leave the girl's side ..."

After a while, people stopped asking.

But for himself, Devin's father carved out a separate and far freer existence. From his private rooms in his own wing of the mansion, the Guildmaster came and went at odd hours while telling his wife that he did only as his duties demanded, that his official business in the guildhall and the courthouse necessitated such an arrangement.

Devin, though, had long had her doubts about her father's true motives for standing aloof from his wife and child. She suspected he hated her, and would gladly be rid of her and the trouble she caused him.

In the midst of this family disunity, Devin all but forgot the scrapbook of the celebrated Beskils. Now, she was forcibly reminded of it, holding in her hands a history of Purity's Sykes, and discovering within that history a chapter devoted to her mother's own people.

The chapter's opening paragraphs dispelled any possible doubt that the two books referred to the same Old Family. The account from Sutter's library echoed what Devin could recall from the Beskil album. Here again lived her larger-than-life ancestors, most of them sporting colorful nicknames to distinguish the generations. "Thunder Thrower" Loring Beskil was the father of "Thunderstroke" Loring. "Eagle Eyes" Nola had a daughter called "Talon." The twin offspring of "Weaver" Winfield went by "Knot" and "Lash."

In Sutter's timeworn volume, however, the story of the Beskils stretched back further than any dates Devin remembered seeing in her mother's scrapbook. This account named the Beskils as prominent members of the Syke clan who had saved the prairie folk from the Great Contagion. In these pages, Devin met the matriarch of the Beskils—a woman called "Indomitable." It was that woman who had first flung up a curtain of mental power to protect the new settlement of Purity. Her kinsmen and offspring took up the task also, bending their powers to sustain the curtain that kept the town safe for many years.

Devin read the chapter twice. Before she had worked through the pages a second time, the incapacitating blankness of the past two days had loosened its hold on her mind. She was not so empty now. She looked at her wrists, at the blue veins visible through the skin, and she saw the blood of her Syke heritage.

* * *

As Sutter had said she would be, Devin was out with the others before dawn the next day, when work began in the fields and pastures. By midmorning, the sun was not yet hot enough to drive people indoors. Even so, Devin began gradually making her way back toward

Sutter's house. No one paid attention to her as she widened the gap between herself and her work crew. They were accustomed to her existing on the edge of the community's life. Even when they included her in their groups, she was so nearly voiceless that she often stood alone in the gulf of her own silence.

Devin reached the back door unnoticed and let herself into the kitchen. Finding the room empty, she took from the open pantry a large, screw-top jar of Angelina's mint-parsley-persimmon spread. The Doña called it *mermelada*. Devin had planned to take only one thing that wasn't hers. But the sight of the mixture tempted her into this additional theft. She had developed a taste for the treat.

Upstairs in her tower bedroom, she stuffed her knapsack with her few belongings—skirt and tunic, comb, toothbrush, underwear. She changed out of the red skirt and embroidered blouse borrowed from the housemaid Raquel, and donned the green cotton pants and T-shirt she had worn upon her discharge from the asylum.

Down in the parlor, Devin hoisted the book that told of the Beskils and slipped it into her pack. The thick volume together with the big jar of marmalade weighed her down, but she was unwilling to leave either of those stolen items behind.

Shouldering her pack, she left through the front door without seeing a soul. Angelina, Raquel, Sutter, or anyone else who might heed her movements were all gone about their day's business. At the compound's main gates, the guards touched their hat brims but said nothing to her as Devin passed through. Many times they'd seen her come and go, usually with a work crew, or sometimes in Sutter's company. If they had ever known that she was a captive, an abductee, they'd forgotten. Devin never spoke to them, never complained to anyone, rarely got noticed by anyone here. Being the least obtrusive member of the community had its advantages. She simply walked out and was gone, her exit unremarked.

By the time the morning sun rose high enough for its heat to beat down oppressively, Devin had crossed the exposed strip of pasture in front of the gates. Beyond that field of grass, she entered the pine and cedar forest that shaded the mountain slopes. Under the boughs, the day was comfortably warm, the air sweet.

She ambled along, in no particular hurry. Purity, to the best of her knowledge, was a long way off. A steady pace would take her there better than a headlong rush that could not be sustained.

After a time, Devin came across a mossy streamlet. She knelt to drink, then followed the watercourse downhill to where it joined a narrow creek that sluiced through a rocky, steep-sided cleft. Warned off by its sharp descent and swift, whitewater current, Devin abandoned the creek and struck aslant through the pines.

Within an hour, her downward progress ended once again, this time at a deep ravine that cut diagonally across the mountainside. Gaping uphill and down for as far as she could see in either direction, the ravine's dry, barren walls were almost sheer. She could not climb down into the fissure, nor jump its width.

Devin found a flat spot well shaded by trees and sat down to rest, for her legs had begun to tire. Around her, the forest was still. Birds had called to her along the creek, but here by the dry ravine no songs broke the silence. Even the insects had grown quiet, lulled to indolence by the spreading warmth of what was now mid-afternoon.

She shrugged out of her knapsack and took from it the jar of marmalade. Devin meant to eat only a little; she must make it last.

For the first time, it occurred to her reawakening brain that food might be hard to come by on her journey. To those bred for the mountain life, this high country might offer much to eat, from berries to roots and wild game. But Devin's knowledge of the natural world was severely limited. Her ten-year cloister behind locked doors had not prepared her to hunt or gather her own food.

She scooped the minty mixture with her fingers. It tasted even better straight from the jar than spread on fresh-baked bread. Again and again she scooped and swallowed—giving in to an urge for the second time today. Walking out of the compound had been her first surrender to impulse. Not stopping herself from eating every bite was her second. The day was going strangely for someone whose impulsive tendencies had been drugged and tortured into supposed oblivion.

When nothing remained in the jar of Angelina's minty herbal magic, when the inside was scraped clean and the last taste licked from sticky fingers, Devin stared into the empty jar, and found that she could truly think. Her mental quickening, nourished it seemed by the marmalade, spawned a hodgepodge of ideas and options, these presenting themselves with greater clarity than any she had known since before her ordeal at the asylum. Her food was gone, but in return she had a full belly and functioning wits.

As quickly as she could backtrack, Devin returned to the creek, just above the spot where it dropped precipitously through cleft rocks. There, she filled the marmalade jar with water, screwed the top on tight, and put the container in her knapsack. With the pack shouldered again, she scrambled back uphill, angling in the direction of the long ravine that had blocked her way, but on a line this time to intersect it higher up. The ravine might be narrower at a point nearer its head, narrow enough that she could jump it.

But when she came again to the break in the mountain slope, her newly gained vantage point proved as impassable as the previous location. Devin crouched on the ravine's rim and pondered which way to turn: Upslope, opposite her desired direction of travel, in hopes of eventually finding a way across? Or downhill, to the sharp drop-off the creek could follow but she could not? Or: back the way she had come from the ranch gates, to search for an easier route? There had to be one. Sutter had followed an easily passable horse-trail up this mountain from the site of the train derailment.

None of those options appealed, however, with anything like the immediacy of the clearly visible far side of the ravine. Straight ahead across the gorge, the mountain fell away in what appeared to be a gentle slope, under pines that reached arrow-straight for the sky. All Devin needed was a way over this yawning obstacle, and her interrupted journey could resume its course.

She straightened and stepped to the nearest tree on her side of the ravine. The thick-boled specimen grew close to the edge. If felled to span the gap, it would make a serviceable bridge.

Devin had no axe or saw to wield against the tree, and too little muscle to use such tools even if she'd carried them. But with only the power of her mind, she had once blasted a hole through a solid wall of the Perridin mansion, sending bricks flying. Before the dust of that destruction was well settled, she'd been brought to her knees: rendered unconscious and loaded on the train, headed for the horrors of the asylum. Up in these empty mountains, though, who would know if she knocked down a tree? Who would care?

Devin stepped back from the brink, far enough from the tree to avoid roots that might rip to the surface as the crown toppled. She squared her stance, digging both feet into the pine-needle litter on the forest floor. She chose a patch of flaky bark a little higher than her head, locked her gaze onto the trunk there, and willed the tree to fall over.

Nothing happened. The tree did not so much as quiver.

Devin blinked, and frowned. With only the force of a thought, Sutter had levitated her body through the air and off a cliff. How was it done? As she stood staring at the tree, Devin realized she had no clue. Every burst of syketic energy ever to issue from her mind had been purely instinctive—a reflex, never a conscious choice. She did not know how to harness the power.

Who could teach her? Sutter?

But hadn't he been trying to do just that, and failing, had lashed out in a way that nearly killed her?

Devin swung the knapsack off her shoulders and rested its weight on the ground while she considered her next move. The westering sun still rode high enough to light her return to the ranch if she turned back now.

But alternately, there was adequate light to read more in the book she had taken from Sutter's library. Now might be the time to begin at the beginning, or perhaps skip to the end. The chapter on the Beskil family fell early in the thick volume, and it was the only part of the book Devin had read. In other, later chapters, maybe she'd find the secret. Maybe the author had included instructions for turning thought into action.

Devin bent to dig in her knapsack, seeking the book. But at the thudding of footsteps, she jerked her head up, and then stood straight, listening, on alert. Though muffled by the leaf mold on the forest floor, the sound of someone's approach was unmistakable on this silent mountainside.

A man appeared, walking toward her, leading his horse through the trees. He paused when Devin spotted him, and secured the reins of his horse to a drooping branch. From there he came on, unhurried, and Devin recognized him. It was Orlando, one of the riders who had taken her from the train.

"You didn't get far, did you, kid?" Orlando, drawing near, spoke with sneering amusement. "Did you think you could hide up here?" He snorted. "I don't know why Sutter wastes time on you. How are you gonna help him take over the world? You're just a spoiled, lazy, rich kid who'd rather run off to the woods than do a day's work."

Devin shook her head. "I don't mind working," she murmured, a little startled by the sound of her own voice, she'd spoken so infrequently of late. "But now, I'm going to see my mother."

Silently, she added, *There's something I have to show her.*

Devin's thoughts flitted to the book in her knapsack, but with her newfound presence of mind, she refrained from mentioning it. Orlando need not know what she had taken from Sutter's house. She resisted the urge to step in front of her knapsack, or nudge it aside with her foot, or make any move that would draw the man's attention to what she carried. She must not lose the precious old book. No one must be allowed to take it from her. It was imperative that she share with her mother the secret history of the Beskil Sykes of Purity.

How much of that history did her mother know, and how much had she deliberately kept from Devin? She had to show Mariah Beskil the book and learn the truth. The urge to do so had driven Devin into this forest and to the brink of the ravine, on foot and without supplies, with no thought for how she would get off the mountain or make her way to the distant town on the plains.

Orlando was quick to scoff at her foolishness in undertaking such an ill-thought-out quest. He threw back his head and laughed, so loudly that his horse shied where he'd tethered it. The animal danced around its tree, pulling at the reins that held it.

"That's a good one, kid," Orlando said between chuckles. "Running home to your mama! Only two things wrong with that plan. First, it's a week's hard ride on a good horse from here to Purity. You'd never make it on foot. Bears or wolves would get you, and buzzards would pick your bones clean." He gave her a wicked grin. "But even if you did make it by some miracle, they'd shoot you dead before you'd cleared the outskirts of town. You're a notorious outlaw, kid. A wanted felon and an escaped mental patient. The news is out that you crashed the train, you syked the crew and wrecked the sleeper car, and then disappeared into the mountains."

As Devin stood staring at him, shocked to hear herself blamed for instigating actions she had only observed as a limply passive witness, Orlando laughed again, and gave her a nod.

"Oh yeah, Sutter was fit to be tied when word went round. 'That girl's stole my thunder,' he said. 'They're giving her the credit for what I did.' But then he saw the beauty of it. As long as they think it was you that tore up their train, they'll figure you're just a lone lunatic who will wander up here until you starve."

The grin faded from Orlando's face, and he gave Devin a look that chilled her. "A lot of us thought Sutter was a damn fool to take you off that train," he grumbled. "We don't want the ordinaries knowing about the ranch, or getting wind of how many Sykes live up here." He looked to the southwest, in the direction of the distant town though it was unseeable past the tree-obstructed horizon. "Rumors have floated around Purity for years about Sykes holed up in caves and hollow trees. As long as they think we're just a few goons living wild, swinging through the branches like monkeys and eating grubs out of the ground, they'll leave us alone."

His gaze swung back to Devin, and she backed a step.

"But who knows," he added, "what they might do if they find out we've got fields and cattle up here, and we've built ourselves houses like civilized folk? That might be too much for them to take, since all of *them* would like to see all of *us* dead."

Devin bristled, provoked once again to unaccustomed speech.

"No, they wouldn't," she snapped. "Wouldn't all of them want us dead, I mean. My parents wouldn't." She paused to silently amend: *Or at least my* MOTHER *might not wish for my death.*

Orlando's evil grin reappeared. "Your parents? The rich Guildmaster and his blueblood wife?" The man hitched his thumbs in his belt and leaned back, shifting his weight to one leg. "I hate to be the one to tell you this, kid"—an obvious lie; Orlando was enjoying himself—"but the illustrious Perridins have disowned their criminally insane daughter. They've denounced her for the villain she is."

He paused to let his words penetrate, eyeing Devin, awaiting her reaction. When she gave him none, he went on, smug.

"As long as you were in the asylum and they were paying through the nose for your 'therapy'"—Orlando took his thumbs from his belt and raised both hands to make finger-quotes around the euphemism for *torture*—"they kept quiet. I guess they were hoping the scandal would die down while you were far away and locked up. But then you fooled your therapist into believing you were cured. You got yourself released, and you trashed the train that was taking you home."

Orlando chortled. "The whole of Purity is scared shitless. If you'd been a little less insane, a little less violent, you might have ridden the train all the way in. No one would have seen the danger coming until it was too late. That's what they're saying. The Perridins could have brought their sweet-faced little monster into the heart of the city. People are saying you would have killed hundreds before the law blew your brains out."

This imagined scenario amused Orlando mightily. He laughed in a way that spooked his horse again, and made the hairs rise on Devin's arms.

"The way I heard it," he continued, "a mob nearly went after your parents. Everybody blamed the Perridins for harboring a rabid Syke and then sending you off to the sanatorium, when they should have drowned you at birth. Just before the rocks and bottles started flying, your daddy made a big public apology for endangering the town." Orlando smirked. "Master Perridin told some cock-and-bull story about you holding your mama captive for years. He had to do what you ordered, he said, or you'd kill the woman. You had her locked behind a kind of mental barricade. To save his wife and himself, the Guildmaster had to go along, he claimed. That was the only reason he pretended to care about you. That was why he paid the asylum to 'treat' you"—again the air quotes—"and why, this past spring, you were put on the homebound train. The Perridins were helpless slaves to the will of their evil Syke child."

Again Orlando dropped his hands to his belt, resting them on the oversized buckle. "Good trick if you could do it, huh, kid?" he sneered. "I hear you packed a powerful punch, back before the psych-surgeons cut out a chunk of your mind. But even *you*"—he leaned scornfully on the word—"even you couldn't have menaced your little mama and your spineless pop all the way from Peaceful Hills. Daddy Perridin was just trying to save his own skin. Smart of him, I guess, since he's still master of the cake-and-biscuit guild or some such as that, and people have quit calling for his resignation. Or his head."

Devin listened to all of this and said nothing, though her agitated thoughts whirled. Throughout, she had looked Orlando in the eye, refusing to drop her gaze. But the heat rose in her face, and her mouth had gone unbearably dry.

Remembering her screw-top jar of water, she crouched to get at the knapsack that rested on the ground at her feet. She undid the flap and dug through her clothes and small possessions, moving the stolen book aside until her fingers closed on the jar.

As she brought up the container, Orlando took a step toward her. He no longer cupped his hands at his waistband, where they had hung from his thumbs and covered his buckle. He had the big buckle open and was jerking his belt through the loops of his denims. He whipped the belt free, and doubled it in his right hand to make a flogging strap.

"I'm going to see to it, kid, that you don't cause trouble for me or anybody else after today." He stepped closer. "You run away again, and this is what you'll get again." He snapped the strap. It made a loud *pop*. "Today I'll leave you bruised. But next time, I'll beat you bloody."

7

DEVIN CAME UP FROM her crouch, gripping the water jar. As Orlando raised the strap over his shoulder, she heaved the container at his face.

It left her hand propelled by more than physical force. The jar had the power of her will behind it. She impelled it with her mind to deliver a stunning blow to her attacker's forehead. Glass shattered with the muted ring of a cracked bell, water spurted in all directions, and Orlando went down. He landed hard, his arms splayed to the sides, the belt flying from his fingers. Blood ran from his sliced skin.

Devin did not check to see whether he still breathed. She shouldered her pack, ran to the tied horse, and mounted.

Her heart was pounding, her breath came short, and her throat felt tight. But she did not vomit, despite the surge of adrenaline. Her spontaneous mental reflex had not triggered the "transient episode of drug-induced stomach upset" that had regularly sickened her since she'd inhaled the orange gas.

Being no horsewoman, and having no idea how to find a passable trail down the mountain, Devin did nothing to guide her mount, only left the horse to its own inclination—which was, as she discovered soon enough, to return to its familiar environs. She was still in the cover of the pine forest, but nearing the treeless strip of grass before the ranch gates, when she sighted two riders approaching. Sutter led.

Devin's stomach dropped and she breathed a little harder at the sight of her rescuer-turned-threat. But she steadied when the identity of the second rider became clear. It was Jack, the attentive young man who had developed the habit of visiting her in the course of those evenings she'd spent reading on the front veranda.

"Here's a rare sight," Sutter drawled over his shoulder to Jack as they met Devin and reined up. "Orlando's horse, but no Orlando."

In a dry tone, he addressed the returning prodigal. "That fellow is mighty particular about who sits in his saddle. How'd you get Orlando's horse away from him, friend? Kill him?"

The question was asked with a smirk, but Devin, having controlled her heaving breaths, answered with businesslike gravity.

"Maybe I did kill him, Mister Sutter. I hit him hard, and he was bleeding bad when he hit the ground."

Sutter's mouth fell open. He gaped at her, uncharacteristically wordless.

Devin looked from him to Jack. Both of the riders sat frozen with astonishment, though Devin wasn't sure whether it was the content of her words that startled them, or the fact that she had spoken out with firm directness. She had answered with no hesitation or faltering, stringing her words together more fluently than either Sutter or Jack had previously known her to do.

She continued in that vein as she pointed to the forest behind her. "I left Orlando back there, after he tried to beat me. He failed in his attempt, and now I suppose somebody ought to see to him."

Sutter roused from his silence.

"Sakes alive, friend! You're *talking*. Really talking. And I do believe you're serious about what you're saying." He motioned for her to dismount. "Hand over that horse, and tell me where you left the fellow."

Devin described the mossy streamlet, the creek that tumbled away through the steep-sided cleft, and the impassable ravine some distance beyond those water features.

Sutter nodded. "Yeah, I know the place."

He turned to Jack. "Take our straying friend to the house," he ordered. "Don't let her out of your sight. Give her to the Doña and tell Angelina to watch her close until I get back."

At a trot then, Sutter rode off through the trees. He took Orlando's horse with him, leading the animal by its reins.

Devin looked up at Jack, who had sat on his horse without speaking during her exchange with Sutter. Now he swung down and stood facing her in the early evening shade of the pines that closed them in.

"What happened?" he asked quietly. "What did Orlando try to pull?"

With her voice working better than it had in more months than she could reckon, Devin did not waste the opportunity to mount her defense, in case Sutter decided to hold her to account for Orlando's injuries. She told Jack of the threatened beating, and how she had thrown the only weapon she carried: the heavy glass jar, full of water.

Devin did not mention the added power that her mental impulse had given to the jar's impact.

Jack nodded approval. "Way to go. Orlando can be a real jerk sometimes. There's not a whole lot of people who'll care if you've knocked his brains clean out. He doesn't have many." Jack indicated the return path to the ranch. "Let's start back, okay? It's generally a good idea to do what Mike Sutter says ... unless there's a real solid reason not to."

For a minute or two then, they walked in silence, side by side, Jack leading his horse. Devin used the time to shape the questions she wanted to ask him. When she'd formed them, she began.

"Before Orlando came at me, he told me ... stuff." She couldn't help relapsing into a slight hesitancy. She found Jack easier to talk to than anyone at the ranch, except for Angelina. The subject she broached now, however, she must approach tentatively, with pauses between her words. "Orlando claimed ... Well, he said I got blamed for wrecking the train from Peaceful Hills. My parents ... they disowned me after that, he said. People are pissed at them, on account of me. Where'd he get all that? ... Is it true?"

Jack slanted her a look. Then he shrugged. "Some of it's true, I guess. That's pretty much the way I heard it, but it's just a rumor going around."

He leaned to the side, and without missing a step he scooped a pine cone out of the forest litter. He rolled it in his free hand in a preoccupied sort of way.

"Maybe you've guessed that Sutter has spies in Purity," Jack went on. "They get news to us however they can, and sometimes the details get a mite muddled by the time we hear what's going on." He cast her another sidelong look. "The part about you being blamed for the train wreck is true enough, though. Sutter wasn't happy about that. He likes to think of himself as the future terror of Purity, the invincible Syke who's gonna come barreling down out of the mountains one of these days and take over the town." Jack grinned. "You'll notice, though, that for all his big ambitions he's just as happy as the rest of us to stay hidden up here on the ranch. When he'd thought it over, he decided it was okay for the ordinaries to believe you were the only dangerous Syke who might be lurking in these heights."

Devin ran a cluster of soft, young pine needles through her fingers as they cleared the last tree at the forest's edge, heading into the pasture. She looked over at Jack. "That's what I've been made to understand since I was five years old—that I'm a dangerous Syke." She shook her head. "But I've never meant to hurt anyone. Well," she amended, "not before today. I wanted to hurt Orlando ... but that was self-defense." She paused, recalling some of the damage she had done as a child. Was there any way to justify that, as well, as a form of defense?

"Don't worry about Orlando," Jack assured her, tossing his pine cone up and catching it one-handed. "You probably didn't kill him. The guy has a thick skull. But no loss, if you did."

Devin cast him a grateful look. She went on talking, stumbling over some of her words, but happy enough to be piecing words coherently together. "Even so, I can see why some people might be scared of me. Back before ... before they sent me to Peaceful Hills ... I tore up some stuff."

Jack laughed—not the reaction she had anticipated. Devin stared at him.

"Sorry." He put on a serious face. "It's just that ... people might call that an understatement, about you 'tearing up stuff.' The way I heard it, you dang near demolished the family estate. And that's a pretty big pile to tear down, they say. Your place is a mansion, isn't it?"

Devin shrugged. "It's big, I guess. I don't really know. After I turned five going on six and they decided I was ... best kept out of sight ... they never took me anywhere. The only other houses I saw were in pictures, in books."

"That's rough. You must have felt like you were in prison. Not a fun childhood, huh?"

Devin looked away. "Oh," she murmured, "it wasn't too awful, not all the time. My mother tried to make it fun."

There flashed upon her memory an image of the library in which Devin and her mom had spent hours reading and talking about books, and staging theatricals in which they would act out scenes from their favorite stories. When they tired of books, they'd head upstairs to the top-floor exercise room where, for half of each day, copious sunlight and fresh air streamed between the iron bars on the windows. They'd feed the birds that often perched on the bars, singing there and chirping. That was all of the outdoors that Devin knew—and all of it that she'd assumed she needed, until she came to the ranch.

After a moment lost in such remembrance, she turned back to her companion.

"I'd like to be as dangerous as people think I am," she declared, her words brittle.

Jack glanced at her, then gazed ahead again, along the path they were walking through the pasture. "What do you mean?"

"I'd stop people from messing with me," she snapped. "That's what I mean."

"You stopped Orlando. Dropped him in his tracks."

"I didn't stop them at Peaceful Hills," Devin retorted, growing agitated. "They had all kinds of ways to make me give in and do what they wanted. Drugs ... poison ... and the worst kind of pain. You can't imagine how bad it hurts when they kill off chunks of your mind."

Jack tossed aside the pine cone he'd been toying with. He reached for Devin's hand, surprising her into leaving off the absentminded tracing of her burn scars, which her fingers had done without her noticing.

"There's nothing wrong with your mind now," Jack murmured. "Those creeps might have shut you down for a while, but you're getting better. You're lots better today. It's like you've woken up today from a long stretch of sleepwalking."

He squeezed her hand. She hesitated only a moment, then squeezed back.

"I know most Sykes don't come out of there alive," Jack went on when Devin gave him no other response. "The things they do to people in that place ... The only way to survive, the way I hear it, is to shut down. Most Sykes can't do that. Not all the way. They keep fighting a battle they won't win."

Devin looked down at the grass that cushioned their steps, some of the blades starting to brown at their edges as summer progressed and less rain fell. When she remained silent, thrown back into memories of the torments she had endured, Jack lowered his head near hers and whispered, "You won, Devin. You *lived.* And whatever damage they did to you, you're healing now. Before long, you'll be just the way you were."

"No."

Her head snapped up, and her eyes met Jack's. All the remembered pain gave force to her words as she found her voice again. "I *won't* be the same. I don't want to be like that." She brushed her bangs out of her eyes. The hair her keepers had cropped to her scalp at the asylum had grown out. "You say I was a prisoner at home ... well, I was. But not just because my parents locked me in the house. I was a prisoner of my ..." Devin made circles with her free hand, trying to shape experiences into such words as could adequately capture them. "I was all instinct, just doing what my gut said. I reacted like a mindless machine." She snapped her fingers. "Like a mousetrap that snaps shut when any little thing touches the trigger. I never had a chance to think things through or make a choice, or make my own decisions."

She looked to Jack for understanding. "You know? I was never in control. At home, my Syke reflexes ruled me. And then at the asylum, those ... people ... made sure they were in control, every second of every day." Devin scowled. "And now, Sutter wants to control me, or use me. He's made that clear enough."

"He can't, if you don't let him."

Devin stopped dead. She yanked Jack to a halt by the hand that still held hers. The horse walking behind bumped them both and snorted.

"He *can't?*" she demanded. "Jack, you told me Sutter was the strongest Syke at the ranch. How do you expect me to stand up to him, if none of you can? He'll do anything to me that he wants. He can pick me up with a thought and throw me off a mountain. That's for sure. He's done it."

Jack's face darkened.

"Listen, Devin." He pulled her close and spoke in a low, urgent voice. "Mike Sutter is a murderer. He killed that other Syke. I'm talking about the one before you, the guy who survived the asylum like you did. No, not like you," Jack corrected himself with an impatient shake of his head. "The other Syke didn't have anything Sutter could use. The guy's mind was wiped. Those butchers left him able to walk and eat, but that was all."

Devin nodded. She knew the feeling. "Then what did Sutter want with him?"

"Sutter's spies told him the guy had been a powerful Syke, once. Mike wanted the same thing from him that he wants from you. He's set on getting a partner who's got enough up here"—Jack tapped his temple with the hand that held the reins—"to help him achieve his grand plan of wreaking destruction on Purity. Nobody from the ranch will do, you see. We're all mental deficients, as far as Sutter is concerned."

Jack broke off as he glanced toward the setting sun. "It's getting late," he murmured. "We'd best get on to the house." He took up the reins and mounted. "Come on up."

Devin accepted the hand he offered and swung up behind him. Jack turned the horse for home. By unspoken agreement, they'd made slow progress after Sutter left them alone together under the trees. On foot, they'd barely cleared the pines and entered the front pasture. It needed only a short ride now, to cover the remaining distance to the ranch's main gates.

In the brief time left to them to continue this private conversation, Devin pressed Jack for more answers. "What happened to the Syke who came before me?" She spoke into Jack's ear. "I mean, it's clear the guy had got arrested and sent to the sanatorium. But did Sutter kidnap him afterward, like he did me?"

Jack nodded. "Yeah. Sutter was convinced the guy must still have his powers. How else could he have survived the asylum? That Syke was just playing possum, Sutter thought. So he hauled the guy up the mountain, and he threw him off. 'If it's wake-up-or-die, that old boy will wake up,' Sutter said."

Devin shuddered, her thoughts flying up the mountain to where Sutter had tested her Syke reflexes in like fashion. "But that man didn't wake up in time, did he. He didn't wake up, ever."

Jack turned to speak over his shoulder, his face nearly touching Devin's. "Turns out, Sutter had it all wrong. The guy wasn't pretending. He didn't have a particle of Syke power left—no way to save himself. The poor bastard didn't even scream as he went over. He hit the rocks partway down, bounced and rolled, and fell the rest of the way. I don't know how far. We never found the body. It's too rugged down in that canyon to search for it."

* * *

Jack did as Sutter had instructed, and delivered the would-be runaway into the care of Doña Angelina. The woman greeted Devin with a tempest of words that defeated her own weak grasp of Spanish. Jack took his leave with a grim smile and a squeeze of Devin's hand.

Angelina saw them touch, but whether she commented on it was beyond Devin's knowing. The flood of Spanish continued with no discernible pause in which Angelina might draw breath.

In the kitchen, the woman fed Devin a supper that more than made up for her having had no noontime meal. Then Angelina settled with her at the table. Slowly and carefully she spoke now, as one might speak to a simpleton.

"Chica," she said, patting Devin's hand, "you must tell me. Did you take from the pantry the big *jarra de mermelada*?"

"Yes," Devin confessed, feeling only a little shamefaced about the theft. "That's the best jam I've ever tasted. I meant to make it last, but then I ate it all."

"All of it? *¿Todo?*" Angelina's eyebrows shot up.

"Are you cross with me?"

The woman clasped Devin's hand. "No, chica. I am not angry with you. But I am frightened for you. I know of no one who has taken so great a taste of *la magia antigua* all at once. It will lead you to visions. Where else it may send you, I cannot say."

Angelina studied her for a moment. Then the woman stood and began clearing the table. "Go wash, chica, and prepare for bed. I will sit with you tonight."

* * *

The visions, or whatever they were—nightmares, hallucinations—began sometime after midnight. Devin roused at intervals to find Angelina sponging her face and arms with cool, damp cloths.

Betweentimes, she drifted amidst spectacularly colorful forms that morphed into recognizable and sometimes welcome shapes, but then dissolved back into chaos and terror.

Her bedroom at home in Purity rose in her mind's eye. She saw the room's sky-blue walls covered with pictures and drawings of the city's features and landmarks, those places she was not allowed to visit—courthouse, library, guildhall. Along with those were pictures of animals she had read about but never seen: deer, elk, black bears, coyotes, mountain lions. Devin glimpsed the tiny mouse she had befriended after catching it in her room. She'd fed and tamed the creature, keeping it for a pet until it turned up dead behind a bookcase. Tears wet her closed eyes as she relived her sorrow at losing the only pet she'd ever had.

In her dream-vision, the tears spread and thinned into an orange mist, and out of the mist rose the torture chambers at Peaceful Hills. Devin retook every "diagnostic test" she'd survived at the asylum. Again she endured the beatings, the blinding lights, the burning pain from venom and flames. Her muscles cried for relief. She screamed as skin tore and nerves fried.

Then she was whisked through the colors of space and time, to land in a tree at the brink of Sutter's cliff-hugging meadow, high above the ranch. He was up there, laughing. An aura of shifting hues wrapped around him. When he took off his hat to flap its brim at her, the motion whipped the colors into a storm that overwhelmed her senses.

When Devin could take no more, he shook her out of the tree and dropped her over the edge. She fell shrieking, and there was nothing to stop her plunge toward death. Just before her body broke upon the rocks, she beheld Sutter's first victim lying shattered on the canyon floor. The man was in pieces, his flesh falling from the scattered bits of his skeleton. But still he raised his smashed skull and wagged his jawbone at her.

"Don't end up like me," the skull mouthed. *"You're a Syke from the Beskil clan. Act like one."*

Devin grabbed for something to stop her fall. The sudden movement jolted her awake. She opened her eyes to find herself clinging to Angelina. Her bed was wet with sweat.

"¡Con calma, chica!" the woman breathed into her ear. "You are safe. The visions, they are bad, I know. But you have strength of mind." Angelina stroked Devin's damp hair. "*La magia antigua* destroys some, but others it makes great. You, *muchacha especial,* the magic will not destroy."

Slowly, Devin loosed her hold on Angelina and lay back on her pillows. "Like Mike Sutter says," she whispered. "What doesn't kill me, makes me stronger."

"Exactamente," her nurse replied. The woman did not smile.

* * *

Through the rest of that night and well into the morning after, Devin slept soundly, her phantoms of the mind exhausted. She woke to the sound of rain beating upon the windows of her tower room.

Downstairs in the parlor in the early afternoon, she found Sutter standing, looking out through the lace curtains. His big-brimmed hat rested on a table. His boots were not muddy. If the rain had driven him under cover, he'd made it indoors before the heavens parted.

He turned at the sound of Devin's steps on the hardwood floor. His face broke into a grin.

"Let me take your hand, friend." Extending his own, Sutter stepped toward her. "Orlando's alive and horror-struck. You made a believer out of him, with that Syke punch you threw." Sutter's amusement carried notes of both relief and delight, audible above the noise of the rainstorm.

Devin accepted the man's offered hand, but with no enthusiasm.

He noticed.

"What's the matter, gal? I thought you'd be delirious with joy today, knowing you're not as brain-damaged as we'd all feared." He released her hand and raised both of his to hold his head in mock distress. "Or do you have a hangover from partaking of so much magic yesterday?" Sutter laughed. "Angelina says you've got a prodigious capacity for *lo sobrenatural*—'the supernatural'," he translated unnecessarily.

"I'm not hungover," Devin hedged. "But I don't know what you mean about me throwing a Syke punch."

Standing alone with Sutter in the storm-darkened parlor, knowing him for a murderer, her every reawakened instinct urged denial and evasion. She'd been conditioned since childhood to deny and hide her powers. And besides: Did she want to give him confirmation that the dormant spark inside her *had* flared to life for a brief instant yesterday? Devin's impulse was to guard that spark as she might protect a hatchling still half in its shell and struggling to emerge.

"Oh, come on." Sutter gave her a disbelieving look as he took her arm and steered her to one of the parlor's well-used armchairs. In the matching chair opposite, he seated himself.

"Orlando's got a concussion," he went on. "Nothing serious, but you did rattle his brains—in more ways than one. That jar you socked him with: Orlando claims you put a whopping big measure of Syke power behind it." Sutter's grin expressed real pleasure, not his usual sardonic humor. "I knew you had it in you, friend. I could feel it in the air around you, sorta like static electricity in a cat's fur." He nodded his satisfaction. "And now they all know it, too. Orlando's telling anyone who'll listen that you sucker-punched him hard enough to drop a bull moose."

Though inwardly pleased to know the blow she'd reflexively landed had been solid, Devin tried to look surprised and offended.

"I don't like Orlando, and I don't like him telling lies about me," she snapped. "He came at me yesterday when I was by myself. He took off his belt and said he would beat me with it. I threw that jar to stop him." She leveled her gaze at Sutter. "I've got some muscle, you know, from working around here, and I threw as hard as I could. That's all."

A frown wrinkled Sutter's brow. "Orlando claims he felt a tremor—that was his exact word, 'tremor'—when you launched that bomb at him. And he sure as hell got the shock of his life when the thing smacked him in the head. He says there's no doubt about it. That jar flew with a powerful Syke mind behind it."

Devin raised her hands in a gesture of bewilderment. "I don't know about that. All I know is it hit him hard enough to stop him, and that's what I cared about."

With a smooth, fluid motion, Sutter reached behind him, grabbed a brass bookend out of the shelves, and pitched it sidearm at her. Devin's hands closed on it without her conscious intent. The brass was heavy enough to give her a jolt as she arrested its flight.

"Good reflexes," Sutter commented. "I'm glad to see they're back. They seem to come and go." He gave her a measuring look. "Running off to the woods by yourself seems to have done you a passel of good. Your head's clearer. You're talking better—not so much hemming and hawing. But are you giving me guff?"

He fixed upon her another moment's skeptical study, then shifted his gaze from Devin's face to fasten upon the bookend. It pulled loose from her grasp and sailed back to him, carried on an invisible mental force.

She let it go without comment, and lowered her empty hands to rest on the arms of her chair.

Sutter hefted the brass weight, then stood it on his denim-clad thigh, one hand holding it upright. "Take it back from me. It's not too heavy for you. That big glass jar likely weighed as much."

Devin started to give him a baffled shrug, but decided that might be overplaying this role she'd intuitively adopted, this pretended ignorance about the power that had glimmered to life within her, yesterday under the trees. He wasn't buying it anyway, so she might as well switch to the truth.

"I don't know how to make it move like that, Mister Sutter."

"Oh, hell," he exclaimed. "Call me Mike. *Mister* Sutter was my old dad ... may he rest in peace."

Mike jiggled the bookend on his leg, a gesture of impatience, but he sounded more matter-of-fact than annoyed when he added: "I don't believe you, friend. Your reputation precedes you. I've got it on good authority, first from Purity and now from an eyewitness right here at the ranch, that you know exactly how to move objects with the power of your mind."

Devin shook her head in vigorous and now-truthful denial. "No, sir. I don't know how. It's true that I moved things around at home. Some of them were heavy—"

"Heavy as a house, I hear," Sutter interjected with a snort.

She ignored the interruption. "—But I never *chose* to do it. Everything was instinct. If anybody had asked me then *how* I did it, I couldn't have told them." She leaned slightly forward, gripping the arms of her chair. "I'm not like you, Mister—er, Mike. You've said so yourself. Persistent Sykes are only 'instincts wrapped in skin.' Isn't that how you put it? You told me the persistent type doesn't think, that we don't have any self-control."

Sutter looked at her through narrowed eyes, his skepticism unallayed.

Devin leaned back and tipped up her hands in a don't-blame-me gesture. "You're right. I have absolutely no control over my Syke reflexes, and never have. If they happen, they happen. I don't know how to *make* them happen."

Her kidnapper, still silent, jiggled the bookend again. Then he began to toss it from hand to hand.

Devin watched its motion with a growing uneasiness. The brass was heavy enough to kill, if it was thrown with that intent.

Moving deliberately, she got to her feet and crossed to Sutter's chair. At her approach, he stopped what he was doing. Devin used the pause to take the bookend from his work-roughened hands. She returned the hefty brass to its place on the shelf behind him.

"I don't know how to move things with my mind," she repeated then, standing beside his chair looking down at him. "I don't know how to make it a choice instead of a reflex. But I'd like to learn, and I think I'm ready now." Devin hesitated as the specter of Sutter's last victim brushed against her mind. But she pressed on. "Will you teach me?"

↻ 8 ↺

MICHAEL "MIGUEL" SUTTER was a talented Syke but a lousy teacher. He could demonstrate, and he did so with such enthusiasm and frequency that his training sessions scared off the other members of the ranch community. No one would come near them when Sutter was showing Devin how it was done.

Explaining how he did what he did, however, was quite beyond him. "Think about it," he'd say. "Get it in your mind, the object you want to move and where you want it to go. Then *send* it there."

His vague instructions did Devin no good. She trained her gaze on all sorts of objects—small as a flower, big as an anvil—and willed them to move. None did.

Frustrated with her failures, Sutter put her back to work around the ranch, assigning her jobs that were far beyond her physical ability to perform. He wanted her raising enormous roof trusses for barn repairs, breaking boulders to clear rocky fields, digging well-shafts in the living rock of the mountain. Such work only got done because other members of the community stepped in to do it.

Jack, especially, risked Sutter's wrath by coming to Devin's aid, and to her defense. When Mike barked at him to "leave her be," Jack growled back: "Be sensible, Sutter. A body can only do what a body can do."

Sykes, however, could push their bodies to far greater physical feats than were possible for ordinary individuals. As the days passed in a haze of summer heat and hard labor, Devin became aware that subtle displays of psychokinetic power were happening all around her, almost all of the time. When she'd first come to the ranch, she'd been too lost in a drug-induced fog to notice how the inhabitants used their syketic abilities to lighten their burdens. But now she saw that men chopped wood and stableboys forked hay, for many more hours in a day than should be humanly possible. The ranch's cooks and their assistants shouldered barrels of water that would have strained the back of the strongest ox. Carpenters floated into place the roof-rafters that Devin hadn't been able to budge.

She stood in the midst of the omnipresent Syke energy, trying to soak it up, to know it as her workmates seemed to know it: as intention rather than instinct. They made the power serve their needs. Whereas Devin, as she had confessed to Jack, had viewed herself as a prisoner of whim, able only to react, and react forcefully, often destructively. But never was she able to take the initiative.

At supper one night, nearing midsummer, when she and Angelina were alone at the table—Sutter seeing to ranch affairs that would keep him outdoors past sundown—Devin's frustration found expression.

"I hate being such a failure," she grumbled through gritted teeth, leaning back in her chair and thumping the table for emphasis. "It's not that I mind disappointing Mike Sutter. He shouldn't complain about me being a poor student when he's such a lousy teacher. But I *want* to learn. I want what everybody in this place seems to have: self-control. *Mind* control."

On the other side of the table, Angelina listened, giving Devin the impression she often had of the woman: the Doña heard more than was said. She heard the unspoken parts that fell between the words.

"Chica," she murmured, "inside yourself you have great strength. Deep within, you need not *learn* of it—you already *know* it. But there is something else inside you, like a wall that hides you from your own mind. The heaviness of that wall weighs upon you, and the weight steals your strength. It is the weight, I think, of guilt."

Guilt.

The word gave Devin a jolt both physical and mental—such a jolt that it opened a crack in the wall Angelina had sensed around Devin's subconscious mind. For so long, she'd thought of herself as a prisoner and a victim: prisoner of her impulses, and victim of a system that punished her for transgressions that were not her fault.

But *guilt?* Angelina saying it made Devin recognize it.

Yes: she'd felt guilty all her life, for being "bad," "wrong," "dangerous," "insane," and every other accusation she'd heard flung at her. From the time she was old enough to comprehend what the words meant, she'd heard herself described in such terms—words only whispered at home, supposedly out of earshot, but shouted in raw fury by a murderous mob in Purity, and then drilled into her hourly by sadistic therapists at the asylum.

She'd come to believe it of herself. Why else would she have been hidden away, never allowed out of the house? She was an appalling creature, abnormal ... sick. That's what Devin's childhood had taught her.

And pounding that lesson deep, like a thorn through her heart, was the rift between her parents. More than once she'd heard them fight over her, and there was nothing of love in her father's attitude toward her. Devin had held herself responsible for the breakdown of the family, and accepted as deserved the Guildmaster's rejection.

But the book she'd taken from Sutter's library, the old book with its pages of praise for the Beskil family: those pages had opened a window through which she could see herself favorably. The Sykes at the ranch also presented her with a fairer picture, although in Purity—and in the Guildmaster's household—every member of this hard-working and productive Syke community would be condemned in the same terms she'd heard applied to herself.

And none of it would be deserved: neither the cruel accusations, nor the condemnation that saw Sykes dying by firing squad or tortured in a pit of horrors.

The realization burst upon Devin like a thunderclap. Where Angelina's words had opened a crack in her mental wall, there now came an explosion. Her deep-seated self-loathing blew out through that exploded crack, shattering into motes that had no substance, disappearing into the ether. The wall fell so completely and Devin's mind opened so wide, the crushing burden of her guilt tumbled out and away, leaving no trace of itself behind.

Never again would she permit anyone to make her feel guilty for being as Nature had made her. Psychokinetic ability was her birthright. She could trace her ancestry back to the preeminent Syke clan. Flooding into Devin's newly-opened mind came her vision, or hallucination, from that night after she'd run off to the woods and eaten a huge helping of "old magic." She heard again the words of the broken man Mike Sutter had thrown off the mountain:

"You're a Syke of the Beskils. Act like one."

In Angelina's kitchen, Devin raised her head from the table. She found she'd been resting her brow on it, and Angelina's cool fingers rubbed the back of her neck.

"How is it with you, chica?" The woman looked worried when Devin met her gaze. "What has happened? Do you not feel well?"

"I feel ... free. Released."

She breathed her declaration in little more than a whisper, for the cracking-open of her mind had left her dizzied. But not so much that she couldn't push back her chair and stand facing the woman—this dispenser of wise truths and magic-infused marmalade.

Devin wrapped her arms around Angelina. "Thank you," was all she could add to the hug before taking herself upstairs for a bath, and to bed. She drifted into sleep feeling weightless as dandelion fluff.

* * *

Before sundown the next day, every inhabitant of the ranch knew that something seismic had shifted within Mike Sutter's newest "victim."

Devin made no announcement, no mention that a wall had fallen, a mental key had turned, or a locked-away place had opened to her.

She only set to work, wordlessly exploring the powers within that place and shaping them to serve her intentions. In the rocky field that was slowly being cleared of plowshare-busting stones, she levitated a dozen boulders out of the ground. With only a raised finger or two to help her focus the power of her will, she sent each enormous rock to find its place in the stone wall that was going up around a nearby corral. Devin smiled as she found herself doing exactly what Sutter had told her to do: wrap her mind—her opened, unburdened mind—around the thing she wanted to move, and then send it where she wanted it to go.

Her smile felt strange—stranger than levitating boulders; strange to use that particular set of facial muscles. Devin hadn't had occasion to smile in a long time. But now she delighted in mental gymnastics that proved surprisingly straightforward, requiring no special understanding of the "how" of psychokinesis or the forces involved. Her mind's ability to move objects was innate—it coiled there like a spring ready to release. But to access that ability at will, and *control* its release, Devin had required what Angelina's wisdom had bestowed: gut-deep, guilt-free, joyful acceptance that she was gifted, not "psycho."

By the time she had moved on from the rocky field, to work with the carpenters who were reroofing the old barn, Sutter had joined the crowd of onlookers. Devin pretended not to notice him as she raised the last two rafters into place, mindfully maneuvering the heavy beams with precise, delicate thought-control—surprising even herself, with how naturally these skills came to her now. It was as if Devin channeled her illustrious ancestress, the Syke called Indomitable, who had raised a curtain of mental power to protect Purity from the Great Contagion.

Though Sutter might have wondered at the overnight blossoming of Devin's abilities, he wasted no words on questions. He only grinned, watched, and waited for the day to draw to a close. Then he put her to his own peculiar test, much as Devin's keepers at the asylum had subjected her to their brand of diagnostic testing.

"Duck!" he yelled as she made her way toward the old house, where Angelina would have the evening meal waiting for them.

In the same instant that Devin heard Sutter's shout, a whooshing sound made her look around. A knife-edged piece of metal was spinning through the air toward her, threatening her decapitation. She had just enough time to recognize the blade as the broken shard of a plow that had not survived its labors in the stone field.

Then the blade was spinning away from her, slapped aside by her instinctive mental swipe. But to her horror, it now whirled directly at Jack, who had come up a little ways behind her on the garden path she was taking to the house.

With an audible gasp, as loud as a shout in the softly encroaching evening, Devin made another mental swipe, catching the metal mere inches from Jack's face. His hands had come up, and Devin's projected power crackled as it brushed against Jack's own syketic response. Hers was far the stronger, however, and the metal rode upon the force of her thought, straight back at Sutter.

Mike stood off to the side, half hidden behind a trellis in the garden in back of the house. He was laughing so hard, he had to brace on the frame to keep from bending double. His laughter continued, even as he slapped the broken metal out of the air. The piece of a plowshare buried deep in the garden's loose soil.

"Shit!" Devin swore hotly. "What the hell was that?" She hurried to check on Jack. "Are you cut?" she asked as she reached him, back along the path.

He shook his head. "Thanks to you, I didn't lose my head." He managed a crooked grin. "Came close to it, though."

"Too close."

Devin whirled, unbridled anger replacing shock as she stalked back through the garden. Sutter had moved from his concealing trellis. He stood now with a boot planted on the back porch steps. His riotous laughter had quieted, but he still chuckled.

"That was an ambush!" she flared at him. "A cowardly thing to do. What the hell is wrong with you?"

The grin vanished from Sutter's face, to be replaced by a fierce scowl.

"Cowardly?" he spat. "Watch your language, gal. That's the wrong thing to say to me."

He swung down from the porch and took a long, menacing step toward her.

Devin's reaction was not within her control. All this day, she had moved through her labors with studied deliberation, reveling in her newfound mastery of mental powers that she could formerly unleash only by unthinking instinct. Sutter's attack with the broken blade, however, had provoked a purely instinctive response—there had not been time for thought or conscious choice.

His advance toward her now triggered a similar reflex. Devin threw up her hands, a spontaneous gesture to ward off a threat, but it was her mind that raised her real defense. Between herself and Sutter's oncoming fury, she hung a curtain of syketic force, invisible but as hard as steel.

In the grip of his anger, Sutter did not stop himself in time. He collided with her steely curtain. It staggered him back a step, so that he tripped on the porch stairs and sat down, hard.

Behind Devin, Jack let out a whoop of laughter. Sutter's scowl shifted from her to the young man who was finding humor in a situation that bordered on the deadly. Devin could not share Jack's amusement, for she'd seen the dangerous glint in Sutter's eyes. One could laugh *with* Mike Sutter, but to laugh *at* him was to invite retaliation tenfold.

"I'm—"

She started to apologize, but the words stuck in Devin's throat. She'd apologized too many times during her years of carrying an unwarranted load of guilt about being exceptional in a world that demanded mindless conformity. But the look in Sutter's eyes, as he glowered at the still-snickering Jack, forced the words past her dry lips.

"I'm sorry, Mister Sutter," Devin murmured. "You startled me, and my instincts kicked in." She tried to smile, to exercise again the muscles she seldom used. "Like you said, I'm just a skinful of instinct. I didn't mean to trip you up."

Her expression of contrition brought Sutter's gaze whipping back to her.

"Don't apologize, ever," he growled. "I've got no use for a panty-waist."

Sutter climbed to his feet, wincing a little from his hard landing on the unyielding porch steps. He yanked the back door open and stomped into the house. Barely had that door banged shut, before the slamming of the front entrance echoed nearly as loud. Sutter had tramped straight through the kitchen and the parlor, exiting out the front and disappearing into the gathering gloom of evening.

"Pissed, isn't he," commented Jack from directly behind Devin. She whirled, to find that he had stepped closer along the garden path. "I shouldn't have laughed," he admitted, "but it was so damned funny, seeing him bounce off and land on his butt." Devin couldn't see much in the growing darkness, but she could make out Jack's wide grin. "Just what is it that he bounced off of, I'd like to know. Whatever you did, are you still doing it?"

Devin realized, with a small start, that she had indeed kept up her inflexible mental curtain, needing no more effort to sustain it than to raise it. She nodded. But conscious that Jack couldn't see her any better than she saw him, she said, "Yeah, it's still here. It's an idea I got from a book. A kind of screen, sort of like a storm shutter on a window, except it goes all the way around."

"May I touch it? —Oh, geez, that came out wrong." Jack's laugh carried notes of embarrassment this time. "Sorry. I didn't mean that the way it sounded. I'm just real curious to know what Sutter ran into, that had the power to knock him on his keister. Maybe I'm not the most sensitive guy around, but I can feel Syke energy when it crackles in the air like electricity. I'd like to know more, if you don't mind me getting close."

"I don't mind," Devin murmured, her voice softer than she'd intended.

Jack's boots crunched on the path's rough gravel as he made a cautious approach. He came so near, Devin could hear him breathing, and she gasped when his fingertips encountered the thought-curtain she had raised around her body. Sparks flew from the point of contact. Flashes of light like miniature lightning bolts, dazzling in the dark night, illuminated his fingers and outlined Devin's form in ethereal radiance.

Jack uttered a sound part whoop, part "Wow!" In the light from the sparks, Devin could see him stiffen, but he did not pull away. With the fingers of his right hand, he stroked the curtain, while his left palm made exploratory circles upon the barrier's smooth, hard surface.

From books she'd read, Devin knew the word "ecstasy," but until this moment she had not grasped the word's meaning. The sensations rising in her body, from Jack's probing of her inflexible shell, were defining, exquisite, and quite unbearable. With a half-swallowed scream, she dropped the defensive curtain.

And then she was in his arms, and they were kissing. Devin had never kissed anyone on the lips before—this was a new sensation to add to all of those she had just experienced. They stood together in the kitchen garden, their bodies pressed close, their kisses greedy and urgent—until the back door opened.

Angelina called into the night, where darkness had again descended with the dismissal of Devin's radiant curtain.

"Supper, chica." The woman managed to sound stern, and at the same time, amused. "Come inside. Eat. Allow the young man to go to his own meal. Hunger *es tormento*, no?"

☙ 9 ❧

DEVIN SLEPT POORLY, and the morning revealed she had backslid in her quest for perfect control of her mind-actions. As she did her assigned work around the ranch, she struggled to focus or execute her intentions. Her grip on her syketic powers was less sure than it had been yesterday, leading to near accidents. A boulder she lifted from the rocky field crashed down short of the retaining wall that was its intended resting place. A water drum meant for the washhouse slipped from her control and went barreling downhill, almost flattening the two men who stood guard at the front gate.

Sutter observed none of this. At least, Devin didn't think he had seen her fumbles. The man was nowhere around. Devin had not caught sight of him since last night, when, fuming, he'd stalked away from her and straight out his front door, disappearing into the darkness. She suspected he was deliberately avoiding her.

As were others around the ranch. Various odd behaviors surfaced among Devin's fellow Sykes and workmates. Some of them ducked around corners, making themselves scarce when she stepped their way. Some found reasons to head for the farthest reaches of the ranch compound, even if their typical chores awaited nearby. Those who couldn't dodge in time, but met Devin in passing, seemed reluctant to make eye contact. Men who had previously ignored her, when Devin walked among them as a barely functioning zombie, now tipped their hats to her, but in a decidedly nervous way.

Only Jack defied the general mood of reserve that gripped the community—Jack, plus one other. A woman Devin barely knew rode up to her, leaned from the saddle, and issued a crisp directive.

"Get yourself together, girlie," ordered the woman, Estelle, a hard-bitten figure of middle years who had a face like tanned leather and could out-ride and out-rope most other cowpunchers at the ranch. "You're a stumblebum today. But when you get your feet under you again, like you had 'em yesterday, you'll do us all a favor if you'll take Sutter down another peg or two. It needs doing. And from what I done saw, there ain't nobody else here can do it."

Before Devin could do more than gape at her, Estelle had reined her horse around and headed off at a long lope, leaving a puzzled stumblebum in her wake.

* * *

"It was quite strange," Devin told Jack. She'd wolfed down her noontime meal and gone looking for him in the stable, the place he most often could be found. "And Estelle's not the only one who's being weird around me today. What gives? Why would she be coming to me about Sutter?" Devin gave Jack a slight frown. "Did you tell anybody what happened with him last night? Sutter's already mad enough, without everybody here knowing he landed on his ass."

Jack put down a can of saddle soap and spread his hands, signaling innocence. "I haven't said a word. But it's hard to keep a secret around here. People see things, and since there's not a lot else to do, they gossip. Tales get told, and sometimes they grow with the telling."

"So you think somebody saw the whole thing? Estelle, maybe?"

Jack shrugged. "The way Sutter was laughing like a maniac, people were bound to peek out of the shadows to see what he was going on about."

"Shit." Never in her life had Devin had the habit of swearing, but since coming to the ranch she'd found herself doing it, and needing to do it, increasingly often. "So now everybody knows he ran up against me and fell down. Is that why people are giving me a wide berth? They think I'm gonna knock them over?"

"That's probably part of it," Jack conceded. "Truth be told, they're avoiding me, too, so I haven't heard a lot of the whispering. But I know folks are rattled. Anybody who was watching last night saw a whole bunch of stuff that wasn't exactly peaceable. Sutter throwing a hunk of iron at you ... you knocking it away like it was made of paper, and then tossing it right back at him. And if they were close enough, they heard you call him a coward. They'd count that a bold move ... kind of insane, in fact."

Devin snorted. "I came from the insane asylum. What do people expect, for pity's sake?" She was moved to sarcasm to hear that her fellow Sykes were pinning the same label on her that the ordinaries would hang on the Sykes. But her thoughts moved swiftly back to the events of last night, which apparently had altered her relationship with every person residing within the compound. "They'd have seen Sutter come at me, and seen him go down," she muttered. "And if they were still watching after he stormed off through the house, banging all the doors in a white fury ... then they saw you and me ... kissing."

Jack draped his arm across the top rail of the horse stall behind him, a gesture of studied nonchalance.

"Before *that* part, they would have seen you light things up with your sparky curtain, remember. I'll wager that's a vision no Syke has witnessed in living memory." He paused as a smile tugged at the corners of his lips. "I can guarantee you, too, that nobody here has ever before seen me lock lips with a girl, either. That was a new and novel spectacle for all who saw us. Some of the guys here, they make nuisances of themselves, pestering the girls." He shook his head. "That's not me. I'm not a hound dog." He paused, his expression sobering as he added, "I apologize if I was ... out of line last night."

"You weren't!" Devin exclaimed.

Before the last syllable was out, she wanted to kick herself. She'd sounded much too eager—pathetically eager. The heat rose in her face. But on she jabbered, unable to stop herself.

"If we're talking about things nobody's ever seen before ... well, I can add to the list. That was the first time I ever kissed anybody. I've only read about kissing in books." Devin hoped the dimness in the stable hid the redness of her face: she was blushing furiously. Not knowing what else to say to Jack about an experience that had kept her awake all last night, reliving it in her thoughts, feeling it again in her skin, she found herself blurting without the least feminine subtlety: "I liked it. I didn't know what I was doing, so I hope I didn't disappoint you. But if you liked it, too, I'd be glad for you to kiss me again."

Jack started to reach for her, but he stopped himself.

"There's nothing about you that's disappointing, Devin," he murmured. "And I'd like nothing better than to kiss you again. But Angelina chewed my ear off this morning. I guess she must have been watching from the kitchen. She reminded me how young you are. You're just a kid ... though I think you've got an old soul." He inclined his head, and smiled ruefully. "Regardless, I've been ordered to keep my hands off you."

"Doña Angelina needs to mind her own business," Devin flared, stung to be called a "kid" by someone who was only three or four years older than she was. And besides: Nobody who endured the tortures of the insane asylum could emerge with the innocence of youth still clinging to them. That snake pit made old souls of everyone who survived its horrors.

Jack smiled again, still a bit crookedly. "There's not much that happens around here that Angelina doesn't know about. Sutter throws his weight around, trying to intimidate everybody with his mighty powers of the mind. But it's really Angelina who runs this place. I don't know her story—she seems to have always been here. She keeps her Syke powers pretty much under wraps, but there's something else about her, too—something mysterious."

"It's magic," Devin declared. "*La magia antigua.*"

Jack raised an eyebrow. "I've heard her use that phrase. Don't know what it means, really, but I respect that she's got it. I believe she's worked a good bit of it on you."

"I'm sure of it. Most of what Sutter has done to me, trying to undo the Peaceful Hills 'therapy'—his approach has mostly made things worse." Devin frowned as she recalled the stupor that had enveloped her after Sutter threw her off the mountain. "But the *mermelada* that Angelina has fed me has done a world of good."

She told of gorging on a huge jar of the stuff during her brief flight into the forest below the ranch. Devin described the nightmares—or visions—that her overindulgence had brought on, and how everything had changed for her after that. She'd found her way back into her right mind, just as Jack had urged.

"I'm not surprised," he said when she'd related this, "that Angelina's magic marmalade works better than Sutter's ruthlessness. What's that old saying? You'll catch more flies with honey than with lye caustic." He drummed his fingers absently on the horse-stall rail. "But don't go mistaking Angelina's kind heart for any sort of weakness. There's another old saying that fits: She's an iron fist in a kidskin glove."

"Then you plan to obey her," Devin said, pouting a little, unable to conceal a certain disappointment, "when she tells you to stop kissing me."

Jack grinned. "I'll obey her—for now. It's what a gentleman would do. And I fancy myself a gentleman." He straightened from his lean against the railing and tipped his hat to her. "But if you'd like, my noble lady, I can be your devoted knight. Like in those old fairy tales."

"Courtly love." Devin caught the allusion instantly, but just as quickly regretted her choice of words. They'd held hands, and they'd kissed—once. That was not a basis for making—or expecting—any declaration of "love."

But Jack seemed to read nothing suggestive in what she'd said. He chuckled. "I see that you and I have read some of the same silly old books, my lady. If memory serves, they decree that the noblewoman must give a token to her knight-errant, as a symbol of the lady's favor. It's customarily a lace handkerchief, or maybe a scarf. Whatcha got?"

This last was delivered in the same tone of voice that a poker player might use when challenging his opponent to lay down his cards. Devin had to laugh.

"I fear I'm fresh out of lace handkerchiefs, Sir Knight," she deadpanned then. "But will you accept this small adornment?" She slipped off her hairband, which she had taken to wearing again as her hair grew out from its near-shearing at the sanatorium.

"With pleasure. In turn, my lady, I pledge to you my service and my sacred honor."

Jack doffed his hat and drew on Devin's gift, tugging the stretchy fabric over his brow as a sweatband. Bending low then, he swept his hat out to the side in an elaborate flourish as he bowed to Devin, looking all the world like a medieval courtier wearing leather and denim.

She came close to giggling, but controlled herself. Matching his pantomime, she dropped a curtsy, though her awkward bob came nowhere near the gracefulness of Jack's bow.

As he came up, Jack crammed his hat back on his head, using both hands, pulling it down over the sweatband. And Devin had to grab a nearby post to keep her balance as she straightened from her clumsy curtsy. They both dissolved into laughter.

Maybe there wouldn't be any more kissing for a while now, but they could flirt. Flirtation, after all, was the whole point of courtly love, as Devin understood the rules of a game she had never played, but was itchingly eager to learn.

* * *

Late on the following afternoon, a rockslide on the mountain above the compound drew every eye to the faint line of the trail that Sutter had marched Devin up, that day when he'd led her high on the slope and dropped her over the edge. When the rockslide stopped short of the ranch perimeter, the inhabitants went on with their end-of-day activities, shrugging it off as if rocks falling from on high were a common-enough occurrence at this ranch that clung to a mountainside.

Devin wondered, however, if Sutter might be up there chucking boulders around, venting his anger where no one would see him. It would be a good thing, she decided, if he spent his fury upon the rocks before he reappeared amongst people who might have seen him knocked on his backside and humbled by the reemerging strength of his protégée.

And reappear, Sutter did, at breakfast the following morning. Devin got the impression that he had been at the table for some considerable time, nursing a cup of coffee while waiting for her to make her way into the kitchen. She was not late—this was her usual breakfast hour. But on most mornings, Sutter would have already eaten and been out the door before Devin reached the table. Whatever else might be said of the man, he kept long hours.

He greeted her courteously enough, but somewhat absently, and seemed to forget she was there while he turned to small talk with Angelina. Sutter praised the woman's cooking ... commented on the beauty of the summer morning ... exclaimed over a songbird that serenaded them from a tree in the garden. In short, he made himself uncharacteristically pleasant and agreeable.

Devin caught Angelina's eye and raised an eyebrow, asking a silent question: *"What's got into him?"* The woman gave a slight smile and an even slighter shrug. But those were enough to say that Sutter's odd behavior had not escaped Angelina's notice, either.

If "Miguel" had wanted to give the impression that he was utterly unconcerned with any aspect of Devin's existence, he failed, for he was on his feet the instant she had put her fork down, swallowed the last of her tomato juice, and given her mouth a final wipe with her linen napkin. He'd obviously been paying attention, even while pretending he wasn't.

"You ready to work, friend?" He looked down at her with an expression far more benevolent—and false—than his usual mocking grin. "The day's not getting any younger."

Though unsure what game he was playing, Devin played along. She pushed back from the table and stood with him, nodding her readiness to begin the day's chores. "That rocky patch in the far field is nearly cleared. Just need to move a few more boulders, and it'll be all set for planting with some kind of late-summer crop. Buckwheat, maybe."

"Listen to you!" Sutter laughed. "The town girl is sounding like an old-timey farmer."

Devin managed to smile at him as they left the kitchen together and walked out through the back garden. "I'm learning every day. I've learned all sorts of things from the people you've got working here. It's a good crew."

"Some of the best," Sutter agreed. "But with a few of the worst mixed in. It's incumbent upon me, I've found, to keep a close eye on both types."

At this, Sutter gave her the side-eye, making Devin wonder which category he had placed her in. She got a clue when he stopped, well beyond Angelina's earshot, and put a hard hand on Devin's arm. She resisted the urge to shake it off, but he must have felt her stiffen, for his fingers dug in tighter.

"Listen, friend," he snapped, all trace gone of his earlier affability. A dark scowl had replaced his grin. "If you ever pull another stunt like you did the other night, suckering me with your sorry imitation of a syked-up wall, I'll kill you." He pulled her close, breathing the threat into Devin's face. "Hear me good, gal, 'cause I won't repeat this. Nobody makes a fool of Mike Sutter and lives to do it again."

Devin did not try to pull away. She met Sutter's gaze without flinching … though in the back of her mind, the vision-ghost of the man Sutter had murdered spoke to her as it had before. *"Don't end up like me,"* the dead man warned.

I'm not aiming to, she silently promised the ghost, and then slung a question at Sutter.

"You'd kill your partner?" she demanded, almost spitting on the plosive letter with which the word began. "When you didn't let me fall to my death up there"—with her free hand, Devin pointed at the slope above them—"I thought you must want me alive to help you make war on the ordinaries down there." She swung her arm the other way, pointing in the direction of far-off Purity. "Have your plans changed, Mike?"

That was the right thing to say. Sutter released her.

He did not step back, but Devin, needing more space between them, allowed herself one long rearward stride. She moved with composed deliberation, never taking her eyes from his.

"My plans haven't changed, not one bit," he retorted. "But I think maybe the schedule just got moved up." Sutter tilted his head and gave Devin a half squint, as if to better see her. "Whatcha say? Let's you and me ride up the mountain and engage in a little Syke practice. You can show me more of what you've got—it all came on sudden-like, didn't it?—and we'll see if you're really partner material."

"Be glad to." Devin kept up the bravado. "I'm sure that buckwheat field can wait one more day."

She was relieved when, minutes later, she reached the stable a few steps ahead of Sutter, to find Jack not there. Her gallant knight would not approve of Sutter returning Devin to the mountain ledge he'd previously thrown her off of. But Devin had accepted this showdown with Sutter as a thing that must happen between them. She had known it was inevitable, in fact, from the moment the man's ass hit the steps of his own back porch. Sutter's wounded pride required salving.

All Devin needed to do was survive. Winning a contest of wills against Sutter would not be in her best interest. But neither would showing weakness.

"I've got no use for a pantywaist," he'd warned.

ଓ 10 ଚ

"START SLOW, OKAY?" Devin raised one hand in a warding-off gesture as she faced Sutter on his chosen battlefield. "Remember I'm still finding my feet."

"Sure thing." Mike's grin—or grimace—nearly split his face. His expression had something of a snarl about it, and within seconds he abandoned any pretext of going easy on her.

He opened their face-off with a game of dodgeball, played with rocks, and played at high speed. Devin was forced to find her mental footing from the first pitch. Sweat trickled down her back, but she successfully syked aside every rock Sutter flung at her, and she managed to hurl several back in his direction, though none struck him.

An observer, had there been a witness to this mind-over-matter competition, would have seen the two opponents off their horses after their ride up the mountain. Both now stood perilously close to the cliff edge that dropped sheer to the canyon below. Such an observer would have clapped hands over ears at the clatter of rocks that rained down upon the meadow and ricocheted over the edge, sending up echoes as the stones rattled downward. The volleys continued fast and furious, filling the air so thickly that the players of this game were barely visible, each of them hardly moving, for there was no point in using their hands. This was not a game of the physical. Every rock was propelled by thought alone.

"Enough!" Sutter eventually shouted. He raised his arms in a gesture that Devin might have interpreted as surrender, except she knew he was far from admitting defeat. Rocks ceased to fly. Each stone tumbled to the earth and dug in where it landed, turning the previously grassy meadow into a churned-up expanse of ruined earth. Sutter looked around at the mess, and shrugged. "This will need reseeding when we're done here. But we're not done."

He allowed a brief break, during which Devin gulped water from her canteen, and Sutter drank tepid coffee from a battered thermos. She watched him, mindful that the man favored surprise attacks. He had ambushed her in the garden behind his house, and before that, he'd thrown her off this very mountainside when she'd been too deep in an instinct-killing numbness to know what was happening.

Her vigilance paid off. With Sutter half turned from her, his attention seemingly on the thermos he was recapping, he sent out a thought so strong, Devin felt it quiver through the air. At the same instant, an enormous *crack* sounded on the bluff above the meadow, a great noise of splintering and rending. She looked up to see a towering pine toppling toward her.

Her response was pure mental reflex, harking back to her natural pattern of instinctive reaction with no thought behind it. Devin sent the huge tree spinning sideways on the heavily wooded slope. It left a swath of denuded mountainside before it finally came to rest, wedged in a stand of pines and cedars even larger than it was.

Sutter's gaze followed the tree's destructive path, his eyes huge, his expression slack-jawed. If he uttered an outcry, the sound of it was lost in the tremendous noise of timbers splitting and crashing. But he had a hand at his mouth as if to stifle a shout, or perhaps an oath or a gasp.

Reveling in this unleashing of her powers, Devin added a self-satisfied flourish. The tree-spinning had been sheer instinct, but her next move was by choice. To demonstrate to both Sutter and herself that she had control over her abilities, she caused the wedged tree to split into uniformly sized logs all along its great length. Further responding to Devin's mental commands, those split logs stacked themselves into neat cords of firewood.

She laughed aloud. Was this not proof that no trace of the Peaceful Hills poison lingered in her blood? Nor did a toxic load of undeserved guilt weigh upon her mind. Devin's glee rang through the hush that had descended upon the mountainside in the wake of her "lumberjacking."

Sutter heard, and he seemed to think she had laughed at him. He whirled toward her, his look as dark as a thundering sky. Savagely, he brought his hand down in a slashing motion.

Devin's instincts answered once more. She wrapped herself in the same steel-hard curtain that had repelled his aggression on that night in the garden. As Sutter's syketic energy collided with the power of her own, sparks flew from the surface of Devin's enveloping curtain. But nothing penetrated it to harm her.

She could not be sure what manner of attack Sutter had intended, whether he'd meant to slap, punch, or stab her, or perhaps obliterate her from the face of the earth. Regardless, the intensity of his attack was sufficient to raise Devin bodily from the ground. Still wrapped in her protective shell, she went sailing off the meadow's edge.

Whether by luck or by Syke instinct, she didn't fall far past the brink of the jutting stone shelf that the meadow blanketed. Devin landed with a lurch in the arms of a gnarled pine growing outward from the sheer cliff-face below the rim. The twisted maze of bare trunk and crooked limbs extended almost horizontally from the rock-face, some fifteen feet below the brink of the precipice.

Devin's hard mental shell had remained intact during her flight into the branches, sparing her skin from the abrasions she had sustained when Sutter had first thrown her over the edge, slinging her high, that time, into a tree that grew above, instead of below, the rim. She steadied herself now and waited quietly, shaken, but trusting in her shell-like bubble. Devin studied the cliff edge above, watching to see if Sutter would appear, or in any way continue the attack.

When half an hour had passed with no sight or sound of him, and no quiver in the air to suggest any bolt of syketic energy heading her way, Devin began to consider what she must do to escape her predicament. Her bubble was cozy enough, and she suspected it would armor her against anything short of a direct lightning strike. But she could not remain within it forever. Not only had she no food or water, she might possibly run out of air. Many of the properties of the "Beskil bubble," as she was coming to think of her protective mantle, were as yet unknown to her.

Experimentally, she willed the mantle to draw back, a few inches at a time. As it gradually dropped away, she secured hand- and footholds in the bristly tree that had broken her fall. Surveying the almost vertical rockface above her, Devin entertained the briefest urge to turn the power of her mind upon the rock, to rearrange the rough wall into a climbable staircase of stone. But barely had she imagined a set of steps leading upward, when a chunk of rock broke loose from the sheer surface and clattered down, striking at the roots that kept the wind-twisted pine clinging oh-so-precariously to the cliffside.

"Not that!" Devin exclaimed. She shook her head to banish the fleeting impulse before it stuck in her mind and reduced the entire cliff-face to rubble, crashing down into the canyon and taking her tree with it. "Impulses are great until they're not," she reminded herself, speaking aloud to the air around and below her.

There wasn't much else below her, only a few knobby branches. Devin had a dizzying view of the canyon floor far below, and it came to her that the bones of Sutter's victim were scattered down there somewhere.

"I thank you for your advice," Devin muttered, casting a vertiginous glance downward, just long enough to direct her gratitude to the ghost, or vision, or whatever it had been that had told her to embrace her Syke heritage. "But now I'm going to follow a little advice of my own, something I'm coming to appreciate more every day. Impulses, at the right time, can save a Syke's neck. But on many occasions, it's way better to act with conscious intent, and curb one's unthinking instincts."

Having so admonished herself, she returned to studying the bare rockface above her, quelling all poorly thought-out urges in favor of calm consideration. Sutter, though he was by no means an exemplary teacher, had shown her that the power of thought could weave a safety net that was strong enough to catch a falling body. The first time he'd dropped her over this edge, he'd caught her in a web that he'd syked into existence. On that occasion, Devin had been too lost in physical pain, mental fog, and drug-induced indifference to perceive the properties of the web that had saved her from a skull-shattering fall. But now she wondered: Could she mold a Beskil bubble into a netlike structure that would stretch from her pine-tree perch and catch secure upon the rim above?

She approached the task as a thought-experiment, imagining a stiff meshwork with crosspieces like the rungs of a ladder. Mentally, she tied the bottom rung to the tree trunk where she crouched, then stretched the top of the mesh upward, adding rungs until the conjured structure snagged on the edge of the stone ledge overhead.

Though the framework was perfectly clear in her mind, Devin's eyes detected nothing—nothing, that is, until she placed her foot upon the first invisible rung and gripped the structure. Sparks flickered everywhere she touched the thought-projected ladder, bright even in the noontime sun of this summer's day. Devin's hands and feet struck sparks just as Jack's fingers had done when he'd caressed the hard shell of her bubble, that night they'd kissed.

At the memory, a shiver of pleasure tingled along Devin's spine. But she forced her concentration back to the task at hand. It wouldn't do to let her attention falter when she was suspended in midair, feeling her way through empty space, climbing rungs made of brainwork and syketic energy.

The ladder held. Devin reached the top and clambered over the brink, gaining the flat expanse of the meadow on her hands and knees. She shot to her feet at once, on guard against any new attack that might greet her rearrival on what had recently been a battlefield.

But Sutter was not lying in wait for her. Wiping the sweat from her forehead, Devin walked to where they had left their horses, in the shade of the mountain flank that soared above the meadow. Both animals were gone, and every piece of gear had gone with them except for Devin's canteen. It was on the ground, near a rock that Sutter had thrown at her during the morning's "Syke practice."

Devin drank thirstily, then sat in the shade to ponder her next move. The only way down from the meadow—short of going over the edge—was to follow the trail back to the ranch. She had little hope that she could reach and then pass through the compound without being seen by Sutter or one of his people.

But why even try to avoid him? If he'd really wanted her dead, he could have continued the attack after he'd dropped her into a tree that barely kept enough of a roothold to support itself in midair, much less her. With one malicious thought, Sutter could have made the rockface give way, knocking her sanctuary loose, sending the gnarled tree—and her—tumbling into the canyon below.

He had not done that. He'd simply left her alone to extricate herself as best she could, and he'd cared enough about her survival to not deprive her of water, should she prove capable of reaching the small store he'd left for her. If indeed he *had* left the canteen on purpose, and the bottle hadn't simply fallen unnoticed from Devin's saddle when he led her horse away.

"In any case, I guess I passed," she muttered into the shadows of her resting spot, hefting the partly filled canteen as she gave Sutter the benefit of the doubt. "I'm still alive, so I guess I passed that lunatic's test for partnership."

Lunatic was not a word she would use lightly. The pejorative had been applied to her too often at Peaceful Hills for it to easily slip from her own tongue. But Devin was increasingly convinced that Sutter was half off his head, the way he swung from fostering to then menacing his protégée, and back again in a split minute, with dizzying unpredictability.

Protégée, however, was not the right word. To Sutter, Devin was a tool. He'd brought her to the ranch for one reason: He wanted revenge on Purity, and he wanted her to help him get it. Devin had picked up enough from stray and overheard comments to know what he was about: He meant to storm the town, make it pay for how he'd been treated there, been forced in his youth to hide who he was, and long ago exiled as a fugitive from its rough brand of justice.

"Will I willingly ride at his side when he goes to seek his revenge?"

Devin spoke the question aloud, for airing her thoughts helped her to order them, and it felt like a conversation with her newly discovered forebears. Each time she had conjured a Beskil bubble, she'd felt herself filled with the spirit of the matriarch, Indomitable.

She considered: Once already, she had tried to go down the mountain and find her way to Purity, to confront her mother with a family history that should have been celebrated, not hidden. Acting on a whim then, she had not been fit for such a quest.

But now?

"Yes." Devin answered the question she'd thrown into the air, and her answer was emphatic. She *would* return to Purity at Sutter's side, for she had her own scores to settle there. Let Mike have his revenge on all in the town who had wronged him. Devin would ride beside him, her head high, flaunting her powers as a Syke; for she had passed the test he'd set her this day, proving she had the strength and the control to be the tool of vengeance he wanted. For her part, she would require only that Sutter leave Guildmaster and Mistress Perridin to Devin's dispensation. Those two must be made to account for what they'd done to their daughter: consigning her to the mind-killing tortures of the asylum, and then renouncing her, declaring her an insane criminal.

There was, however, another reckoning that must be made first: the Peaceful Hills Sanatorium and Rehabilitation Center for the Treatment of Persistent Mental Disorders. That place must be annihilated, razed to the ground. Sutter had made a start when he'd wrecked the train that carried hapless victims from Purity up the switchbacks into that hellhole. Now Devin would make him *her* partner in a campaign of destruction against the asylum. He'd likely not need much persuading to take on that nest of vipers as their first target. The report he'd read, of the treatment Devin endured there, had set him frothing.

The sun, passing its zenith, was well along its downward arc by the time Devin slung the canteen's strap over her shoulder and began the long descent of the trail to the ranch compound. She'd made it down about a third of the way when she heard a horseman approaching. It was Jack, riding up toward her.

"Devin!" he called. "You all right? What did Sutter pull this time?"

As Jack reined up and dismounted, his face full of concern, Devin hurried to reassure him.

"I'm okay." She took her knight's free hand in both of hers. "Sutter was, um, impressed, the way I defended myself the other night. He wanted to see more of what I can do now."

Jack snorted. "He wanted to win a pissing contest, more like, and prove he's still king of the mountain. You rattled him that night." Jack squeezed Devin's hand as he studied her face. "Did he rough you up?"

She shook her head. "Not much. He tried. But I've got my feet under me now, and I'm holding my own against him." Devin shrugged. "Which doesn't mean we're pals. I've got my doubts, really, that the man is completely sane."

"He's a crazy twisted devil." The vehemence of Jack's reply brought a flush to his face. "You'll have to watch your back," he warned as he shortened his hold on the reins in his other hand, bringing his horse up, preliminary to him remounting. "No one here has ever stood up to Sutter before. There may be no end to the payback he'll want."

Devin edged away from the horse, tugging at the hand of Jack's that she still held. "Don't ride. Let's both walk." She tilted her head, indicating the downward trail.

Jack grinned. "Your knight wasn't planning to leave you afoot, my lady. My trusty charger can carry us both, easy."

Devin acknowledged his gallantry with a smile and another hand-squeeze, but she still didn't let Jack put his foot in the stirrup. "That's an offer I'd gladly accept, Sir Knight, if I was in any hurry to get back to the ranch. But I'm not. There's something I've been wondering about, and I'd rather us talk here"—she gestured at the silent pinewoods around them—"where there aren't ears to overhear."

Jack nodded assent, and together they started down, the horse ambling along behind them.

"What's on your mind?" he asked.

"Public opinion, I guess you might say. I'm bothered about the people down there"—Devin nodded in the direction of the compound, the main buildings of which were hidden by a sloping curve in the trail—"all those people who were obviously avoiding me after the blowup in Sutter's backyard, when he came at me that night."

"And got knocked on his ass for his trouble," Jack interjected, smiling. "Yeah, I remember you said folks were keeping their distance afterward."

"But you said the same." Devin looked at him as they walked side by side. "About yourself, I mean. You told me people had been dodging you, too." She chewed her bottom lip. "Is that on account of me? Have I put you in a tight spot?"

Jack shook his head. "Nah. No more than usual. Truth be told," he added, "most everybody here is in a tight spot. All of us are caught between a town that would kill us for having powers, and a murderer who has killed at least one Syke for not having *enough* power." Jack sucked his teeth, conveying angry disgust. "People at the ranch are just trying to survive. They keep their heads down and don't cause trouble. But now they've seen you—Sutter's new recruit—give the boss a heap of trouble." The smile returned to Jack's face. He practically beamed at her.

"They heard you laugh about it, too," Devin muttered, her attitude serious in the face of Jack's amusement. "They've ostracized you as a troublemaker, along with me. Is that it?"

"'Ostracized!'" Jack's grin widened. "That's a big word for a little leeriness. Leery ... yeah, that's what they are. People are looking to see how the land lies. They don't know whose side I'm on."

"Side? What do you mean? Every Syke has got to be on the side of our own people, right?"

With Devin holding his right hand, and the reins grasped in his left, Jack's capacity for gesturing was limited. But his horse followed close at his shoulder, putting enough slack in the reins that he could bring up that hand to scratch his ear.

"If war breaks out between you and Sutter—you being the only one here who *can* challenge him," Jack replied as a thoughtful frown replaced his grin, "people don't know if I'll throw in with Mike or with you. I've always gotten along fine with Sutter. He doesn't hassle me much, and I seem to be on his short list when he wants a rider or two with him."

Devin nodded, recalling Jack's presence at her rescue—or kidnapping—from the prison train, and again when Sutter found her in the forest after her confrontation with Orlando.

"You've confused them," she surmised. "People thought you were tight with Sutter."

"And now they've seen me gettin' comfortable with you." The smile had returned to Jack's lips, and it was touched with a hint of a secret warmth that made Devin's heart flutter.

"So will everybody just wait to see which side of the fence you come down on, and then maybe follow suit?" she asked, trying to ignore the heart-tickling flutter and deal instead with her startlement at Jack's suggestion of impending warfare between herself and Sutter. Though perhaps she should not be surprised that some such rumor was floating around the ranch. Estelle, after all, had deliberately sought her out to suggest she "take Sutter down" a peg.

Jack stopped walking, and pulled Devin to a halt beside him. Turning to face her, he released the hand he held so he could grip her shoulder.

"If you are planning a war, my lady," he murmured, his voice as soft as if he feared being overheard on the deserted trail, "don't count on the folks at the ranch joining the fight. Most will try to stay out of it. Doesn't matter what *I* do. Everyone is too scared of Sutter to turn on him. Even with all you've seen from him, you haven't seen a fraction of what he can do—and has done—to people."

"But you've really got the wrong end of the stick!" Devin exclaimed, deciding it was past time to put Jack straight—and through him, every rumormonger he could reach. "Haven't you heard? I'm Sutter's partner. If there's going to be a war, he'll be the one bringing it. And now that I've passed his test, by not falling to my death up there"—Devin pointed back up the trail, in the direction of the sheer drop-off—"he'll have me riding into battle with him, not against him.

"But that's not all, Jack," she added, privately wondering how the ranch folks' aversion to conflict might affect her and Sutter's intended vengeance against, first, Peaceful Hills, and then Purity. Bringing her hand to her shoulder, she covered Jack's fingers with her own, and a note of insistence crept into her voice as she asked: "Don't you suppose he'll want you and every other ranch Syke to join his fight against the ordinaries? Staying out of it might not be an option for anybody here."

"Yeah," Jack muttered after a brief pause in which he looked to the southwest, in the general direction of Purity. "I guess I always knew I'd have to make a choice someday. If Sutter ever found his partner, that is."

When Jack turned back to Devin, his gaze was clouded. But he tried to renew his smile as he gathered his reins and put a foot in the stirrup.

"Let's ride, my lady. These boots are no good for walking."

☙ 11 ❧

JACK PULLED HER UP behind him on his horse, and Devin locked her arms around his waist as they rode down the mountain. Their descent was the crowning part of a day that, overall, had been exceptionally satisfying. Devin was still thinking about his sweaty back, and how her body had felt, pressed up against it, when she climbed the steps of the back porch and entered Angelina's kitchen, arriving back at the main house in the late afternoon.

The Doña exclaimed over her, exhibiting a marked degree of consternation, but Devin barely paused to offer the woman vague reassurances. It was only when she ascended to her bedroom and caught sight of herself in a mirror that she understood what had excited Angelina's fluster. The "Syke practice" Sutter had put her through that morning had left Devin beyond disheveled. Her hair was a rat's nest, her face and arms were streaked with dirt, and her sweat-stained clothes looked to be unsalvageable. Jack was a gentleman indeed, to have mentioned none of this when he found her on the mountain trail. Devin had been so pumped up to find her Syke powers equal to Sutter's test, she had imagined that the whole experience had left her unruffled. The image reflected in the full-length mirror told a truer story.

It was bad enough that Jack had seen her like this. But Devin would be damned, she silently swore, if she'd give Sutter the satisfaction of beholding her so bedraggled. She set to work, and more than an hour later, came down to the evening meal washed, brushed, and as close to starched as she could manage with the few toiletries and amenities available to her.

She found Sutter waiting in the parlor. From Angelina, he had undoubtedly heard that the "protégée" he'd thrown off the cliff had survived, and was now under his roof once more. Sutter's attitude of studied indifference telegraphed that he was eager to see her, even while he pretended otherwise.

"How was your day, friend?" he asked, oily-voiced and smirking, when Devin was down the stairs and turning toward the kitchen.

She would have ignored him, but for her plan to wheedle Sutter into joining with her to attack the asylum first—while letting him think it was all his idea. Thus, Devin paused, and even managed a small smile as she replied: "Eventful." Her smile gained sincerity when she added, "And successful."

He tipped his hat and gave her a nod of acknowledgment that bordered on respect. Saying no other word about what had happened up on the ledge-meadow, he escorted her to supper and held her chair as she sat. He made small talk over the meal, and Devin contributed a few innocuous comments while Angelina looked from one to the other, frowning at each of them in turn. But the woman asked no questions.

When the table was cleared, Devin followed Sutter out into the back garden and into a dim, rapidly cooling evening. As she'd expected, the man lost no time in pressing ahead with his scheme for revenge.

"A week," he said, propping one booted foot on a stone that marked the corner of the vegetable plot. "It won't take longer than that, I reckon, to round up the horses, pack supplies, and get lined out on the trail to Purity." He leveled his gaze at Devin, seeming still to challenge her. "Whaddya say, partner? You ready to help me teach that place a hard lesson?"

Devin rested one hand on a tall wooden stake that anchored a bean trellis. She dug the toe of her boot into the soft earth, pretending to ponder. In truth, she had planned her words hours ago, up in the rock-strewn meadow when she'd decided her course.

"Um," she faltered, feigning a hesitancy she did not feel. "Will it just be you and me? I mean, I'll back you all the way, Mike, but maybe we could use some extra help. How many from the ranch were you planning to take?"

Sutter stared at her, and laughed.

"All of them!" He grinned in his devil-may-care way. "Did I forget to mention that part? You and me, gal, will ride at the head of an army of Sykes. Purity won't know what's hit 'em."

Devin continued to press her boot-toe into the dirt. This was the potentially delicate part, when she had to convince Sutter to direct the initial attack elsewhere, while ensuring that he perceived no threat to his ego.

"When I was a kid," she said, still not meeting the man's gaze for fear he'd detect her lying, "they made me memorize poetry and famous speeches. Boring stuff. My parents stood me up on a chair and made me recite from memory, letter-perfect. To guarantee no mistakes, I had to rehearse first. I had to practice."

She looked up now, trusting to the deepening twilight to veil her gaze. There hadn't been a grain of truth in what she'd just said, but it laid the groundwork for the perfectly rational argument that came next. Devin hurried to make her case; Sutter was showing signs of impatience.

"For something as big as an assault on Purity," she said, regarding him earnestly, "I'd be afraid of mistakes if I don't practice. What would you think about Peaceful Hills as a first rehearsal, Mike? It's smaller than Purity, and closer, and it's a more immediate threat to us. Isn't it? I don't remember much from my first days after you rescued me, but I remember telling you about the orange gas they used on me. And I recall you saying that every Syke here could be in danger if that poison reached us on the wind."

It was almost completely dark now, but the stillness that had settled over Sutter was enough to tell Devin she had captured his full attention. Softly at first, the man began to chuckle. The chuckle erupted into a full-throated, rather maniacal laugh.

"I like the way you think, friend," Sutter exclaimed when his guffaws subsided sufficiently that he could speak. "Looks like I've got myself a fine partner. You throw timber around like it's kindling, and when you're not gone in a brain-fog you make good sense. The butcher shop it is! And from there, we're on to Purity. We'll ride out in a week."

* * *

Everyone at the ranch was given to understand that the war plan was entirely Sutter's. Devin said nothing to the contrary, not even to Jack. She did not want the troops speculating about who was really in charge. Let them go on obeying Sutter, as was the habit of almost every Syke at the ranch. To get her way, Devin need not disrupt the established order of things.

Sutter drafted the entire population to help with outfitting his army. But as he oversaw the preparations, he had to concede that some of his people must stay behind. At least a quarter of the ranch residents were too old or too young to be useful in a fight.

Exemptions also went to those who had spent decades building houses and barns, fences and corrals. Driven by a desire to keep what they had made, they argued that the ranch must maintain a garrison of able-bodied and strong-minded Sykes for protection. The homebodies—as Devin dubbed them—got their way through flattery, hinting it was Sutter alone who had defended the place all these years, and his prolonged absence would leave the ranch vulnerable to everything from wildfires to cattle-killing wolves.

Sutter listened, nodded sagely, and agreed to discharge the builders from his mounted army. He told them their battle would be on the home front, and warned that he had better not return to find the place in ashes.

Thus it was that fewer than half of the residents rode out through the gates on the morning of the army's departure. Devin found herself on the same horse she had ridden like a mindless sack of potatoes during her rescue from the prison train. Much practice at the ranch had improved her riding skills. Her status was also higher now. She rode close behind Sutter, and occasionally brought her horse up beside his when the forest opened out sufficiently to permit two riders abreast.

This state of affairs was not lost on Orlando. That fellow also had a spot in the vanguard, but he had been demoted to fourth place. Coming third, behind Devin, was Jack. Devin took care to show her knight no special regard or favor, for fear of making him a target of Orlando's spite. That fellow had not forgotten or forgiven Devin for clocking him with a heavy glass jar. He shot her many looks of resentment, but was at pains that Sutter did not see.

They followed no discernible trail, for the ranch residents had been assiduous through the years about covering their tracks whenever they ventured into the forest, maintaining their mountain compound's secrecy and seclusion. Devin did her best, however, to memorize their route along the high ridges and rocky shoulders that Sutter guided them up and over. It was terrain chosen to reveal little sign of the riders' passing, and for the most part they journeyed in silence, picking their way single-file through shadowed stands of towering pines and occasional stretches of treeless, sun-blasted scree.

The army had neared the end of its second day of travel before Devin found an opportunity to speak privately with Jack, even as closely as he rode behind her. Their position in the vanguard placed them under the eye of both Sutter and Orlando, and those men watched like hawks when the riders took a breather or made camp. Devin had been surprised, at first, that Sutter had included Jack among the lead riders. The young man had surely earned his elder's enmity, laughing as he had when Devin's Beskil bubble landed Sutter on his backside.

It's a case, I imagine, Devin silently surmised, *of keeping friends close, but enemies closer.*

Whichever of those categories Sutter placed her in—she was thoroughly unconvinced by his trick of calling her "friend"—the man couldn't reasonably object when Devin announced, at their second nightly camp, that she was going to find Angelina, back amongst the ranks.

"I didn't know she had come with us," Devin said as she dug into a saddlebag for her day's ration of dry bread and pemmican. "But this afternoon along that high ridge we crossed, the way it swept up and around that long bend, I could see the whole army stretching out behind us. And there was Angelina, riding at the very end." Devin put her hand on her stomach, and grimaced. "I need some of her special marmalade. This stuff"—she wrinkled her nose at the oily pemmican—"is making me queasy again."

"Shit," Sutter swore, though Devin wasn't sure what he meant by it. Was he concerned about her possible relapse into a disabling, drug-induced nausea? Or was he vexed that Angelina had joined the expedition? Devin had had the impression, back at the ranch, that the woman would stay behind and take no part in the attack on the asylum.

She did not question Sutter's displeasure, only dropped the pemmican back into her sack of rations, and wiped her greasy hands on her trousers. Without a by-your-leave, she turned to head off in the direction she had seen the woman.

"It's getting on toward dusk," Sutter growled at Devin's back. "You oughtn't go wandering around this mountainside in the dark, especially if you're bilious." He sighed, a sound of deep annoyance. "Take Jack with you. And when you find Angelina, tell the Doña I'd like a word with her, at her earliest convenience. Tonight, like."

"All right," was Devin's only reply. She did not look around, and she spared no glance for Jack as he shouldered his own saddlebag and followed her out into the twilight. They wended their way through a camp that was surprisingly orderly, given that the "troops" had little or no military training and had been allotted only one week to prepare for this expedition. It seemed, however, that the members of Sutter's army were inclined to do in the mountain forests what they'd done at the ranch: wranglers took care of horses, woodchoppers fed campfires, cooks cooked, bedrolls were laid out under the trees instead of in bunkhouses.

Despite the neatness of the arrangements, Devin did not immediately locate Angelina in the stretched-out encampment that wound below the ridgetops. Nor did she wish to end her search too quickly. The gathering darkness, and the hum of conversation from the groups around the cooking fires, provided cover as she led Jack out of sight and beyond anyone's hearing.

"Orlando is—" *giving me the creeps,* Devin started to say, needing to voice her resentment of the fellow who had stared holes in her back over the past two days. She'd barely got his name out, though, before Jack seized her arm with a suddenness that made her break off and gape at him.

"Are you all right?" he demanded, his tone low and anxious. "Are you feeling sick to your stomach?"

"What?" Devin had a moment's confusion until she remembered. "Oh. That." She shook her head and smiled. "My stomach is fine. I don't have that problem anymore. It was just an excuse to go looking for Angelina, to get away from Sutter and Orlando for a while. And maybe grab a chance to talk to you. Have you noticed how they're watching us?"

Jack nodded, relaxing his grip on her arm. "I'm surprised Sutter let you wander off on your own. And sent me to keep an eye on you."

"Well, he couldn't exactly have Orlando follow me in the dark. If that guy saw a chance to push me off a cliff, I believe he'd take it." Devin's chuckle was short and mirthless.

"Orlando would have to go through me to do it," Jack vowed. "But won't Sutter fret now, that you and me together might steal a couple of horses and ride on out of here. Make good our escape."

"Huh?"

For a moment, Devin could offer no other response to this proposal that had come out of the blue. Was he serious? Jack had never before suggested they run off together ... had not even come close to proposing such a venture.

For the space of three breaths—the first of them sharply indrawn—she turned the idea over in her mind ... and found it held great appeal. But to desert Sutter and this expedition would mean abandoning her own quest for revenge, and that was not something she could do.

"I ... don't know ... don't know about that, Jack," she half stammered, finally managing to overcome her surprise enough to answer him. "Taking off, I mean. Where in the world could we go? There's only the ranch, or Purity, or Peaceful Hills."

She laid her hand on Jack's where he continued to hold her arm. His touch was light now, but she felt a quiver of tension in it. Driven to defend her prior silence about her own plans—her failure to admit, before now, that she had inspired Sutter's current goal and rode willingly with him—Devin hurried to add: "I guess I never got a chance, before we left the ranch yesterday, to tell you that attacking Peaceful Hills was my idea. Sutter wanted to lead his avenging army straight to Purity." Devin shook her head. "Too ambitious, right? For a straggle of untested troops, the asylum is a better first target. More isolated ... fewer people. But really, Jack, there's nowhere else *I* personally can go, until I see that hellhole obliterated."

She was rushing to explain, to have him understand why she had not leapt at the offer he had seemingly made her, to spirit her away from the coming conflict. Her voice dropped to a whisper, barely audible above the sighing of the breeze in the pine trees. "*Evil* doesn't begin to describe what they do to Sykes at Peaceful Hills. You can't imagine what goes on in that chamber of horrors, because it's worse than anybody's worst nightmare. I want it destroyed, Jack. And I want to be the one who does it, the one who makes sure those devils never hurt another Syke, never ever, for as long as the world lives on."

Jack's grip on her arm had gradually retightened, and now he pulled her to him. Only when she was within his embrace did Devin realize she was shaking. Not from cold, although the night air was chill on the mountainside. She shook from rage, and from remembered fear ... and above all, from a gut-deep determination to raze the asylum to the ground.

The two of them remained like that for some moments, their arms around each other, saying nothing. But then a movement in the trees made them pull apart. It was only one of the troops, a man come out in the dark to relieve himself. His presence bestirred them, however. They started back toward the encampment, pausing briefly before they reentered the light of its many fires.

"I won't follow Sutter to death and destruction," Jack murmured into Devin's ear. "But anywhere *you* lead, my lady, I will go."

Then they were walking among their fellows in Sutter's army of Sykes, and there could be no more whispering or hand-holding.

☙ 12 ❧

"MIGUEL WILL NOT SEE me this evening," said Angelina, when Devin and Jack had found her at the far end of the encampment and delivered Sutter's message. The woman was spreading her blankets on a cushion of pine needles, ready to turn in. "I have ridden far today, and now I wish to rest. You"—she pointed at Jack—"may tell Señor Sutter that I will speak with him in the morning, if he cares to come to my fire. You"—Angelina swiveled briskly to point in turn at Devin—"shall stay here with me. It is not right that a young woman sleep unguarded in the company of unmarried men."

Devin felt herself redden, but trusted that the flickering light of Angelina's campfire hid the rush of blood to her face. She started to reply that she'd already spent one night of this journey wrapped in her blankets near the snoring forms of the three men of the vanguard. She could say with absolute certainty that two of the three had zero interest in her—not in the way that Angelina was suggesting, anyhow. As for attracting that kind of attention from the third ...

Devin took care to not glance in Jack's direction as she accepted the clean wool blanket that Angelina handed her.

"I'll be glad to stay here," she said, opting for the simplest and most innocent response she could make. "It's hard to sleep with those fellows sawing logs all night."

Out of the corner of her eye, she saw Jack smile as he turned away, to commence retracing his steps to the head of the encampment. He swerved to brush past Angelina's shoulder, close enough to mutter something to her. Devin couldn't be certain, but it sounded a lot like, *"She's never unguarded, now."*

* * *

As surprised as Devin had been to spot Angelina riding at the rear of the army, she was even more startled when awakened at first light by the aroma of fresh-made bread. The rations carried by every rider included a bag of hardtack. The dry and tasteless sustenance was made with basic ingredients—flour, water, salt—and would last for years, keeping a body alive, if not satisfied. But the bread that Angelina fried in an oiled pan was yeast-risen and fluffy. Devin was barely out of her blanket before she was biting into a golden-brown puff, its crust delightfully crisp, with insides soft and flaky.

"How in the world?" she exclaimed upon seeing the barrels of flour, yeast, and cooking oil that had appeared, as if by magic, at this end of the encampment. People were coming and going from the barrels, dipping up what they needed for themselves, and passing extra portions up the line. At one campfire after another, as far as

Devin could see in the predawn light, cooks turned out small mountains of skillet-fried bread. The air was redolent with the mouthwatering aroma.

"You need *mermelada* with that, chica." Angelina paid Devin's question no mind as she handed her a large jar of the mint-parsley-persimmon spread. "Nothing better for breakfast, *¿sí?*"

"Mmm." Devin offered only that response as she slathered marmalade on another crispy puff—her third—and practically inhaled it. She had thought, last night, that she was lying about her stomach, using her past troubles with nausea to get clear of Sutter for a while. But as she stuffed herself with bread-and-spread, her belly seemed to relax, like a deep knot untying itself. Whatever magic this was, she needed and wanted it.

The thought brought her back to the question of the barrels. How had Angelina got them here? They were too large for packhorses to carry, and no wagon could have traversed the mountain's slopes and ridges, following the convoluted route the army was taking. As Devin pondered the problem, she could reach only one conclusion: Angelina had syked them here. According to Jack, the woman seldom displayed her syketic powers at the ranch, and no one seemed to really know the extent of her abilities.

Did the "no one" include Sutter? As Devin wolfed down yet another marmalade-topped bread-puff, she wondered if the man who claimed the title of strongest Syke at the ranch might, in fact, be deluding himself.

When she'd eaten all she could hold, Devin took a pan of warm water under the cover of the trees to attend, in private, to a needed washup. She scrubbed marmalade stickiness from her hands and face, rinsed trail dust from the rest of her, and returned to Angelina's fire to find Orlando crouched there. The fellow had one fried puff between his teeth, and was filling a sack with a dozen more.

"Mike wants you, pronto," he growled at Devin, speaking with his mouth full. "At the front. Don't keep him waiting." Orlando straightened from his crouch, flung the bread sack over one shoulder, and stalked off, elbowing people aside as he strode toward the head of the army that, with the sun now risen, was breaking camp.

"Idiota estúpido," Angelina muttered, perfectly echoing the thought that had come to Devin's mind.

* * *

While Devin had begun her day well-fed and content, Sutter started out grumpy. He scowled as she rejoined his vanguard, but he said nothing to her, only helped himself to the bread from Orlando's bag. He still had one puff clenched in his teeth when he swung into the saddle to lead his army onward.

Whereas he had taken a route that had kept the riders high in the mountains for two days, on this third, by late afternoon, they were noticeably dropping. The pines thinned, the forest opened out, and they picked their way down dry gullies that were half choked with brush. As the sun dropped low in the west, the riders tethered their horses in a copse of scrubby trees and made camp where the terrain was relatively flat. The area was large and open enough that the army could gather in a rough circle instead of stringing out lengthways along narrow ridges.

The more compact arrangement made it possible for Sutter to step across the circle and seek out Angelina, without him having to pass through the entire army and lose face—as he would have done had it been more obvious to the gathered company that *he* was going to *her,* instead of her coming to him as he had ordered the night before. Leaving Devin and Jack at the fire that Orlando tended, Sutter joined Angelina where she'd settled nearby—with none of her barrels in evidence, this time. Though the woman was again frying bread in an iron skillet, she was making only enough, this evening, for herself and a few fortunate guests.

Sutter was among that number, Devin saw as she glanced over, surreptitiously, and saw the man accept the crusty brown puff that Angelina offered him. They were too far away for Devin to hear what they said, but she could not miss the scowl on Sutter's face as he squatted at the Doña's fire. Angelina, by contrast, was her usual composed, dignified self. The woman went about preparing supper with unhurried efficiency, appearing to speak little as she arranged bread and marmalade on a trencher, while letting Sutter go on talking at some length.

Eventually, the man threw up his hands, bolted to his feet, and stalked across the circle, to rejoin the chosen riders of his vanguard. One of those riders—Devin—he summarily dismissed.

"Angelina wants you," he snapped. "She seems to think you need special care and feeding." He snorted, his scowl having never left his face. "I guess maybe you do, seeing what that woman's *bruja* stuff has done to wake you up from the poison and all-else they did to you." At the word *they,* Sutter gestured vaguely beyond the circle of troops, out in the general direction that Devin took to be "down" from the raised terrain where they were camped. "Just be sure you're ready, friend. Be wide awake tomorrow, and ready to wreak havoc. I expect we'll arrive in sight of Peaceful Hills by midday."

"We're that close?"

Devin's stomach clenched, and for an instant she forgot she was returning to that hellhole to take her revenge, not to endure more "therapy."

Sutter nodded. "You'll be at my side when we attack that butcher shop, and I'll expect fireworks from you."

Devin smiled, and her stomach relaxed. "You'll have them, Mike."

* * *

As the sun rose on the new day and Devin left Angelina's fire to rejoin the vanguard, to begin the final push toward their objective, she plied Sutter with the questions she'd never thought to ask before. How was the asylum situated? How should they approach it? Did armed guards patrol on foot or keep watch from high towers? During her time at Peaceful Hills, Devin's tormentors had kept her so closely confined and heavily drugged, she never saw or knew anything of the facility beyond her cell, except for the torture chambers and testing rooms.

Sutter proved unable, however, to shed much light on the setting or circumstances of their target. He had reconnoitered the place only once before, riding to it alone years ago, back when he'd first devised his scheme of rescuing—kidnapping—an imprisoned Syke, in hopes of that person possessing the mental strength he wanted in a partner.

At the time of his first reconnaissance, Sutter had concluded that stopping the transport train would be easier than breaking into a facility that, from the outside, appeared to be little more than a concrete box.

"You'll see what I mean, when we get over this next hill." Sutter gestured ahead to a rise that grew more rocks than trees.

They were still below the crest of that rise when he reined up. He signaled to those who followed, indicating that the main force should wait. Only the vanguard advanced to the hilltop, and there the foursome paused again, to survey the bleak scene that spread before them.

The hill sloped downward to a wide depression in the earth, a depression shaped like a huge bowl with uneven sides of bare, chalky rock. Directly across from the riders, the bowl's opposite rim rose much higher, forming a nearly vertical cliff. A railway track entered the bowl off to their right, where the rim was lowest. The track traversed the sand-floored depression, to disappear in a tunnel that had been cleanly bored into the base of the towering cliff opposite. Near the tunnel's mouth, pressing right up against the foot of the cliff, a concrete building squatted.

The structure was, as Sutter had said, a nearly featureless box. From the hilltop where she sat on her horse, eyeing the lifeless prospect below her, Devin could see no windows in the building, and only the vaguest hint of what might be a door. The concrete was uniformly gray, as was the face of the cliff overshadowing the building. Equally colorless were the inner walls and floor of the chalky-white dustbowl that held the structure and its attendant rail track.

Those were the rails Devin had ridden, twice. The prison train had carried her from Purity and entered the tunnel on those dusty tracks, but she'd been unconscious upon her arrival and never saw this desolate outpost of misery. Then, when they put her on the return train, she'd been so poisoned by mind-altering drugs, though technically "awake" she had heeded nothing and known nothing of her surroundings.

"Peaceful Hills!" Devin spat after a long moment of silent study of the place, a powerful disgust rising in her breast. "Peaceful like a graveyard. This is the land of the dead." She gestured at the barren landscape. "There's not a blade of grass or even a shriveled cactus down there."

"It's an old mine," Sutter said. "That'd be my guess. They strip-mined this gap a long time ago. Back before the Contagion, somebody must have been out here digging this big pit in the ground."

"How poetic," Devin snarled, her voice dripping sarcasm. "Where they used to ruin the earth, now they ruin minds."

She sat for another moment, rubbing the burn scars on her arm as she glared at the godforsaken desolation. Then Devin was digging her heels into her horse's flanks. Down from the hilltop she streaked, whooping like one of the ancient warriors who had peopled this land before her own forebears arrived in the mountain-and-plains country. Before Sutter could do anything to stop her, she was off the slope and arrowing for the concrete box, her horse at a gallop, Diego's hooves throwing up gritty clouds of white as she crossed the pit's dusty bottom.

The wind in her ears prevented her hearing what Sutter and his army might be doing behind her, but Devin assumed they would follow. It was immaterial, anyway. With or without the support of other Sykes, she meant to reduce this place to rubble. She'd grind it into the same white powder that coated everything here, most noticeably the railroad tracks, which she found herself racing alongside as she approached the building. To judge by the accumulated dust, no train had run upon those rails recently. Which meant that Peaceful Hills had neither received nor discharged any new victims.

Only belatedly, as she reined Diego to a sliding stop in front of the tunnel, did Devin think to look for armed guards. There was no fence or wall around the concrete building, and no guard towers nor any obvious sign of a security detail. Devin spared a quick glance upward, looking for a possible sniper on the roof of the boxy building. When she saw no movement there, she swept her gaze down and across the structure, seeking the door that had appeared, from a distance, as an indistinctly scribed line in the concrete.

There. She saw it—a wide doorway set flush with the exterior wall. Devin didn't bother with a handle or a doorknob. There appeared to be nothing of the sort set into the concrete, only a chunk of brass affixed to the wall, gridded with a dozen small buttons. The buttons went flying as Devin bent the power of her mind upon the incised line that marked the doorway's edge. With no more than a wish—an intention—she flung the thick slab of concrete back upon its unseen hinges. The door clanged open with such violence, it cracked the wall behind it and broke the thick support jambs, leaving the door to sag askew beside a prison entrance it would never again seal shut.

"Hold up!" came Sutter's yell from behind her.

Devin turned to see him riding toward her at the head of his entire army. On either side of him rode Jack and Orlando. Jack's lips were set in a grim line, and Orlando scowled. But Sutter practically foamed at the mouth.

"Wait!" he bellowed again.

Devin did not wait. She'd slid from the saddle without being aware of dismounting. And now, only feet away from her, the broken, gaping door beckoned.

She was inside it in a flash, barely hearing Sutter's distant roar as he repeated his command. Rage wrapped her like a red mist as, unseeing, she sought to fulfill her vow of revenge. Had she encountered a "therapist" or an orderly at that moment, nothing would now remain of the individual except smeared blood and entrails.

But Devin met no one in the darkness inside the door, and the rush of her momentum had carried her only eight long strides down an unlit hallway before she was wheeling around, to race back outside. She retreated with both hands over her nose and mouth, trying hard not to gag.

The stench. The god-awful stink of the place. Devin had never smelled anything like it ... except once when she was very young, and an animal got trapped in a chimney of her parent's mansion, and it died there ... and that room was unusable for months, until the stink finally cleared.

"Oh my god," Devin whispered behind her cupped hands. She did not lower them from her face until Angelina came to where she stood braced against the exterior wall, in the hot sun well outside the gaping door.

"It's death," Devin murmured to the woman. "It reeks of death."

Angelina pressed a bandana into Devin's hands. "Do not let it fill your lungs, chica, or take from you your courage. The evil odor is *testimonio* that a terrible *catástrofe* has befallen this place."

ଓ 13 ରু

THE ENORMITY OF THE catastrophe became steadily apparent as Devin reentered the structure, accompanied now by Sutter and small teams of Sykes who pushed past the broken door and into the building's depths. All wore bandanas or scarves over their noses and mouths, but for many the stench was too overpowering. They withdrew to fresh air before they'd even reached the inoperable elevator that stood abandoned at the end of the dark hallway, its doors stuck open. But other Sykes scouted past the elevator and found a staircase, its treads of steel spiraling downward, descending floor after floor into deep gloom.

Sutter, upon catching up with Devin outside, had berated her for storming into the building alone. "That was a damfool thing to do," he fumed, "charging ahead like that. Don't go off half-cocked. You'll get yourself killed."

Now, still seething, he went ahead of her, leading the way down the seemingly endless flights of steps while Devin and Jack followed close behind, their hard-soled boots ringing on the metal treads. The stairwell was a windowless black hole, unlit and unventilated, although the battery-powered lanterns in the hands of the two men revealed air grilles and light fixtures on the stairwell walls.

The men's lanterns were a luxury that Devin had never seen used at the ranch, where kerosene lamps and homemade tallow candles prevailed. Only one building at the Syke compound, the dining hall, had electricity, supplied by a small rooftop wind turbine and sufficient to run only the lights. Batteries were in equally limited supply among the exiles, and were reserved for times of extraordinary need.

This was such a time. Without the lanterns, they might never have located the electrical closet in a hallway that opened off the bottom of the long-descending stairway. There could be no doubt that this remotely situated building was wired for electricity: the stairwell light fixtures were proof enough, and Devin's memories of the place added weight to the supposition. She'd seen very little of the facility during her stay here, but she remembered the incandescent lights that had shone in her face without letup for days and nights at a time.

"Here it is. Finally!" Jack exclaimed with undisguised relief as he flung open the nondescript closet door and closed the main breaker switch. As the switch snapped into place, light flooded the hallway, making all of them blink in the sudden glare. Power restored, the building's ventilation system kicked on with an audible hum of fans and whoosh of air.

"I'm willing to bet the ranch and every horse," Sutter declared from behind the bandana that wrapped the lower half of his face, "there ain't nobody left alive in this catacomb. We've broken into a tomb. But now we're down here, let's figure out who died, and how.

That starts with finding the bodies." He clicked off his lantern and motioned for Jack to do the same. "Just follow your nose, 'cause you sure as hell can smell them."

The odor of decomposition had been a little less noticeable in the stairwell, but down on this bottommost level of the deeply dug structure, the stink was overwhelming. Devin tried not to inhale as the three of them began forcing open every door they found, gradually working their way back up the stairs and along each off-branching hallway.

Despite her determined efforts, Devin's shallow breaths turned into full-throated gasps when doors opened to reveal rooms that she remembered. She recoiled with a visceral reaction of horror when she reentered the place of burning. This had been the site of her final test at Peaceful Hills, when her tormentors girdled her in fire to be certain she no longer cared whether she lived or died. And indeed, by that point in her treatment, life had meant nothing to her.

Seeing the fire room set Devin trembling. Her nerves screamed as if flames seared them, and she quivered so violently, Jack could not fail to notice.

"You don't need to be down here," he muttered, pausing to let Sutter go on ahead of them, farther along the hallway they were exploring. "Let's get up topside, into the fresh air. I'm choking."

"So am I," Devin whispered back. "The smell is sickening. But I need to see this, Jack. I need to see every room." By willpower alone she controlled her shudders as she went on in a low voice, "This place has haunted my nightmares. Coming here from Purity was like crossing from the living world into the mythical abode of the damned. I was trapped in a horror story. Even as bad as it hurt, it didn't seem real to me most of the time. Just a macabre fantasy ..." She trailed off, struggling to explain. "I don't know how to describe what it felt like then. But now, I can see that this place is solid and real. It's not a myth or a fantasy, or only something from a nightmare. It's a building that somebody buried and kitted out for torture." She gestured around her, then slapped the wall, needing to feel its bulk. "To understand what happened to me here, I have to see every square foot of this place."

So saying, Devin gritted her teeth and banged open the next door down the hall.

Revealed was the snake pit where her keepers had provoked a viper into sinking fangs into her flesh. She froze in the doorway, her arm stretched across it to be sure Jack stayed clear while she probed for any sign of a poisonous, slithering creature. But the room was empty except for two chairs, one of them overturned. The space was otherwise featureless, apart from the glass receptacles that lined the back wall.

Cautiously, Devin stepped from the doorway to examine the containers, and found terrariums stacked on shelves. Within each clear-walled enclosure lay the shriveled form of a dead snake. The creatures had been left to perish in the dark bowels of the building, caged up and buried alive in a subterranean room where sunlight never penetrated.

And that was when Devin knew. She knew, even before other wandering teams of Sykes began to seek out Sutter to make their reports. As surely as if the ghosts of the dead had whispered the awful truth in both her ears, she knew what those scouts had found in other parts of the building. The erstwhile "patients" had been locked in their cells and left to die of hunger, thirst, and despair, same as the snakes in their glass cages. No searcher would stumble across the rotting remains of a therapist, an orderly, or any other Peaceful Hills hireling. Those had cleared out, abandoning this place and every Syke imprisoned here.

This was indeed a catastrophe, as Angelina had said, but what had been done here was also a crime. A monstrous crime that Devin would stop at nothing to avenge.

* * *

It took days to locate and bring up the bodies of all the murdered Sykes. Devin marveled that so many individuals had been condemned in Purity and put on the train to this hellhole. During her time here, she had met no other inmate. The isolation must have been by design. Two Sykes together, even if mind-damaged and drugged, would have stood a chance of overpowering their captors. To guard against any kind of coordinated resistance, the jailers at Peaceful Hills would have taken pains to keep their prisoners not only separated, but ignorant of each other's very existence.

Once all of the victims' bodies were on the surface, every living Syke who looked upon the faces of the dead were agreed that the remains must not be buried in the desolate pit of the old mine. Those who were strong enough would transport the corpses into the pine forests higher up the mountain slopes, and would inter each body in a separate grave, rejecting the cold anonymity of mass burial.

The transportation was accomplished by no physical removal, but by psychokinesis, relying on the few Sykes in the company of Sutter's troops who had the necessary mental potency to move that much dead weight over so great a distance. Amongst these, Angelina took the lead. It was the only time that many in the company had seen a display of power from the enigmatic woman who was clearly a great deal more than Sutter's housekeeper.

Out of respect for the Doña, as well as reverence for the dead, most of the Sykes who were not part of the burial detail directed their attention elsewhere, granting privacy to the woman and her cohort of assistants as they went about the grim work that required their absolute concentration. The few who were minded to stand around gawking at the levitated remains were castigated roundly by Sutter, and sent back into the bowels of the building, or tasked with clearing the tunnel that cut the base of the cliff behind the structure's uppermost level. Their job was to retrieve any usable supplies that might have been left in the abandoned death-trap.

"I think Sutter's right. This place must have started out as a mine," Jack commented one evening when he and Devin took a break on the surface, where they could breathe freely and escape the odor of death. Removing the bodies had not eliminated the stench of decay. The smell clung to the building's walls as though it had seeped into the pores of the concrete. Getting the ventilation system operating had helped, but the depths of the structure still reeked of putrefaction.

"I'd say the place has gone from bad to worse," Devin replied. "After the miners killed the land, murderers came to kill our people."

"But in between, I think there was a bunker here." Jack gestured with the canteen he held. "That building"—he pointed at the concrete box which capped the buried substructure—"is way bigger than any mining camp would have. Even if the mine operated long enough that they needed a year-round bunkhouse for the workers, why build it with such thick walls? Why sink it so many stories below ground?" He shook his head. "That place is built like a fortress. No windows ... all concrete and steel ... only the one heavy door in the front, and another door just as thick in the wall from the tunnel."

"You've been in the tunnel?" Devin made a mental note to explore that passageway herself, before she fulfilled her pledge to destroy this place.

"I was curious to see where it led, if it went all the way through. Turns out it dead-ends, but it goes deep enough into the foot of the cliff to have held a locomotive and a few train cars. There's a turntable at the back"—again he gestured—"where they would have spun the locomotive around to send the train back to Purity after it had dumped out its prisoners."

"So the inmates probably entered the building through the door from the tunnel," Devin surmised. "If every Syke came here the way I did—knocked unconscious—I don't suppose anybody but the devils who ran this place ever saw the building from the outside."

She paused, thinking of Jack's characterization of the place as a fortress.

"Ever since we left the ranch," she mused aloud then, "we've been pushing deeper into the wilderness. There's nothing out here, and I suspect there never has been. Why would anybody sink a multistory fortress into the ground under a played-out mine?"

"You'd want the isolation if you were trying to get away from the Great Contagion." Jack scratched his chin, which was showing a week's growth of beard. He had not shaved since the ranch. "I think what we have here"—he flicked a finger toward the building—"is a survivalist's bunker. Somebody with the money and the means built this in hopes of keeping a big bunch of people safe. It could have held most of a small town. Especially if people were in a panic to escape the contagion, and didn't mind sleeping six to a room."

Devin nodded. It made sense. The cell block where most of the Sykes had been found dead, locked up like animals and abandoned without light or food or water, was laid out on the pattern of hotel rooms or tiny apartments sharing a common corridor. Those rooms might once have housed frightened individuals who came willingly to a bunker in the wilderness, hoping to survive the plague that swept lethally around the world. The hallways might once have echoed with children's innocent laughter, instead of the screams of Sykes whose minds and spirits were destroyed by tormentors determined to break them.

And if the bunker had been built in the pit of an old mine, that could explain the railroad tracks which connected this place to Purity. The present-day town on the plains lacked the industrial might to build a railway into the mountains. The tracks and the train could be leftovers from the defunct mine. At the time of the Great Contagion, the people who sought shelter in the bunker might very well have ridden the rails to get here.

"Well," Devin said, standing and stretching the kinks from her back, "maybe the place wasn't always evil. Maybe it offered hope, once upon a time. But I'm not letting anybody move back in and resurrect the house of horrors. When Sutter's through stripping it of everything he wants, and I've been in every room, I'm tearing it down to the foundations."

* * *

On the day that Sutter finished cannibalizing the building for anything he could haul away on horseback, he made no objection to Devin's declaration that she meant to obliterate what was left. He was curious, she supposed, to see how much destruction she could wreak on her own, with no support from him or any other Syke. He only warned her not to rupture the tanks that held the orange poison.

She had found those during one of her final sweeps of the building. The tanks had been locked behind a door so unobtrusive and out of the way, the room had been missed by other searchers. When Devin forced it open—mentally wrenching the door off its hinges—she discovered a space that must once have served as a shower room. But it had been enlarged and substantially refitted to accommodate two hulking, upright tanks. Both were elevated on steel supports, and each tank bore the symbol for acute toxicity: the universally recognizable skull-and-crossbones.

Devin needed slightly longer to identify the other dominant feature of the room: a cylindrical chamber of clear glass, more than head-high. She had never before seen the chamber from this side of the glass. Or if she had, she'd been too drugged-up to know what she was looking at. Now, however, as she studied it, the thing became obvious. The see-through cylinder that had trapped her bruised body while her "therapist" poisoned her with mind-killing orange gas: it was a shower stall.

Devin snorted at the absurdity of it. But then she stepped closer, to examine the modifications her tormentors had made, and her derision turned to a quiet, gut-deep fury.

The top of the shower stall had been sealed with a cone of aluminum. A hose from the nearest elevated tank fed in through the top of that, through a hole in the cone's center. Wide strips of rubber sealed the cone to the glass, continued down the edges of the curved shower door, and wrapped the base of the cylinder where it sat on the tiled floor. Those who had opened valves to release gas into the chamber wanted none of that poison leaking into the air *they* breathed. The operators—Devin's therapist and attendant technicians—had kept their distance, occupying a space on the far side of the room behind a second, wider, but similarly sealed glass door. From that control room, electrical wires snaked along the walls to feed current to a grid covering the shower stall's floor. With the push of a button or flick of a switch, Devin's tormentors had used that metal grid to deliver their own brutal variety of electroshock therapy.

The room reeked of pain and despair, deepening the all-pervading stench of bodily rot. After discovering the grid, Devin had lingered only long enough to pull every electrical plug from every socket. What the orange gas was, and whether it was flammable, she had no idea. The tanks might even be empty. But there was no sense risking a spark that might set off an explosion when she pulverized the building. Mindful of the enormous quantities of shattered concrete that would soon tumble down into this room with crushing force, falling from the multiple upper stories, Devin summoned a Beskil bubble to enwrap the two tanks in impenetrable rigidity. If she did everything right, rubble would bury the tanks at least a hundred feet deep, but they would not rupture. The poison they held would be entombed under tons of concrete and steel.

The time came for the entombing. Sutter's troops were out of the building—Angelina insisted upon a headcount to verify that all seventy-five were topside—and Devin had completed her walk-throughs. Often with Jack's steadying presence, but sometimes on her own, she'd set foot in every room of the structure. She'd found the pool room where two orderlies had nearly drowned her, and the dungeon-like space where, chained by handcuffs, she'd hung suspended from the ceiling. She'd walked the perimeter of the chamber with the spikes on the floor and the balance-beam in the air. The set-up had been designed to provoke a fear response, but by that point in her ordeal, Devin had had none. She'd endured it all through mindless indifference.

Now as she revisited each of these spaces, she spat on the floor and cursed her tormentors. But when she moved on, to explore the underground cell block, her mood changed to one of near-reverence. Devin stepped softly from room to room, wondering which had been hers. It was impossible to know, for the prisoners' cells were all identical. She searched in vain for any trace of individuality, any personal effects, perhaps a name scratched into a concrete wall. No vestige appeared. The people who had perished in this place had left nothing of themselves behind.

That was as it should be, she decided. If all the prisoners had been treated as she had been, their personalities were stripped away, all emotion denied to them, any zest for life sucked out of them. At the end, those who died here were empty husks. The graveyard high in the forest where clean breezes sighed through the pine boughs: that was their memorial. This place held no memory of them, and it should not be suffered to remain for an hour longer.

Up in the sandy pit of the old strip mine, Devin waved everyone back. Jack retreated with clear reluctance, only leaving her side when she insisted that his nearness would be a distraction. He didn't give in until she explained about the tanks of toxic gas, and what that gas would do to the mind and body of a Syke if she allowed it to be released.

Sutter needed no persuading to get clear. He waited off to the side, well away from Devin and somewhat distant from his troops. He stood with his thumbs hitched in his belt, looking bored. But at the first sharp *crack* that resounded from the building, echoing across the pit as Devin began the demolition, his head jerked toward the noise. For the next few minutes, his gaze did not leave the collapsing concrete.

The disintegration of the whole thing took surprisingly little time. Devin's sweeps through the building had given her a detailed mental map of the structure's interior. Now, behind closed lids, she called up that map, and she pictured the ceilings coming down, toppling the walls with them. Shouts rose from the onlookers behind her, but Devin paid them no mind. She was too intent on maintaining the collapse, dropping one floor in upon another, the implosion picking up speed as the upper stories pancaked down, crushing and filling the levels deep belowground. She lent a part of her mental strength to brace the Beskil bubble around the tanks, holding that shield rock-steady while tons of rubble thundered down upon it.

The noise of concrete cracking, splitting, and shattering rose to a deafening roar, but Devin's attention did not waver. Although, distantly in a corner of her mind, she seemed to hear Sutter's inadequate description of how syketic power could be brought to bear upon an object, and thus turn thoughts into actions. *"Get it in your mind, and send it where you want it to go."*

If Devin could have sent the asylum straight to hell, she would have done so. Lacking any real conviction, however, that the Hades of mythology could be any worse than the horrors of Peaceful Hills, she contented herself with ramming the facility's crushed remains down deep into the subterranean space its dozen lower levels had occupied. When she opened her eyes and looked to where the single above-ground floor of the building had once been visible, its front facade windowless and featureless, there was now no structure to be seen.

There wasn't even any dust rising from the implosion. Devin had so thoroughly collapsed the building in upon itself, even the smallest motes and specks of residue had been squeezed down into what was now a quite deep hole in the ground. Already, Sutter's troops were clustering at the hole's edge, peering into the depths and exclaiming their astonishment at the finest display of Syke artistry any of them had ever witnessed.

Sutter did not join the crowd at the hole. He stood frowning, radiating displeasure at being upstaged by his junior partner. As Jack came up at Devin's elbow, and together they sauntered over to stand with him, Sutter tipped his hat to her, but it was a courtesy that communicated more sarcasm than respect.

"Neatly done. You tidied that right up." Sutter's smile was humorless. "Gotta say though, friend, I expected a wilder show from you. Something a mite more scrappy. When we get to Purity, you'll likely not have time to be tidy." The smile became Sutter's usual cynical smirk. "Folks aboveground and still breathing ... well, those kind of folks—*alive,* like—tend to fight back. Things in town may get messy for you."

Sutter clicked his tongue as if relishing the thought of the messiness. Then he strode away to break up the crowd at the hole and order his troops to get ready to ride.

☙ 14 ❧

SUTTER'S ORIGINAL INTENT had been to advance his army straight on to Purity as soon as Peaceful Hills was dealt with. He and his troops had looted so much from the asylum, however, it was now necessary that they return to the ranch, to unload the spoils from the overburdened horses. They carried sheets of aluminum, panes of glass, steel lattices, and canned goods from the asylum's kitchen. The troops had also liberated precious boxes of flashlight batteries. When the devils who ran the asylum cut loose and cleared out, they had evidently done little more than throw the main power switch and lock the front door behind their retreating asses.

"You know why, don't you, friend? Why they abandoned the place?"

Sutter twisted in his saddle to shoot the question at Devin. They were climbing away from the ugly desolation of the open-pit mine, and as she rode alongside him, she had remarked on the evident hastiness of the evacuation.

"You do understand," he persisted when she did not immediately answer him, "why they shut the place down and buried those poor sods alive, leaving them to rot in the dark?"

Devin winced at this reminder of how her fellow inmates had languished in their final days, when all hope was gone and they could only lie in their cells and passively await a death that would have been a welcome release, if they'd still had the emotional capacity to yearn for release.

"I've got an idea of why the devils cut and ran," she conceded, giving Sutter a sideways glance. "But I'd like to hear what you think."

Almost since Devin's first meeting with the man, Sutter had evinced a cruel streak. It was clear to see now, in the way that he grinned at her hesitancy.

"You want me to say it, so you don't have to?" Mockingly, he indulged in his habit of tipping his hat. "I'm glad to oblige you, friend." He settled the hat back on his head as he continued. "Here's how it went: Your old pals at Peaceful Hills got the order to bug out as soon as Purity heard you'd stopped the prison train and tossed a railcar around like it was a toy."

"I didn't stop the train," Devin pointed out. "You did."

"That's right." Sutter's grin widened. "That was all me. When I got you off that train, you were as useless as tits on a rooster. You could barely stand and walk." His eyes flickered with unsuppressed amusement. "But the good folks of Purity don't know that I exist. Oh, maybe they've heard a rumor or two about runaway Sykes living wild in the mountains. But they don't know about the ranch, and they don't know about me. All they know for certain is that *you* were declared 'cured' and put on the train home. Your keepers were so damned convinced they'd cut the heart out of you, they figured you to be about as dangerous as a crumpled paper doll."

"And now they believe I came to life on the train." Devin shifted her gaze from Sutter to stare ahead at a ridge the Syke army would soon wend its way upward. She was recalling what Orlando had said on this same subject. "I fought off the effects of the drugs, defied all of my soul-killing conditioning, and syked the train off the tracks. I climbed out of the wreck, and I ran off. That's what they think."

"There's nothing else they *could* think." Sutter gave a short laugh. "You getting free of their poisons and their mind-control flipped a middle finger at their whole Peaceful Hills setup. Why should Purity go on paying for 'treatment' that doesn't work? Keeping that bug-house fueled, staffed, and supplied must have cost the town a pretty penny over the years." He pulled his hat lower over his eyes as he added, "It had to have been the rich folks yanking the purse strings so they'd always have a place to send their psycho children. Just the way Perridin sent his dear little dangerous daughter to the sanatorium to get her tamed." Sutter snorted. "Nobody ever paid for a 'cure' for the kids on my side of town. Sykes from poor families just got stood up against the wall and shot."

Devin wiped her sweaty forehead with the back of her hand.

"And now, they'll shoot every Syke they can smoke out," she muttered. "They won't even pretend to offer 'humane treatment' anymore, because I've convinced them there's no point in continuing. They see my escape as their proof that our sort cannot be permanently cured. They killed every inmate at the asylum because murdering *all* Sykes is now the official policy of the town of Purity."

The only acceptable Syke is a dead Syke. Devin could almost hear those words like an echo off the mountain slopes as she imagined the mayor issuing the edict from the courthouse steps.

"Welcome to my side of town, friend," Sutter almost crowed. When Devin went on staring straight ahead and gave him no answer, he continued in a gloating vein. "I've heard it said that the gears of government grind slowly. But you saw how fast the boss medico and all the hirelings vacated Peaceful Hills. They didn't even stop to pack their peaches before they were out the door and hightailing it home to Purity." He chuckled as he patted a saddlebag that bulged with the canned fruit he'd purloined.

"They were scared," Devin muttered. "If I could pull my mind out of the fog and find the will to derail a train, then maybe those Sykes they had locked in the cell block could shake off the stupor. The asylum boss and all the hirelings were terrified that the inmates would rise up, syke the doors off their cells, and break the neck of every ordinary they could find."

The fingers of Sutter's rein-less hand curled into a fist where they rested on his thigh. "I'd have paid to see that. Hell, I'd have jumped in and helped with the neck-wringing. But those poor sods were no threat to their jailers. Not a one of them died on their feet. They never got off their cots."

He sighed in a way that sounded almost sympathetic. It was so out of character, Devin couldn't help but glance at him.

"You saw how it was." He returned her gaze, no trace of a grin showing on his face now. "I warned you, friend, not to look, but I know you saw how we found the bodies, the way they were laid out behind all those locked doors, all of them flat on their backs, just rotting in their beds."

Devin nodded. "I saw. I'll never forget it, or forgive." She managed a grim smile. "The ordinaries may think they escaped the menace of the Sykes when they barred the asylum door and lit out. But maybe they've overlooked the fact that I'm still out here. I'm the one who got away—thanks to you, Mike."

And thanks especially to Doña Angelina, Devin added silently. True though it was that Sutter had rescued her physically from her captors, Angelina's old magic had restored her in the more profound way, mentally and emotionally. The woman had healed Devin's soul.

"I'm going to see if Angelina needs any help," she said, dropping back behind Sutter's horse as they gained the high ridgeline, and the way narrowed. "For some reason, she likes to bring up the rear, and she stays so far back, I can't see her. I get worried about her."

Sutter snorted. "Angie has been taking care of herself for a long time. She doesn't need you fretting over her. But go on if you want." He waved Devin away. "Check on Orlando while you're at it. He's supposed to be watching that nobody loses their load. If half of our salvage winds up scattered on the slopes between here and the ranch, I'm not going to be happy."

As Devin reined away, she gave the man a small wave of acknowledgment, but she had no intention of seeking out Orlando. That worthless fellow had made himself scarce all the time they were at the asylum, finding ways to shirk his share of the work in bringing up the bodies and scavenging for supplies. Devin was quite content to continue seeing little of the louse.

But she caught Jack's eye where that member of the vanguard was riding at Sutter's flank. With a tilt of her head, she invited him to trail along after her, toward the army's rear.

Jack waited for a curve and a dip in the ridgeline to block Sutter's view so he could turn his horse and follow without unduly attracting the man's notice. The vanguard foursome—Sutter, Devin, Jack, Orlando—was not holding together on this return journey to the ranch. Orlando had lost his spot for having been delegated to watch over the loot the troops carried, and Sutter no longer kept an eagle eye on Devin. He allowed her a far greater degree of independent action than when they'd been riding toward, instead of away from, Peaceful Hills. And he seemed to have forgotten Jack was around. Even so, the lady and her knight remained circumspect about being seen too much in each other's company.

"I'm glad to be heading home," Jack exclaimed softly when he caught up with Devin about halfway down the line of riders that snaked along the ridgetop. "That back there"—he gestured in the direction of the strip mine and the obliterated asylum—"was pretty damned horrible." He reined his horse alongside hers, and leaned from the saddle to search her face. "How are you, my lady? You doing okay?"

Devin passed a hand across her mouth.

"Honestly," she admitted, allowing herself a moment's vulnerability now that Sutter wouldn't see, "I've been better. Being down in that hellhole again, and seeing what they did to all those Sykes after I got out of there ..." She trailed off, and shuddered.

"But you paid 'em back." Jack's voice and his eyes expressed admiration tinged with concern. "The way you flattened that place and slammed it right down into the bowels of the earth ... there's not one in a million of us could have done that. You got your revenge."

Devin shook her head. "No. I didn't. I didn't get revenge. The murdering devils got away scot-free. All the signs point to it: the power deliberately shut off at the mains, the front door locked ... and no dead bodies except in the prisoners' cells." She ran her hand through her hair, encountered tangles, and realized she had not brushed it in days. She'd had a mind for nothing except stalking the halls of the asylum, trying to lay her personal demons to rest while anticipating what must be done to avenge all those innocents who had died in the airless dark.

Jack studied her. "You're going to Purity with Sutter, aren't you." He kept his voice low as they rode slowly down the line of mounted troops, skirting past the column in the opposite direction of the army's travel. "You're going to help him attack the town."

Devin faltered over her answer, finding no words adequate to say how profoundly their discoveries at Peaceful Hills had affected her. Yes, she was going to Purity, and she would burn the town to the ground, if that's what it took to bring every murderer to justice: not only those who had left the imprisoned Sykes to die, but all of their accomplices. She would take revenge on anyone who had issued the order, or had supported in any way the decision to lock the asylum and bury her people alive.

"Jack ...," Devin began. But she seemed to choke on the remembered stench of the corpses, and the words would not come.

He lifted a hand, forestalling her efforts to say more.

"I don't think you or Sutter even noticed how close I was riding behind you both, while ago." He gave her a lopsided smile. "I'd got curious to hear what you two were saying. That's probably the longest conversation I've known you to have with the man, and it seemed serious. So I crowded on up." He shrugged, unapologetic about his eavesdropping. "I didn't catch it all, but I heard enough to get the drift. Criminals have got to be brought to account."

Devin shot him a look of gratitude. He understood, and she would not ask more of him than his understanding.

"You don't need to come with us to Purity." She gave him a slight shake of her head. "When we get to the ranch, you ought to stay there. There'll be plenty for you to do, what with the crops ripening and the cattle that need to be worked."

He stared at her as if she'd suggested he sprout wings and fly to the moon.

"Did you forget what I promised?" he exclaimed. "What I said before, I still mean. I won't follow Sutter into any battle of his ... but wherever *you* lead, my lady, I will go."

* * *

Angelina was not of the same mind as Jack. Three days after the army returned to the ranch, with the Doña riding rearguard the whole way back through the mountains, Devin asked the woman if she meant to accompany the troops when they rode out anew, heading for Purity.

"No, chica," she replied. "I will not make that journey. I will not be needed. The spirits do not summon me there, as they bade me go to the bad place where so much evil had been worked."

"Spirits?" Devin studied the woman. "Do you mean the, um, the ghosts of the people who died at the asylum?"

Angelina did not look up from the pastry dough she was kneading.

"I do not know, chica. Perhaps it was their soul-voices that I heard. Perhaps I was called by the spirit of the land itself, *la tierra* that had been savagely violated. I only know I was needed at that terrible place." She shook her head. "Though you and Miguel may be drawn to make another journey, I am not."

Devin leaned across the kitchen table to place her hand on Angelina's fingers, which were sticky with dough.

"I'm glad you know how it feels to be drawn to a place, Doña, and how you can't ignore the feeling. I am called back to Purity. I'm obligated to seek justice there. Not just for myself, but for all those dead Sykes you buried under the pine trees." Devin paused as Angelina's hand turned palm up to grip hers, hold it gently, and then slip free after a moment to continue working the dough.

"I'm not sure I'll return to the ranch," Devin mused, speaking slowly as she wiped bits of transferred dough from her fingers. "I suppose it depends on what happens at Purity. In any event, Doña, I want to thank you for everything you've done for me. In case I don't see you again after I ride out next with Sutter, I want you to know how grateful I am for your kindness, your wisdom, and the *magia antigua* you mix into your marvelous persimmon marmalade."

This made Angelina smile. The woman left off kneading the dough to round the table and wrap Devin in a hug. The arms around her felt so warm, so much like her mother Mariah's had once felt, Devin had to choke back tears.

* * *

Orlando had erred in more ways than one, that time he'd caught Devin playing truant in the woods and had paid with a concussion for his presumption in attempting to punish her. He'd claimed it was a week's ride from the ranch to Purity. Sutter's army, however, would need longer than that to cover the distance, for they could not ride directly there. An absence of waterholes on the plains, parched by the summer sun, dictated a detour. When they left the ranch and descended gradually into the foothills below the high peaks, Sutter set a course straight westward.

"We're heading for the Contagion River where it leaves the mountains," he explained without Devin having to ask. "You'll know the river, I suppose, down where it loops around Purity. I imagine rich kids get to play in it, same as the poor ones do."

Devin, riding beside him, shook her head. "I don't remember ever seeing the river. Except one time I climbed on the roof of our house, and when I looked past the courthouse I could see a stretch of dark water." She shrugged. "I never asked my parents what it was, whether it was the river or maybe only a drainage ditch. They were upset with me for making a hole in the roof so I could get up there and look around."

Sutter laughed. "Well then, friend, you're in for a treat. The way we're going, you'll get to see the river where it drops down from on high, at the prettiest spot there is."

The man did not exaggerate. Four days of riding brought the army to the base of a towering cliff that rose sheer above the foothills. A double waterfall tumbled from the heights. No—it was a triple falls, with a smaller but still impressive cascade spilling down at a slight remove from the twin, central torrents which roared over the cliff with magnificent power. The tops of the falls were lost amidst sprays and clouds of vapor. At the base of the steep cliff, the combined force of the three cascades had carved a pool of such size, it could properly be called a lake. Deep and wide, the plunge-pool brimmed with the bluest water imaginable. But not blue only: the water had green tints also, the colors blending into a transparent, gemlike turquoise.

"It's clear as glass!" Devin exclaimed when she dismounted and led her horse to drink from the pool. "It seems as deep as the sky is wide, but I can see the bottom, even so."

"It's snowmelt." Sutter had joined her in admiring the lake and the broad, fast-running river that issued from it, the river flowing southward through a deep-cut notch in the foothills. "There's glacier ice in that water, from mountains so high they're covered in snow year-round." Sutter craned his neck to gaze upward, squinting as though he hoped to glimpse those distant ice fields. "When I ran away from Purity in the desperate days of my youth, I followed the river up this far, and I tried every which way to get on up higher. I wanted to find the headwaters." He sighed, a sound almost wistful, as he gestured at the soaring cliff. "Never managed to get around this thundering anvil of the gods ... but the search led me eventually to the ranch."

Devin stared at him. Accustomed as she was to Sutter's often earthy language, she experienced a moment of astonishment, hearing a phrase from his lips that skirted close to poetry. But *thundering anvil of the gods* perfectly captured the majesty of this immense, unclimbable cliff and the waterfalls that roared from its unseeable heights.

The noise of the triple cascades filled what would have been an awkward moment of silence, during which the man dropped to a crouch on the rim of the crystalline pool. As though embarrassed to have shown any hint of a softer side, he whipped off his hat and plunged his head into the ice-cold water, flinging drops Devin's way when he came up sputtering. He did not again look at or speak to her.

She took the hint. In search of Jack, she wandered off through the army of Sykes. Sutter's troops were making camp, building cooking fires on the wide meadow that bordered the lake and greened the nearside riverbank. The river's clear water frothed white as it raced toward the gap in the foothills, dashing against upthrust rocks that partly filled the channel but could not impede the water's swift flow.

The power of the surging river awed Devin. Back at the ranch, she'd seen plenty of streams and creeks, but this roaring river was orders of magnitude greater than any watercourse she'd previously set eyes on. Likewise, the lake almost overpowered her senses. The lower ranch pastures had only stockponds fed by windmills that lifted water from deep wells. On the slopes above the compound, small lakes dotted the high meadows, also providing water for the ranch's grazing livestock. But none of those mountain lakes held such a vastness of coiled power as emanated from the turquoise plunge-pool. Devin was forcefully reminded of how impoverished her childhood had been, with no access to nature's magnificence beyond what she'd had in her top-floor sunroom.

Any kid of mine will grow up outdoors, Devin silently vowed as her searching gaze found Jack near the base of the great cliff. He worked clear of the crushing might of the waterfalls. With the other wranglers, he was staking the army's horses where the animals would have good grazing and water—a task not difficult to accomplish amidst such plenty. But as she walked through the encamped army to join him, Devin caught snippets of conversation which suggested the troops expected to ride into less hospitable country when they left this awe-inspiring, blue-green Eden.

☙ 15 ❧

IN THE EARLY LIGHT of the new dawn, the army followed the roaring river southward, keeping to its banks and threading a way through the rocky gap that separated the mountains from the plains. As they descended the final slopes of the diminishing foothills, what stretched ahead of the riders, and to either side as far as Devin could see, were miles of empty prairie.

The land lay entirely open. No trees grew except immediately along the riverbanks. Away toward the far-distant horizon, dark spots suggested clumps of vegetation—scrubby brush that found enough moisture to survive in occasional seeps and low places. Otherwise, this was a world of grass. Under the late-summer sun, the endless expanse of trackless prairie looked more yellow than green.

"How many miles to Purity?"

Her question carried a note of urgency as Devin rode alongside Sutter. The emptiness on all sides set her head spinning. Her life until now—imprisoned first in her family home, and then in the nightmare confines of the asylum—had not prepared her for this vast openness. Devin felt immeasurably tiny, a mere dot upon this plain that appeared to go on forever.

Sutter shrugged, apparently unawed by their surroundings. "We've got about a hundred and fifty miles to cover. Maybe a little more. We should get there in a week if we don't push the horses."

A surge of appreciation for the animal she rode had Devin bending to pat the gelding's neck and comb her fingers through his chestnut mane. Like Sutter, her horse Diego seemed undisturbed by the all-encompassing emptiness. As the animal clopped along, Devin took heart from Diego's solid, muscular form and his steady pace, and she began to regain a sense of her own substantiality. She might be a dot in this grassy immensity, but she was not powerless, and she was not alone.

She twisted in her saddle to gaze at the ranks of the riders who followed behind her and Sutter. The Syke army was strung out along the river, riding two and three abreast for what looked like a mile or more. The headcount had grown since their Peaceful Hills campaign. On the army's previous expedition, through the mountains to the asylum, many of the exiled Sykes had made excuses to remain behind at the ranch that was their sanctuary.

Perceiving their reluctance to join in that earlier foray, Devin had privately wondered how loyal to Sutter his troops might prove to be. Indeed, she'd suspected that after Angelina had caught up with the army and stationed herself at the column's rear, the woman had facilitated the desertion of some of Sutter's less-committed troops. At least a few of those who had ridden out through the ranch gates, on the first day of that prior excursion, had not gone on to witness

Devin's destruction of the asylum. They'd quietly slipped away and made it back to the ranch before the main body of riders reached the hellhole in the played-out strip mine.

But from the returning army—those who had stayed the course and made the full circuit—the defectors heard in graphic detail what Peaceful Hills had yielded: the pitch-black cells and the locked doors, the stench of death, the corpses of murdered Sykes. Enraged, and as desirous of revenge as Sutter could wish, every man and woman who was fit to ride had rushed to join his army of vengeance. Only the children and a few infirm individuals among the eldest had remained behind this time, tended by Angelina and a handful of the woman's helpers. Mountain wolves were bound to take cattle during the army's absence from the ranch, but every Syke deemed that to be a necessary sacrifice. Years of pent-up resentment had exploded into a furious demand for justice.

As Devin ran her gaze over the formidably large body of troops, she spotted Jack riding a little aside, some yards distant from the ranks that snaked close to the riverbank. With his head turned toward the column of riders, he appeared to be studying the troops as she was. Or more likely, Devin thought, he watched for any sign of stress or lameness among the horses. Eager though his fellow riders might be to reach Purity and avenge the murdered Sykes, Jack would not tolerate the abuse of any horse as the army pursued its objective.

"I'm going to ..." Devin didn't finish the sentence, but jerked her head to tell Sutter that she meant to fall back, leaving him alone at the head of his army.

He made no response beyond a grunt and a vaguely uninterested wave. The man had long since ceased to monitor Devin's movements.

Her annihilation of Peaceful Hills had raised her from "junior" to full partner in his campaign against the ordinaries.

Still maintaining some level of discreetness, however, where Jack was concerned, Devin did not ride straight to the wrangler's side. Partway down the column of troops, she fell in with Estelle, the tough-as-leather woman who had encouraged Devin to undercut Sutter's authority. Estelle had never repeated that request, nor especially sought Devin's company, since. But neither had the woman actively avoided her, not in the way that many in the community had steered clear after Devin knocked Sutter on his ass. Estelle's unimpressed indifference to both Sutter and Devin was refreshing when stood against the arm's-length caution that many in the company displayed toward the two Sykes of superior strength.

"What are you planning, girlie, when we get to Purity?" Estelle asked in her blunt way after she and Devin had exchanged brief greetings. "You gonna tear the place down?"

"I don't know," Devin answered truthfully. "I guess it depends on how many of the townsfolk share the blame for the killings at the asylum. If the whole town knew and approved of Sykes being left to starve in the dark, then ... yeah. I'll help Sutter tear the place apart."

Estelle nodded. "That's what I wanted to hear. I've got no love for the town." She scowled as she added, "My parents died trying to get me out of Purity and somewhere safe. That was a long time ago, but I remember like it was yesterday." With an angry gesture, the woman flicked her hand at a gaunt willow growing on the riverside. Branches snapped with a noise like bullwhips cracking, and the top of the small tree toppled into the water. It was a rare demonstration of syketic power from someone who displayed her abilities sparingly. "Maybe I can't pulverize a whole big building like you can, girlie," Estelle growled, her eyes narrowing, "but I'll sure as hell break some ordinaries' necks."

Devin found she'd unconsciously knotted her fingers in her horse's mane, as if to brace against a suddenly gusting crosswind. Aware that her handhold made her look like a greenhorn—like she was hanging on for dear life—she eased her fingers from the wiry hairs. Musing upon the feeling that she'd been abruptly buffeted by the unexpected, Devin pushed back her straw hat and wiped a sheen of sweat from her forehead. The sun at this hour was well along its downward arc, but it still shone hot in a wide, cloudless sky.

After another quarter mile of riding beside the scowling but now-silent Estelle, Devin took her leave of the woman and drifted farther back along the column, nodding to a few acquaintances but not stopping to speak to any rider until she fell in with Jack.

"This evening when we make camp," she informed him as she reined alongside, "I'd like to help you take care of the horses." She patted her gelding's neck. "I know you wranglers don't need my help, and you'll think I'm in the way. I'm town-bred, after all, not a country girl." Devin smiled at her denim-clad knight. "But Diego has been the picture of patience since I first slouched on his back, not knowing what I was doing, or, in those first days, even being aware that I was sitting on a living, thinking animal."

She shifted in the saddle and the leather creaked under her, a sound that underscored how radically her life had changed since Sutter, Jack—and yes, she must credit Orlando, too—had taken her off the prison train and conveyed her to the mountain ranch.

"I'll be glad for your help, my lady." Jack touched a finger to his hat's wide brim. "It's the mark of a true horsewoman, taking on the care of her mount."

Devin blinked back the tears that suddenly, ridiculously, moistened her eyes. She was not prone to crying—never had been, since childhood—but Jack's comment went to her core. It seemed silly to be so moved by a simple word: "horsewoman." It was what that word conveyed, however, that brought the tears. Coming from Jack, the title conferred respect on a new, higher level. It moved her from Sutter's realm—where she was valued only for her Syke powers—into Jack's world where loyalty, compassion, and patience ruled. But could she stay in that world while pursuing a quest for revenge?

"You okay, Devin?" Jack rode close, bending to look at her face.

She tried to wipe away the tears, but her eyes were still damp when she looked at him.

"It's the dust," she mumbled. "Out here on the flank where you like to ride, there's more dust than grass. Let's get to the river. It's cooler by the water."

"As you wish, my lady." Jack again tipped his hat to her. Together they rode to insert themselves into the long column that snaked along the riverbank, finding a break in the line of troops where a few of the Sykes straggled behind their comrades. "Better?" he asked as they matched their pace to that of the other riders.

Devin nodded, still drying her eyes. They rode on in silence for a bit, her thoughts restless but tending always toward their destination.

"You ever been in Purity, Jack?"

As soon as she asked the question, she wondered if she shouldn't have. Jack had never mentioned his origins. Perhaps it was a topic he avoided.

But he answered her easily, displaying no discomfort.

"Nah. Didn't you know? I was born at the ranch. That's what they tell me, anyway. I don't remember." He crooked a grin. "I don't remember ever having just one mom or pop, either. Every grownup on the place helped to raise me."

"It takes a village," Devin murmured, recalling something she'd read somewhere. A little louder, she asked, "But you really don't know who your mother was, or your father?"

Jack shrugged. "It never seemed to matter—not to me, or to anyone else. I was told that the woman who gave birth to me got killed when a tree fell on her in a thunderstorm. I was just a baby, and I have no memory of her. Of course, I don't remember the storm either. There's been lots of those since—thunderboomers in summer, blizzards in winter."

"That's sad," Devin murmured. "I'm sorry you never knew her. … Or your father, either?"

"My father …"

Jack trailed off. He stared straight ahead, and long moments passed as he rubbed his thumb on his chin, pensive. Then he glanced at Devin, but only fleetingly before looking away again.

"Nobody's ever said, but I suppose it was just one of the cowboys. I don't know if he's even still around. If he is, he's never made himself known to me."

That's terrible, Devin started to say. But she stopped when she thought of her own parental situation: a father who had never shown her the least affection and held to a separate wing of the family home so he need never see her; and a mother who had reportedly disowned her. And those two had not only shipped her off to an asylum that specialized in torture, they'd paid big money to fund the torments Devin had endured.

Compared to all of that, Jack's childhood sounded idyllic. Who needed parents when you had a village and a ready-made family of your fellow Sykes?

"It's been a hot day," Jack said then, returning to matters more immediate. "If Mike Sutter doesn't call a halt soon, I'll be reminding him that we're all flesh and blood out here. He may think he's an iron man, but that horse he rides needs rest."

* * *

Jack was spared the necessity of questioning Sutter's judgment, which was certainly how the older man would have viewed his intervention. Before the sun sank much farther toward the horizon, Mike brought the column to a halt and ordered his army to make camp. Exclamations of relief rose like a soft chorus around Devin as the troops dismounted and relinquished their horses into the care of the wranglers.

Devin was now a member of that crew. Whereas she'd been accustomed to swinging out of the saddle and going immediately to the river to refresh herself and wash away the day's dust, she now had the horses as her first responsibility. Head wrangler Jack assigned her to help unsaddle the animals, rub them down, and lead them to water.

It was, she discovered, a pleasant way to end the day, for it gave her a solid reason to absent herself from Sutter's company at the army's head. She'd increasingly found grounds to avoid the man. Joined though they were in a common cause, and regardless of what she owed him for rescuing her from the prison train, Devin distrusted the man's mercurial cruelty. To what depths of ruthlessness would Sutter descend, when they reached Purity?

"I talked to Estelle today," she told Jack when she found herself working beside him, brushing dried sweat from a horse's coat while he picked pebbles from the hooves of the animal picketed alongside. "She got me thinking. Maybe I haven't seen past my own arrogance."

"How do you mean?" Jack did not look up from his work.

"Well ..." Devin hesitated, trying to order her thoughts concerning the unexpected crosswind she'd felt, coming from Estelle. "Ever since I told Sutter I'd help him get revenge on Purity," she continued slowly, "I've sort of assumed it would be just him and me rooting out the guilty and dispensing Syke justice. I had it in my mind that we'd do it in a kind of orderly way—a way that would spare the innocent." Devin paused in her brushing to ease a cramp in her hand. Horse-tending used muscles she did not typically employ. "But all of these people who've come with us ..."

She trailed off as she stretched her fingers in a vague gesture that encompassed the army. With dusk closing in, the troops busied around their evening chores of cooking, eating, and washing-up, the latter involving their bodies and clothes as well as pots and pans.

"What about 'all of these people'?" Jack straightened from his task to stare at her, somewhat incredulously. "Have you been thinking the rest of us were just along for the ride?"

Devin hung her head, shamefaced.

"Actually, in a sense, I have. I've kind of imagined that when we reach Purity, the troops will ... I don't know ... cheer us on, I suppose. Kind of like the onlookers cheered when I demolished Peaceful Hills. Maybe they can knock down some doors in Purity and help drag out the murdering devils who try to hide in basements and cellars. But it'll be up to Sutter and me to decide what happens to anybody who shares the guilt for massacring Sykes." A brief and uncomfortable pause ensued before Devin added, "That's what I've been thinking, anyway."

Jack snorted. For a moment, he looked angry. But then the scowl left his face, and his tone softened.

"I think you've got a lot to learn about human nature, my lady. I take it that Estelle gave you a lesson on the subject?"

Devin nodded, remembering the woman's smoldering anger. "She told me her parents sacrificed themselves, getting her safe out of Purity. She didn't go into detail, but Estelle made it clear that she wants her own revenge for what the town did to her folks." Describing for Jack the woman's unexpectedly strong display of syketic power, Devin added, "She was so angry just thinking about what had happened years ago, she snapped a tree in two. And she vowed to break a bunch of necks the same way."

Jack passed a hand across his mouth. He gave a short, low laugh, a sound devoid of humor.

"So now you're worried that every Syke who's come along on this trip has their own private axe to grind. Their own old score to settle. And no one's likely to wait for you or Sutter to give them permission. That it?"

"Like I said," Devin muttered. "Blinded by my own arrogance." She paused again, searching his face in the gathering dark, and then whispered, "What are we riding into, Jack?"

He locked eyes with her for a long moment before he answered.

"My guess? It'll be a bloodbath. I think that's what Sutter wants. But now that the blinders have come off your eyes, you'll have to decide for yourself what *you* want, Devin. And what you're prepared to do to get it."

☙ 16 ❧

THEY RODE FOR DAYS through a landscape that did not vary from the flat and featureless. A palpable ripple of relief passed down the line of troops when, at last, they came to an area of low hills that forced the river to veer from its heretofore direct course southward. The channel broadened as it meandered through the hills and dales, the river's lessening current stroking the feet of each low rise.

In one shady bend of the sinuous watercourse, the army's lead riders came upon a lone individual, the first human they had seen since leaving the ranch. A man sat in a small wooden boat that he had tied to a long-limbed willow on the near riverbank. He was fishing. The moment Devin laid eyes on him, the boat rocked gently, as though the approach of herself and the other riders had startled him into shifting his weight on the cross thwart, as if he had prepared to stand. But the man did not stand or otherwise react, except to raise one hand in a casual greeting.

At the front of the army, just ahead of Devin, Sutter reined up, and so did those who followed. This afternoon, they were again a vanguard of four. Devin, Jack, and Orlando rode with their leader.

"Stay here," Sutter ordered them. "I'll speak to that fellow. If he's come upriver from Purity in the last few days, he may have news that we need to know."

So saying, Sutter rode down the riverbank and into the shade of the willows, halting his horse no more than a foot from the bow of the man's rowboat. He tipped his hat to the fisherman, and as the two conversed, Sutter remained mounted but allowed his horse to crop the green grass on the bank where the boat was tied. Despite the fisherman's initial apparent startlement, both men now seemed at their ease, and their conversation stretched on for nearly ten minutes. Not a word of what was said reached those whom Sutter had ordered to wait.

"Say," Orlando muttered after looking upon this scene for a time. "I think I recognize that fellow. I think he might be one of Mike's moles."

Jack nodded agreement but said nothing. He only shot Devin a look that prompted her to recall what he'd told her earlier about Sutter having spies in Purity. If the fisherman was among that number, it tracked that Sutter would wish to speak to him out of anyone's earshot.

This supposition was bolstered when Sutter, having at last concluded the parley, returned to the vanguard and ordered half of its number to stand watch over the fisherman. "Orlando, you and Jack stay with that fellow until the army is past him and out of sight around that next bend." Sutter pointed ahead to where the river curved around the foot of another low hill. "I don't want anybody bothering him. He's not hostile to us."

Jack and Orlando grunted agreement, and as they reined their horses down the riverbank to do as they were bid, Devin joined Sutter in leading the other troops on ahead. During Sutter's lengthy huddle with the fisherman, the Syke army had crowded up behind its leaders, packing in as close as the terrain allowed. Riders had climbed the gentle hillslopes, gaining vantage points from which they could see what had occasioned the delay. Now the army had to re-form its long column, falling in behind as Sutter led them onward. Jack, Orlando, and the fisherman were soon out of Devin's sight as the river wound its way through the hills.

By late in the afternoon, the undulating landscape was dropping away once more toward the unbroken flatland that surrounded it on all sides. But where the river channel curved one final time, the Syke army ended that day's march in a wide meadow sheltered by the last of the hills. Up until now, the army's nightly camps had been fully exposed, strung out along one bank of the river and made visible for miles by the cooking fires the troops kindled. This was the first time the army had camped in any sort of concealment, and Devin wasn't sure if that was by design, or simply because the grass was greener and lusher in this protected bend of the river. The prairie in late summer provided plenty of dry forage for the horses, but the animals went after this fresh grazing with a gusto that communicated their approval of the change.

"Did you get anything out of the fisherman?" Devin asked when she joined Jack and the other wranglers in tending the horses that evening. "Did he have news from Purity?"

Jack shook his head. "The man didn't say a word, except to complain the fish weren't biting. That might have been a dodge, though. The fellow could have had a creel full, and he just didn't want to share any of the bounty."

Devin laughed. "That was smart of him. All those Sykes riding past would have cleaned him out, pilfering his whole catch if he'd admitted to having any. I imagine people are getting tired of beans and beef jerky by now. I am." She lifted her hat and pushed her sweat-dampened hair back from her face. "Have you ever tried to syke a fish out of the water? Seems to me that'd be easier than catching one with a hook and line."

"Yeah, I've tried it a time or two in the trout streams in the mountains. Those buggers are slippery, and they're fast. I generally scoop up more water than fish, and manage mostly to just soak my head."

"Ah," Devin said, nodding. "That could explain why I haven't seen anyone try to fish this river when we camp at night. Until we came across the guy in the boat, it hadn't even occurred to me that the river might have fish in it. With a name like 'Contagion,' I would think it might be barren." She rubbed her lower lip. "Doesn't sound appealing. I'm not sure I'd want to eat anything that swam in that water."

Jack shrugged. "The river got its name a long time ago, back when people ran scared from the sickness. After all these years, it's flushed clean. And unless you're drawing from a well I don't know about"—Jack's wry expression suggested doubt—"you've been drinking it steady, right along with the rest of us and the horses. That's why Sutter came this way, so we'd have good water. Out away from the river, there isn't much. Not many fish, either. Catchable, edible, or otherwise."

Devin stared at him until he broke out grinning. She had to chuckle, then, at her momentary display of outright stupidity regarding the wholesomeness of the river water. But immediately, she wondered if it *was* only a moment.

"Ever since we left the foothills and rode out on this prairie," she admitted, "I've felt as small as a bug. Like I could get lost out here and disappear in this endless grass, and I'd be nothing but another tiny, nameless insect. As I suppose you can tell from some of the things I've said lately, it's messing with my brain." Devin tapped her temple.

"Join the club!" Jack exclaimed.

He put his hand on her shoulder, sending a gasp-inducing quiver along Devin's spine. He'd been careful about touching her since declaring that their age difference—narrow though it was, from Devin's perspective—demanded a platonic relationship. The warmth and weight of Jack's touch held her enthralled as he added, "Being out here in the middle of so much 'nothing' mucks with a person's head."

He raised his hand from Devin's shoulder to gesture at the vast openness of the grassland that stretched westward into the distance, beyond the river's far side. "All this *bigness* plays tricks on your mind and muddles your thinking."

"It gets to you, too?" Devin's astonishment vied in her breast with all of the feelings his touch had aroused in her. "I thought I was the only one. It's overpowering out here. This much space, all around ... it shrinks a person."

"You're not alone. I feel it," Jack assured her. "Up in the mountains, I've got plenty of room and plenty of sky, but there's still a kind of shelter to it, like there's walls around me. But here ..." He gestured again, then said softly, "Out here, it's so damned *exposed*. I feel as naked as a turtle without a shell."

Devin wanted to kiss him. For weeks she'd thought she might be in love with him, and now tonight, in this moment of shared confidences, she was certain of it. It did not matter that she'd known only the walls of her parents' house, and then the walls of the asylum, before arriving in Jack's wonderfully alien, open-air world of ranching, riding, and cowpunching. Despite their disparate origins and ways of life, he understood about walls, and he understood her.

Had the moment lasted a second longer, she would have made good on her impulse. The look on Jack's face told of similar urges rising. But he was holding firm in his determination to "keep his hands off her," as Angelina had commanded. He turned away, and began grooming the next horse in the picket line.

"So, like I said," he declared more loudly than necessary, and without looking at her, "that guy in the boat didn't breathe a word about Purity. Why don't you go on and find Sutter, and ask what they talked about, all that time." Jack, brush in hand, gave the horse a particularly long, sweeping stroke, which ended with him facing away from Devin. "I'm curious, and he's more likely to talk to you than he'll tell me anything."

"All right," Devin muttered, accepting her dismissal with a pang of disappointment. As she walked off in search of Sutter, she put her hand on her shoulder where Jack's fingers had briefly rested. She would hold to the memory of his touch. It would have to do, for now.

* * *

Orlando had prepared the vanguard's usual supper of beans, jerky, and hardtack, which Sutter ate without apparently minding that it was the same thing they'd had for days. Devin filled her plate only partly, though. She could hardly stomach the fare anymore.

"Mike"—she spoke from opposite him at the campfire, choosing her moment when Orlando went to the river to wash the cooking gear—"what did you find out from the fisherman? Does Purity know we're coming?"

Sutter lifted his shoulder in a shrug of indifference. "The fellow hadn't caught wind of it when he left town a few days back. But he's been upriver long enough that he wouldn't know the latest from Purity. He'd been fishing in that same spot, there under the willows for a while, and he hadn't seen a soul until we showed up." Sutter looked across the campfire at her. "What does it matter, partner, whether they know we're coming or not? You ain't afraid of their firearms, are you?"

Devin shook her head. "I'll rip the rifles out of their hands. No problem there," she promised as she returned Sutter's gaze. "But I'd rather we didn't give the guiltiest among them enough advance warning that they can slip out of town and disappear. I'd like to catch them by surprise so we'll be sure to get them all—every single devil who murdered those Sykes, and every person at the top who ordered it done."

Sutter grunted. "Don't you worry, friend, about any of them getting away. If some of those bastards go on the run, they'll have nowhere *to* run except down the river. Heading off in any other direction, they'd die of thirst." He pulled out his knife to carve another chaw of jerky, and took the meat between his teeth. Speaking around it, he added, "We'll chase 'em down the river as far as we have to, until there's not a one of them left standing. You'll get your revenge. And I'll get mine. Me in my way, and you in yours."

The man grinned savagely, and again Devin saw it—that hint of madness she'd earlier detected in him, a lunacy born of his obsession. She looked away.

When Orlando returned, burdened with the washed cookpots and grumbling about his lot in life, she slipped away from the firelit circle and walked to the river. Dumping her barely touched supper in its waters, she scrubbed her plate with a handful of sand, while her thoughts drifted to what Jack had said about them riding into a bloodbath. The constant murmur of the fast-running river seemed to whisper a question: Just how badly did she *want* her revenge?

Before she could compel herself to examine that question and form a conclusive answer, something brushed against her fingers where they dabbled in the water. Instinctively, she grabbed, not with her hands, but with a flash of her will. She netted the thing in a mental construction and flung it up on the riverbank, a sizeable gout of water coming with it.

What she'd caught was a fish. Silver-scaled and weighing at least six pounds, it was a feast—or would be one, if she could find anybody who knew how to clean and cook it.

Devin rejected her usual cook—Orlando—out of hand. She wished to share this prize with someone she liked. Someone special.

Not physically touching the still-flopping fish, she levitated it off the grassy riverbank and headed in search of Jack. But covetous eyes followed her every step as she steered the fish past scores of campfires on the riverbend meadow, and strident voices called out to her from people she could not identify in the dark beyond the flickering firelight. It came as a relief when Estelle's distinctive near-growl reached her ears.

"Where you going with that, girlie?" the woman demanded. "Bring it here. There's none of these muggins knows how to cook fish. If you don't want that beauty ruined, hand it over."

Beelining to the woman's fire, Devin complied. In short order, Estelle had the fish scaled, gutted, and sizzling. Devin ate better that night than she had since leaving Angelina's kitchen. She was satisfied when Jack also got a share, as, done with the horses, he passed Estelle's campsite on his way to join Sutter and Orlando at the head of the company.

Devin did not follow him. She stayed with Estelle. The woman made no objection to her bedding down where she was. And all things considered, Devin thought as she drifted into sleep under a vast, star-filled sky, it would be easiest on her and Jack both, if she put a little extra distance between them tonight.

☙ 17 ❧

"THE FELLOW IN THE BOAT drifted down the river right past us last night, past our whole camp, quiet as a leaf on the water," Jack reported, low-voiced, when he found Devin the next morning as she saddled her mount for the day's ride.

"He got by without being seen? Except by you, I mean?" Devin paused in snugging up the cinch. Jack was already mounted, and she looked up at him, frowning. "Is the guy hightailing it to Purity to tell them we're coming?"

"That was my first thought." Jack scratched his ear under his hat. "I was on my feet, starting to raise the alarm, but Sutter grabbed my arm and swore at me. He told me to keep my mouth shut and leave the fellow be."

"Sutter saw him, too?" Devin rubbed her forehead above her raised eyebrows. "Sneaking past in the dark of night, not making a sound, is what a person would do if they were up to no good. What did Sutter have to say about it?"

"Nothing. He told me to go back to sleep and mind my own business."

"Your business! If we're being betrayed by someone Sutter was wrong to trust, that concerns every one of us." Devin's frown deepened. She tapped her thumbnail on her teeth. "Maybe he'll tell me more. I'll make out like I saw the man last night. Sutter can't keep his partner in the dark."

* * *

Devin rode close to Mike all that morning, looking for a chance to question him. But with Orlando sticking stubbornly to his own assigned place in the vanguard, she had no opportunity until Jack drew the fellow away with a probably invented concern about one of the packhorses showing signs of lameness. Jack and the wranglers gave all of the horses such care, the pack animals as well as the saddle mounts, a debility in any of them was unlikely. But the ruse worked. Orlando rode off with Jack toward the rear of the army, where the packtrain followed.

"I'm glad they're gone," Devin said truthfully when she was finally alone with Sutter, the two of them far enough ahead of the trailing troops to be out of everyone's earshot. "I saw something last night, and I wasn't sure I should talk about it in front of other people. You seemed kind of friendly with that man in the rowboat, so I didn't feel right accusing the guy until I'd checked with you."

"Accusing him? Of what?" Sutter peered at her from under the brim of his hat. "What did you see, friend?"

"It was late last night, and dark, but I'm sure it was him. The fellow drifted past us, not using his oars, not making a sound." Devin watched for Sutter's reaction. "It was suspicious, him waiting until we were all asleep and then slipping like a shadow down the river toward Purity. I didn't like the look of it, and thought you should know."

Sutter eyed her in silence, his gaze shadowed by his hat. Finally he nodded, and gave her his usual sardonic grin.

"You're a pretty good nightwatch, aren't you. Yeah, that fellow was real quiet. Did a good job of not getting noticed. By anybody besides you and me, I mean."

"You saw him, too?" Devin exclaimed, continuing the pretense that she'd seen something she hadn't, and didn't know something she did. "What did you make of it?"

"I concluded," Sutter said, and traced a finger along the brim of his hat, as though sweeping aside an invisible cobweb, "that the man is good at following instructions."

"What?" Devin stared at him, puzzled into a near-stammer. "Wh-what do you mean, 'instructions'? Whose?"

"Mine, of course."

"Umm ..." She faltered, then raised one hand palm up, a gesture of bewilderment. "You'll have to explain, Mike. I'm not following this at all."

Sutter laughed. He threw a glance over his shoulder, as though to be certain they were still out of anyone's earshot.

"I guess there'd be no harm in filling you in, partner, this far along." Sutter trained his gaze on her again. "But let's make it our little secret. Safer that way. Spying is a dangerous business, I'm sure you'll agree."

Getting Devin's hesitant nod of assent, he went on.

"Over the years, I've built myself a pretty wide network of spies in Purity. You might be surprised how many Sykes have avoided detection by the ordinaries in town. I'm told it's not that hard to do, 'abstaining,' hiding your abilities and living a lie for the sake of saving your neck." Sutter smiled again, but grimly. "I couldn't do it, mostly because I've got my pride. And you couldn't do it, because an instinct-driven powerhouse, what they call a *persistent* Syke, could not pretend to be an ordinary little nobody. Not for the life of you, you wouldn't be able to fake it. Not forever." He clicked his tongue. "Those poor sods we found dead in the lockup must have been at least a little like you, too quick with their Syke reflexes to have a hope of going undiscovered. Or maybe they just got careless." He shrugged. "Slip up, get caught, and you're doomed."

"But you've got spies in town who are really good at not getting caught," Devin put in. "That right? Like the guy in the boat."

"Like him, yeah. And even better than him. They've fed me information for years, and they've hustled my people out of town when things get hot and one or two of our friends need to run."

"So the fisherman was someone you trust." Devin's head tilted quizzically as she took all of this in. "But you told the guy to go downriver in the dead of night and stay quiet until he was past us. Why?"

"Because he's going to warn our folks, and I didn't want anybody holding him up with questions they don't need to be asking." Sutter looked at Devin like he thought her brains had fallen into her boots. "We're bringing thunderbolts, blight, and ruin to Purity, right? I told the fellow to get on down to town, quick as he could, find someplace safe to hole up, and make sure his spy buddies lie low, too. They have to understand: there's no guarantee I'll know friend from foe, once the fireworks start."

Orlando chose that moment to return to the vanguard, grumbling about a waste of his time. Then, looking to the fore past Sutter, he threw up one arm and exclaimed, "A sheep, boss! I see a sheep. How 'bout I kill it for our supper?"

"It's not wild," Devin protested, distracted from what Sutter had been saying about friends and foes. "Somebody owns it. It's pastured. See the fence? And isn't that a shed in the distance?" She peered ahead, trying to make out details of the first signs of habitation they had come across in days of following the river. "There's a house, too, and more sheep."

"More sheep means more meat." Orlando shot her a greedy leer. "We'll *all* eat mutton tonight."

"So now you're a sheep rustler?" Devin countered, looking scornfully at him. "Didn't your mother teach you it's wrong to steal?" She pointed at the fence that cut their path. It was more of a wall, a rubbly construction about four feet high, made of stacked stones and mud bricks that blended with the landscape so it looked nearly like a natural formation. Except the wall ran too straight, arrowing eastward across the plains, its near end anchored upon the riverbank at the water's edge. That end was noticeably eroded, evidence that the river could flood with a rising, rushing current strong enough to eat away at hardened bricks of mud and the even harder foundation stones, reducing them to gravel.

Orlando was bristling at Devin's having called him a thief. But whatever response he might have made was lost in the loud bang of an explosion.

Both of their horses startled and tried to bolt, requiring Devin and Orlando to control their mounts as, shocked out of their argument, they jerked their heads together in the direction of the noise. A great hole had been blasted in the wall, directly in their path. Sutter, now several steps ahead, rode through the dust-choked opening and drew rein in the no-longer-enclosed sheep pasture. Not a single ewe or ram remained nearby. But toward the shed in the distance, a flock of sheep sprinted away, putting acres between themselves and the architect of the explosion.

"You did that?" Devin gasped as she mastered her horse and trotted through the wide break to join Sutter. "I guess it must have been you, since I don't see anyone else around." She scanned the surrounding area, glancing especially toward the cluster of low buildings that suggested a farmstead, barely in view southward. "I think there may have been quieter ways of saving Orlando from the shame of sheep-rustling."

Sutter laughed. "We'll stick to beans and beef. Even if I didn't hate the taste of mutton, there's no time now to be butchering a bunch of sheep." He gestured toward the farmstead, and the look on his face grew serious. "That's our first sign of civilization. We're not too far from Purity now, and I aim to discover whether the sheepherder is friend or foe. Whoever lives there will have to convince me they don't hold with murdering Sykes in their beds."

Devin, with the tip of her tongue, moistened her lower lip. The threat implicit in Sutter's words had come through clearly. His rampage against ordinaries was about to begin, if he found the shepherd blameworthy.

The Syke army followed the vanguard through the breach in the brick-and-stone wall. As the riders streamed through, raising clouds of dust from the strewn rubble, Devin abandoned any thought of waiting where she was until all of the troops had passed by. She'd had a fleeting inclination to bend the powers of her mind upon mending the wall, once the army was through the break. But if she meant to show goodwill to the shepherd—if any goodwill proved to be warranted—she needed to be up front with Sutter, ready to save the farmsteader from Mike's crusade of vengeance ... but, again, only if such saving was merited.

As Devin reined her horse around, preparing to close the gap that she'd allowed to lengthen between herself and Sutter, she spotted Jack with the packtrain, coming through the wall breach. She beckoned him to her, and when he rode close, she muttered, "Let's hurry on up to keep an eye on Sutter. I think he's aiming to make a start on what he came to do."

Jack raised an eyebrow, but spoke no word as he urged his horse forward. Together, he and Devin loped to the front of the column, catching up with Sutter and Orlando while the vanguard was still a half mile from the farmstead.

The low buildings—constructed, like the boundary wall, of stone and sun-dried earth—blended with their surroundings and were not obtrusive, but were still unmissable on the bald prairie. As the army neared the farmstead, a single individual emerged from the largest of the modest structures and stood outside its door, apparently weaponless, awaiting their arrival with arms crossed and no sign of alarm.

The person was dressed similarly to Sutter and every rider in the ranks: wide-brimmed hat; long-sleeved, button-front shirt; denim trousers tucked into boots. Devin assumed the whipcord figure was a man, until she spotted the loose braids that tumbled from under the hat and fell nearly to the person's waist.

"Howdy, strangers," the waiting figure greeted them, her voice confident, huskily mature but distinctly female, almost magnetically so. Devin, studying the woman, could not begin to guess her age. Her braided hair looked silvery-gray until she stepped away from the door and came out into the full sunlight to offer Sutter a handshake. In the slanting rays of afternoon, the silver transformed into gold. The thick braids, one on either shoulder, gleamed like ropes that were woven of precious metals.

"Golly," Jack whispered, barely loud enough for Devin to hear. But his reaction confirmed that she was not the only one impressed, and perhaps a bit awed, by this supremely self-possessed woman with the dazzling hair and an aura of incontestable authority. As Sutter leaned from his saddle to shake the hand the woman offered, even he seemed a little dazed. He stared at the woman, and managed no other response to her greeting except a slightly breathless, "'Afternoon, ma'am."

After a pause in which Sutter recovered enough to at least release the woman's hand and straighten in his saddle, he added, "This your place?" He nodded toward the sheep, which had bunched into the farthest angle of the enclosed pasture, catty-corner from where he'd blasted a hole to bring his army through the woman's wall. "Those your animals?"

The woman inclined her head with the dignity of a sovereign bestowing the favor of her notice upon a yeoman of little merit. "Yes, to both your questions." She looked from Sutter to the long column of troops that had invaded her property, their two hundred horses trampling the grassy stretch of pasture along the river. Her smile was icy as she added, "You are all welcome to sit and rest a spell, but you'll pardon me if I don't invite you to supper. I don't have near enough grub to feed so many visitors."

The way she said "visitors" was entirely civil and polite, but the coolness of the woman's smile communicated what she really meant: *intruders, trespassers.* Devin flushed with embarrassment, feeling that she'd overstepped all the bounds of propriety to push her way uninvited into the domain of this regal woman. She gathered her horse's reins, preparing to ride on, and saw Jack do the same.

Sutter, however, had regained his composure and remembered his purpose.

"That's mighty kind of you, ma'am." He clipped his words as if impatient to get past the civilities. "We won't stop, but before we ride on, I'll need the answers to a couple of questions." The stare he leveled at the woman held more menace now than bemusement. "Do you know what happened at Peaceful Hills?"

The woman frowned thoughtfully, and raised one hand to push her hat back on her head. Her face, thus revealed more clearly to Devin's study, did not disclose her age any more obviously than her hair had. She was deeply tanned, her complexion an earthy brown, but her skin was smooth, not burnt to leather by the harsh sun of the plains. Her eyes were a surprising shade of deep turquoise. When shaded by the brim of her hat, the woman's eyes had appeared almost black. With the sun glinting off them, however, their gemlike blue-green tints shone forth. Devin found herself catching her breath once more. Who *was* this woman?

"The only 'peaceful hills' I know of," the shepherdess said after a moment's consideration, during which she met Sutter's threatening stare without the slightest twitch of nerves, "are those hills that lie a little north of here, in that broken country where the river bends." She shrugged. "I've not heard of any happenings up that way, so I assume they're still peaceful. If you've come through there, you'll likely know more than I do." She smiled again, but wryly. "The fact is, you folks"—she gestured at the long line of troops that were waiting, with increasing impatience, for the signal to move on—"you folks are the only thing to disturb the peace on this river for a couple of years or more. It's generally always quiet out here."

Sutter continued to hold the woman's gaze, as if locked in a staring contest. When neither blinked, he asked his second question.

"Do you know any Sykes?"

The woman's chin came up. She raised a finger in warning. "That's not a question many people will dare to ask, not this close to Purity. But maybe you're a stranger to these parts, and you don't know the ways of that town. If you'll take a little friendly advice, you'll keep quiet about 'Sykes' once you hit town." She pointed south, down the river. "If that's where you're meaning to go, anyhow. I don't know your business, and I don't care to."

"Answer the question." Sutter's temper flared. "Do you know any?"

The woman's turquoise eyes narrowed. "You're mighty insistent, mister, on knowing my business when I've got no interest in yours." She lifted one of her long, shiny braids from her shoulder and ran it through her fingers. The late-afternoon sun struck sparks from its silver and gold. "But since you're so keen on the subject of Sykes, I'll talk about them as freely as you do. Sure, I've met some." She flicked the end of her braid toward the river. "From time to time, adventurous souls make their way up here from Purity, fishing the river, or just wanting to get out of town and away from all those people."

The woman shot another glance down the line of troops as she added, pointedly, "I've no use for crowds, but I don't mind the occasional visitor. If someone's caught out on the river at nightfall, I'll give them supper and put them up for the night." She gestured at a shepherd's hut that sat on iron wheels among the other farm buildings, near the open shed. "Some of my guests have given me to understand they have certain powers of the mind. No one comes right out and says they're a Syke, but they make their meaning clear."

"And you're fine with that, are you?" Sutter demanded. "Sykes don't scare you?"

The ice returned to the woman's smile.

"Not much of anything scares me, mister. And now"—she took a step aside from where she had stood talking to Sutter—"if you'll excuse me, I need to get the sheep in. There's prairie wolves out here that'd love to relieve me of half my flock." At this, the woman looked directly at Orlando, filling Devin with a feeling that she knew exactly what the fellow had proposed, in the way of killing and eating her livestock.

Sutter eyed the woman a moment longer, but then touched the brim of his hat. "It's been a pleasure, ma'am. We'll be on our way now." He lifted his reins and urged his horse forward, heading south along the riverbank once more.

His troops followed, but Devin held back when she got past the farthest farm building, and Jack reined alongside her.

"Interesting," he muttered as they waited off to the side, watching the army file past. "Whoever that woman is, she's got nerves of spring steel. Sutter could have killed her with a thought, but she didn't give an inch."

"I'm not so sure," Devin whispered back. "That he could have killed her, I mean. Not with his mind, or his fists, or in any other way." She shot a meditative glance in the woman's direction. The lady of steel had produced a horse from somewhere on her farmstead, and now rode the animal without saddle or bridle, heading to the corner where her sheep huddled.

"Let's try to hurry the army along," Devin said as she turned her own horse toward the rear of the column, which was lagging behind as the final two dozen riders cast curious looks at the only sign of human occupancy they'd seen on the prairie. "Those sheep will stay skittish until we've cleared out, and I think we've already tested that woman's patience about as much as she'll tolerate."

"You believe she could be dangerous?" Jack's eyebrows twitched up his forehead as he fell in beside Devin to urge the stragglers along. "How could she be any threat, by herself, to a whole army of Sykes?"

"I've just got a feeling about her." Devin groped for a way to explain her gut-deep instinct. "There's something about her that reminds me of Angelina."

"And you think Angelina is *dangerous*?" Jack stopped short of scoffing, but his incredulity shone clear. "Angie's about the safest person I've ever been around. You've seen the way she takes care of everyone at the ranch."

Devin gave an impatient nod. "She's the soul of kindness, but I've also seen that she's got power. Great power that she doesn't often reveal. Remember how she lifted those corpses from the mine-pit and laid them to rest, under the pines halfway up the mountain? She did it because no one else could. No other Syke from the ranch had the strength of mind to do what she did." Devin tucked a loose strand of hair behind her ear as she studied Jack, looking for a sign that he understood the point she meant to make. "I'd never say that Angelina is dangerous, but she's undeniably powerful. And with great power comes the potential for big danger."

Jack returned her gaze, and slowly nodded. "You think that woman back there"—he jerked his thumb toward the farm buildings that lay a short distance behind them—"you think she's got hidden powers. Is she a Syke?"

"Maybe. Or I'd say probably. She sure didn't flinch when Sutter asked if she knew any. I don't have that much experience with ordinaries, outside of the asylum," Devin admitted, thinking of her cloistered childhood and the isolation it had imposed. "But from what I've seen, ordinaries tend to fly into hysterics at any hint of a Syke around. You have to admit, she was amazingly calm and casual about Sutter's questions, when most people would have been alarmed."

Their conversation was interrupted by the boom of an explosion up ahead. Both Devin and Jack jumped, as did their horses. But the blast was far enough away this time that all the horses settled quickly, including the pack animals at the end of the column. Devin and her loyal knight were bringing up the rear, for reasons that now went beyond hustling the army clear of the farmsteader's property, ensuring that every rider got out before nightfall, which was now fast approaching. The conviction had grown in Devin's mind that she must make amends, at least in part, for the damage Sutter had done—and was doing—to the mud walls of the mysterious shepherdess.

"I was expecting that noise," she said as Jack craned his neck, trying without luck to see very far ahead. "I figure that came from another wall, or fence, or whatever the right word is for the way the woman sets her property lines. That was Mike blasting his way through, like he did the other wall."

"Shit," Jack muttered. "Sutter doesn't seem too bothered about testing the woman's patience." He threw a glance over his shoulder as if worried the shepherdess might be racing toward them in a towering rage.

The way behind remained clear, however, and did so until the entire army had covered the distance to the second wall and every rider had passed through the new-made breach. The moment she and Jack crossed to the outside on the packtrain's heels, Devin drew rein.

"Wait." She dropped from the saddle. "I can't leave it wrecked like this."

"Hurry." Jack looked ahead to the army that continued moving steadily down the river. He shot a glance, as well, toward the setting sun. "I don't fancy hanging around here after dark."

Devin made a vague reply, more a wordless noise in the back of her throat. Her attention was on the break in the wall, and the many stones Sutter had blasted out of his way. She bent her mind upon the stones and ordered each to find its former place in the structure's foundation. The fragmented mud bricks were trickier to return to their previous states and locations, for the force of Sutter's syketic blow had pulverized many of them. But Devin found she could use a modified Beskil bubble to mold the loose debris into the form of bricks that would hold their shape, as she mentally commanded the broken bits to pack themselves back together and be solid blocks once more.

She was levitating the final brick into place, centering it like a keystone in the repaired wall, when a woman's calm, husky voice spoke from the twilight.

"You do fine work, Miss Perridin."

Devin dropped the brick. She bit off a scream of surprise and jumped backward, away from the wall and straight into Jack's arms.

He caught and held her, keeping them both on their feet while swearing under his breath. "*Shit!* She moves like a ghost."

The woman came into view across the restored wall, her shimmering hair her most visible feature in the gathering dusk. She did seem a ghost, for her arrival had been utterly silent. The wall was far enough from the main buildings of the woman's farmstead that she had almost certainly ridden here, not walked. But neither Devin nor Jack had heard any sound of an approaching horse, and there was now no snuffling or stamping to indicate that any stood tethered nearby.

"Pardon me for disturbing you," the woman said, chuckling softly as she glided up to the wall on her side and touched the spot that would have held the final brick, if Devin hadn't dropped it. "The sounds of your work stirred my curiosity." The woman no longer wore a hat, and the gleaming crown of her hair sketched the movements of her head as she bent to study the repairs, then straightened to address Devin. "I thank you, Miss Perridin, for patching the hole your impudent companion made in my sheep fence."

"How ... how do you know my name?" Devin half stammered, startled into finding her voice. "I'm sure I didn't tell you, back there." She gestured in the direction of the farm buildings where they had last seen the woman.

The ghostly figure laughed.

"Oh, my dear young lady!" The woman's teeth flashed white in a broad smile. "You are famous. Everyone this side of the Contagion River knows your name. You're the one who got away."

Devin pondered this, her finger rubbing at her lower lip. "Then you do know about Peaceful Hills," she said after a moment, careful to not sound accusatory. "You know about the prison train, and the Sykes it carried to their deaths."

"I've no direct knowledge of any part of that atrocity," the woman responded, firm-voiced. "But I've heard stories. My visitors from Purity have told me what they know of it. They've spoken of a powerful young woman who derailed the asylum train and disappeared high into the mountains."

"Do you approve?" Jack interjected, the first words he'd directed at the shepherdess. "Of her wrecking the train, and getting free?"

Dusk was folding into the deeper darkness of night, making it impossible to see the deep turquoise hues of the woman's eyes. But enough starlight shone down and reflected off the nearby river to pick out a small movement of the woman's lustrous-haired head. Devin felt as much as saw that the woman's gaze had shifted to Jack where he stood with one arm around Devin's waist, continuing to offer her his welcome support.

"I'm surprised that you need to ask," the woman replied. "The fact that I am standing here speaking to Miss Perridin in the open, not hiding from her in my root cellar, should be answer enough for you, young man. But to be perfectly clear about my views on the matter: yes, I do approve."

Jack let out an audible sigh of relief. Devin sensed some of the tension leaving him, and her own taut nerves relaxed a little. Whoever and whatever this woman was, they might reasonably count her an ally.

"If you've no more questions for me," the woman said, with a smile they couldn't see but which sounded in her voice, "I shall bid you good-night. Your companions have gone on without you, and although I am not sorry to see them off my property, I expect you will wish to rejoin them before the night is far advanced. As I mentioned before, prairie wolves prowl these parts. The flames of many campfires, however, will certainly deter them. I advise you to delay no longer. Your work here is done."

Jack accepted this dismissal with alacrity. He stepped away from Devin and gathered his horse's reins, preparing to swing into the saddle.

Devin, however, lingered a moment to offer an apology.

"I'm sorry," she said, approaching the chest-high wall to face the woman who stood on the other side of it, "that I didn't get a chance to rebuild your other fence." She gestured in the direction of the first damage that Sutter had inflicted upon the woman's property. "My ..." *partner*, she started to say, but decided not to associate herself so closely with the man. "The fellow who knocked it down is a bit of a hot-head."

"So I gathered." The woman's murmur was low enough to not reach Jack's ears. "Do not trouble yourself about my fences, Miss Perridin. While I am grateful for your efforts, I must needs restyle your work to suit my peculiar tastes." She dipped her head, and at Devin's feet a foundation stone shifted.

Devin jumped back, getting clear in case the entire structure was about to crumble. But only a few bricks slumped where the foundation had been disturbed, sending out a little spray of dust that made Devin sneeze.

"That's a start." The woman lifted her head to gaze directly at Devin once more. A gleam of starlight picked out a droll smile on her lips. "You needn't have built your rows so straight and neat. I prefer a fence that's a tad dilapidated. Rustic, I suppose you'd call it. But I'll set my mind to further 'rustication' after a night's rest. Now the hour grows late, and your young man is eager to be gone." The woman gestured in Jack's direction.

The taste of dust made Devin aware that she was standing, gawking, with her mouth open. The *who* of this woman remained a mystery, but Devin was now sure of the *what.* In this unexpected spot on the banks of the Contagion, just a day's ride from Purity, a Syke was living freely, openly, with no apparent fear of discovery by the ordinaries.

"Devin." Jack's call broke into her thoughts. "If you don't want Sutter sending Orlando to look for us, we need to be getting on."

That was the right thing to say, to get her moving. Devin assuredly did not want Orlando prowling after them in the dark.

"Goodbye," she said to the woman across the wall from her. "I hope we'll meet again."

"I'm certain we shall. You are always welcome here, Miss Perridin. But," the woman added, with a clear note of warning in her voice now, "I would discourage your Mister Sutter from returning here. That is the name of the hotheaded fellow, I take it? Once I've remade my fences to my liking, I will not look kindly upon him knocking new holes in them."

"Yes, ma'am," Devin murmured, not knowing what else to say to the ghostly figure who held herself like a queen and exuded power like a goddess. "Goodnight."

Jack handed over her horse's reins, and Devin hurried to mount, as ready now as he was to catch up to the others. The army had undoubtedly made camp by this hour, and from the troops' supper there might be nothing awaiting Devin and Jack except scraps and leftovers. But she'd eat whatever there was, even if only hardtack and cold beans. Her stomach was growling.

As they reined away to follow the river southward, the woman's voice reached them once more.

"A final word, Miss Perridin," the shepherdess called from beyond the wall. "Whatever you have in mind for Purity, don't prove the ordinaries right about you. Don't be a monster."

ଓ 18 ଛ

EXCITEMENT CRACKLED IN the predawn air like ethereal electricity when the army rode out at first light the next day. If they allowed nothing to delay them, Sutter said, they could be assaulting the heart of the city, Purity's courthouse square, before nightfall.

Devin interpreted Sutter's "nothing" to mean *no one*. The man made it clear he would not willingly engage, this day, in any conversation as long—or as polite—as yesterday's talk with the gem-eyed shepherdess. Sutter meant to sweep all aside as he led his troops into the middle of Purity.

But by early afternoon, when the riders reached the first thin fringes of habitation on the farthest outskirts of the populated area, they'd seen no one who might question, oppose, or delay them. The outlying farms and isolated cottages looked entirely deserted. Behind the hedgerows, kitchen gardens appeared neatly tended, and farmers' fields showed no sign of neglect. Clearly, the abandonment was not of long standing, but a thing that had happened recently. Quite possibly, this very day.

"Where is everybody? Where are the rifles? Where's the sheriff?" Devin voiced the questions that all of the ranch Sykes had in their minds, and several besides herself had already asked out loud.

She turned to Jack, who rode, as usual, at her side. "I've been worried about Sutter going off like a bomb when we get among people. If he loses his head, he'll kill the innocent along with the guilty." Devin kept her voice low to avoid being overheard by Sutter or Orlando. The latter had reasserted his right to the second-place spot in the army's vanguard, and he rode now on Sutter's flank, with Devin and Jack lagging purposely behind so they could talk. "But now," Devin added under her breath, "I'm afraid Mike'll just start flattening everything in sight. Somebody better show up pretty soon, and they'd better have the right answers for him."

"Could be, there's nobody in Purity or the whole vicinity who has the guts to stand up in front of an army of Sykes and name names," Jack commented. "We may never know exactly who issued the order to turn off the asylum's lights and lock the doors with all the 'patients' still inside. Whoever's responsible may have doomed the whole town and most of the spittin'-distance neighbors to feel Sutter's wrath. And yours," he added, looking sidelong at Devin.

She pushed back her hat to rub her forehead, then shrugged. "I don't know that anybody in Purity is really innocent. After what we found at Peaceful Hills, I'm inclined to blame them all. It's hard to believe there's any soul east of the river who didn't know what went on in that hellhole, because the tortures lasted for years. Even if the final crime has been kept secret, and most of the ordinaries aren't aware of what happened when they shut the place down." She paused, rubbing her lower lip. "But if there *are* some who do not share in the guilt of the authorities, they ought to be spared. I don't want to turn into a murderer like those devils at the asylum."

"Don't be a monster," Jack muttered. "Isn't that what the lady said?"

Devin sighed. "It's like she knew exactly why we were riding to Purity. I wonder if that man in the boat stopped to tell her on his way down the river. Judging by this"—Devin gestured at the depopulated suburbs through which they rode—"I'm thinking he tipped off everybody he saw."

She had earlier told Jack about the boatman carrying Sutter's warning to his network of spies in Purity, but now it appeared that many others besides the spies had gotten the message. "Everybody around here is lying low. The word has spread."

"Or maybe there's something else ..."

Jack trailed off as he stared ahead, in the direction of the city center. They were close enough to the heart of things now to see the tops of the taller buildings, including the bell tower on the schoolhouse, and the law court's cupola. These were backlit by the afternoon sun, obliging both Jack and Devin to squint and shade their eyes as they peered at the skyline.

"Look there!" Jack exclaimed after another moment's study. "Is that smoke? Past the towers on the tall buildings. It looks to be over on the far side of town."

Up until now, their ride into the fringes of Purity had largely been accompanied by an empty silence—a stillness that was untroubled by people, anyway. Chickens clucked, dogs barked, and cattle lowed in the paddocks. Among the latter were unmilked milk cows, left in a state of some distress by their absent owners.

What came to Devin's ears next, however, were not barnyard sounds. She heard a noise like far-off thunder, with a great clanking and clanging, and then a rumble that put her in mind of many voices shouting and crying out, their cries muffled by distance.

"That's the sound of trouble." Jack cocked an ear to listen. "I think we might be riding toward a riot."

"That could explain why we haven't seen the sheriff gunning for us with a regiment of riflemen. The marshal's busy quelling an uprising. Maybe that's where everybody's gone." Devin gestured at the deserted homesteads nearby. Then she urged her horse to a quicker pace. "Let's go see!"

Sutter had had the same idea. He and Orlando were off at a trot before Jack and Devin had closed the space between them. But their horses brought them speedily up, and with the four members of the vanguard riding together once more, all broke into a gallop. Devin spared a glance over her shoulder, and saw the Syke army come pounding after them, the sound of their horses' hooves ringing off the cobblestones underfoot.

The dirt roads and country lanes were behind them now. They'd ridden from the thinly populated outskirts into a more close-packed neighborhood of genteel homes lining cobblestone streets. But these houses, too, appeared deserted. As Devin raced past, she saw no one standing in a doorway or tending flowers in a window box. The only signs of occupation were the dogs in the fenced-in front yards, each barking furiously at the passing riders, along with a few cats that streaked for cover, disappearing to either side of the street.

Such was the speed of the army's advance, and the modest size of the so-called city, the riders could have crossed from one end of Purity to the other before the sun had dipped perceptibly lower. That had evidently been Sutter's intent: to lead his troops through the middle of town and arrive in a thundering rush at the far edge, into the middle of whatever fracas had sent smoke rising into the sky.

But at the town center, Sutter was obliged to rein up sharply, his vanguard riders with him, and the pursuing troops as well. The army came to a ragged, disorderly, and noisy stop, for some of the horses had the bits in their teeth and were set on continuing the race. While the riders shouted and cursed their unruly mounts, the horses neighed their frustration at the abrupt halt, and some reared, adding to the chaos.

A scene not too different played out on the opposite side of the town's central square, where an army of a different sort had amassed in such numbers, they had effectively blocked the way of the in-riding troops. The army that milled in a shouting, angry throng across the plaza from Sutter's forces was not a mounted cavalry. They had no horses, and they couldn't properly be called an "army" any more than Sutter's riders could. Neither side wore uniforms. Sutter's troops were in boots, hats, and denims: the standard garb of ranch hands, for such they were. The opposing "army" wore clothing typical of workmen and shopkeepers.

Devin picked out the white aprons and paper hats that characterized butchers. Others in the throng looked to be mechanics or painters, to judge by their overalls. One impressively large, rawboned woman appeared to be covered in flour, as though she'd stepped away from a bakery's kitchen to join the riled-up throng in the courthouse square.

The crowd across the way was not only angry, it was armed. A few individuals carried rifles, but most were equipped with makeshift weapons. Glinting in the sun were knives, axes, and shafts of various lengths, the latter with sharp points like spears. There were also pitchforks and garden implements: spades and shears brandished by people who looked like they'd never done violence to anything bigger or more threatening than a rabbit they'd caught stealing from their vegetable patch.

"It appears," Jack shouted to Devin over the noise that filled the plaza from both sides, "the rioters have come to meet us halfway. Or is this a different bunch from whoever did the burning on the far side of town?"

Devin raised one hand palm up, signaling her confusion.

"But they're not here for us," she shouted back. "See? They're hardly looking our way. It's the courthouse they're screaming at." She gestured at the three-story building which dominated the plaza, the building with the cupola that had been visible from the outskirts. "Can you make out what they're shouting over there? Sounds like, 'Come out killers'!"

Jack nodded, but before he could voice a reply, a particularly piercing outcry from the ranks of the rioters claimed his attention and Devin's, and also Sutter's. The three of them reined their horses close together at the edge of the plaza, where they'd pulled up short upon seeing the huge crowd packing the square across from them. Devin had no idea where the fourth vanguardian was. Perhaps Orlando's horse had carried him off in the initial chaos of the army's aborted crosstown race. She hadn't spared a moment to look around for the fellow, and she certainly would not do so at this instant, for something surprising was happening on the courthouse roof.

Every eye in the plaza—whether that of a congregated rioter or a Syke in Sutter's company—was trained now on the cupola atop the building. A small door like a shuttered window had been thrown open there, and a man was leaning far out, holding on to the sill with one hand while shaking his fist at the crowd with the other. Devin couldn't hear the man's shouts over the rioters' cacophonous cursing and screaming, but she assumed the fellow was raining abuse upon the crowd. His face twisted with unconcealed rage and loathing.

"Sheriff!" Sutter bellowed suddenly from just in front of Devin, so unexpectedly that she jumped.

Up until now, Mike had seemed as confused as she was by what they'd ridden into. He'd anticipated being met by armed officers of the law, a direct and clearly identifiable threat that would have been easily dealt with by an army of Sykes. By thought alone, and from a safe distance, he and his troops could have wrenched the rifles out of every deputy's hand, and probably would have snapped the necks of those officers to boot, before the deputies could do more than feel the rage and the syketic power behind the violent thoughts that killed them. Sutter had been wholly unprepared, however, to encounter a riot in progress—a riot staged by townspeople who, it would seem, had beaten them to the punch in making war on Purity.

But now, the appearance of the man on the courthouse roof jolted Sutter out of the bewildered stillness that had gripped him. He spurred his horse forward, trotting out onto the stone-paved plaza and sparing no glance for the crowd that cursed the man from below.

Sutter looked only upward, craning his neck to keep the man in sight as he rode nearer.

"Sheriff!" he roared again, and the man heard, for Sutter's shout had cut through the clamor of the crowd. The man on high shifted his gaze to peer not at the throng below, but to search in the direction from which the shout had come. Sutter raised an arm to secure the fellow's attention, ensuring that the man would know who had hailed him.

"This is for Tony!" Sutter screamed up at him. "*Die,* pig!"

Sutter's raised arm came down, and the sheriff came down with it. The force of Mike's mental attack yanked the man out through the cupola's small window. The sheriff slid headfirst down the steeply sloped courthouse roof, and his descent picked up speed when he tumbled off the roof's edge. He fell screaming, and his screams were clearly heard, for Sutter's attack had shocked the big crowd into near silence.

The silence lasted until the sheriff's body hit the plaza's pavement. But at the sound of the man's skull shattering upon the unyielding stone, the crowd went wild. They cheered for Sutter as they might cheer a conquering hero.

Sutter, however, wasn't finished. He gazed for a moment at the sheriff's broken body and the widening pool of blood that stained the white flagstones a grisly red. Then he looked high again, squinting with concentration, his face contorted in a savage grin. Sutter dispensed with an arm-wave this time: nothing beyond his strength of mind, his potent syketic power, was necessary to smash the cupola atop the courthouse. He did it with a thought. Pieces of the structure rained down, and the crowd below erupted in new turmoil, but no longer cheering as people dodged the falling tiles and timbers.

"Stop!" came a yell from the crowd. A man raced out of the throng and beelined toward where Sutter sat on his horse with about half the width of the plaza between him and the fellow who had shouted.

Devin recognized the individual: it was the boatman from the river. The man waved his arms frantically, trying to get Sutter's attention. But Mike was intent on doing more damage to the courthouse. From the building came a sound like a deep groan, followed by an ominously sharp *creak*.

The sound brought Devin's gaze snapping upward. Instead of watching Sutter and the agitated boatman, she looked for the source of the creaking. The cupola's collapse had left a hole in the center of the courthouse roof, and Sutter seemed determined to widen that hole until the roof's entire structure fell inward, crashing down inside the building. Terrified screams came from the crowd across the way, and Devin looked over again to find the boatman at Sutter's stirrup, both of his hands raised as if beseeching Mike to cease his attack.

She acted. With a flash of her will, Devin cocooned the roof in a Beskil bubble, halting the collapse mid-crumble, holding each overstressed rafter and roof beam frozen in time, precisely where it was. For good measure, she wrapped the entire building in a second impenetrable bubble. She could remove both of those bulwarks, if she so chose, and allow the building to continue its collapse, after she'd heard what the boatman was desperately trying to convey to Sutter.

As Devin encased the building in syketic safeguards, she encountered no resistance from Mike. He'd been distracted, his attention drawn elsewhere. At the same moment she summoned the bubbles, Jack had spurred away from her side, urging his horse onto the plaza's slick pavement and riding straight at Sutter, giving Devin the time she needed to enforce her own intention upon the courthouse.

Now, she saw Mike stiffen. His gaze whipped around and he jerked his hand up in a gesture of warning as he glared at Jack.

Not taking her eyes from the pair, Devin swung out of her saddle. As she walked out onto the plaza, she was peripherally aware that majorities in both armies—townspeople to one side, ranch hands on the other—were watching her stride toward Sutter, Jack, and the boatman. The latter individual was still trying to have his say, but the former ignored him. Sutter was too busy looking daggers at Jack.

"You interfere with me at your peril, son." Sutter's growl reached Devin as she came to the boatman's side and stood with that man at Mike's stirrup. Around Sutter and his horse, syketic energies flowed and fought. Devin could feel the forces contending, one against the other. Jack and Sutter were engaged in a battle of wills. The mental contest brought the blood to Sutter's face—he flushed with anger. Jack, however, had gone pale under his outdoorsman's tan. As he'd readily admitted to Devin during one of their first conversations, his Syke powers were a shadow of Sutter's. Jack would not long be able to keep this up.

Devin intervened, but in a way that would allow both men to save face. This was clearly a "pissing contest," and she'd had firsthand experience with Sutter's reaction to the perceived loss of such a battle, up on the mountain-ledge meadow when her unbridled display of Syke prowess had bruised his ego. She did not wish to further enflame the man's short, hot, unthinking temper. Sutter was angry enough already.

She did the only thing she could think of, therefore, that did not involve her own incursion of mental force into the syketic fray. Devin took a step back, away from Sutter's stirrup, and then threw herself hard at his horse. She slammed into the horse's shoulder, startling the animal off-balance so that it had to fight for footing on the plaza's slippery pavement.

"Shit!" Sutter swore. His attention broke from Jack and fastened on the slewing, skidding animal under him.

Both Devin and the boatman backed up while the rider fought to control his mount. For a long moment, the outcome remained in question: would horse and horseman stay up or go down? Sutter's riding skills prevailed, however, and he steadied his mount.

"What the *hell*—?" His furious gaze fixed now on Devin.

With an impatient gesture, she brushed it aside.

"Shit, Mike," she swore as vehemently as he had. "Aren't you the least bit curious to know what in blazes is going on around here?" Devin indicated the agitated crowd. The rioters were agitated now in two directions, both toward the courthouse and toward Sutter. "This isn't exactly playing out like we expected," she observed, rather unnecessarily.

Not waiting for him to answer—he glared, but his mouth worked without producing a sound through clenched teeth—Devin turned to the boatman.

"Sir," she began.

But that man cut her off, eagerly grabbing this chance to make himself heard at last.

"It's the children!" he cried. "The children are locked in the courthouse with the killers."

Devin gaped. "Someone's killing children in there?"

The boatman waved his hands helplessly. "The kids are their shields. They're using the children as human shields to protect themselves from us"—he gestured at the noisy crowd—"and now from all of you, too." The boatman indicated Sutter's troops, many of whom had followed Devin onto the paved plaza. Like her, wary of a surface too slick for horses' hooves, they'd left their mounts on grittier ground at the edge of the square and entered the plaza afoot.

Many of the hesitantly roving troops were met halfway by people who slipped out of the crowd thronging the plaza's opposite side. Devin saw handshakes exchanged, and more than a few embraces as, on both sides, people reunited with those they had once known. This was a homecoming, she realized, for many if not most of the Sykes who had ridden here from the ranch. Most of Sutter's followers were fugitives from the harsh justice of Purity that declared all Sykes to be dangerously insane criminals.

She took all of this in with a sweeping glance, but it was the boatman's declaration of children in danger that held her.

"Who's 'they'?" she demanded. "Who's using the children as shields?"

"The killers," the boatman repeated.

He took a deep breath and visibly forced himself to a semblance of calm as he tried to explain. "Already by this morning, before you folks got here, we'd rounded up 'most all of the medicos who legged it from the asylum. We've, umm, *dealt* with that lot." The boatman turned his head and spat, and there was a gleam of satisfaction in his eye when he went on. "After they'd locked the doors behind their sorry asses, the asylum staff came home to Purity on the last train down from the mountains. None of the medicos would admit what they'd done, abandoning the Sykes to rot, but the kitchen drudges knew it. They gave us the names of everybody at the snake pit who was directly part of the massacre—the ones who pulled the trigger, so to speak. We've dealt with those devils."

Devin stared at the boatman, and then shot a glance at Sutter. Mike was still frowning, but he no longer glared at her or Jack. As he sat on his horse, the animal now calm, his gaze bored into the boatman. Sutter had to be realizing, as Devin was quickly coming to understand, that the rioters in the plaza were united in common cause with his army. Both groups sought justice for the murdered Sykes of Peaceful Hills. The crowd had resumed its chant—*"Come out, killers!"*—and Sutter's troops now shouted with them. Evidently the ranch folk had heard this same report from the townspeople who had met them.

"Those devils have been dealt with, you say?" Devin asked, turning back to the boatman. "Then who are the killers who are holding the children hostage in the courthouse?"

"Them's the authorities," the boatman exclaimed. "Officialdom, you might say—the people who told the medicos to leave the inmates to die. It was cleaner that way, they said. Neater. Final. All of it out of sight and out of mind." He spat again as he gestured at the sheriff's cooling corpse. "The town council is holed up in the courthouse with the sheriff's deputies and the judges. All the powers-that-be are in there, with the heads of the guilds, too."

Devin blinked. "The guilds?" she echoed. "Is my father—Guildmaster Perridin—in there?"

The boatman blanched. Perhaps he had not known to whom he was speaking, or perhaps he knew and had forgotten her identity in his concern for the captive children. In the minds of most Purity residents, Devin could not be closely associated with Master Perridin, for father and daughter had never been seen in public together—except the once, Devin supposed, when the man threw her, unconscious, onto the prison train.

"Why, yes," the boatman faltered, hesitant and pale. "Perridin is in there with the other shot-callers."

"And he knew?" Devin pressed the boatman. "He knew about the massacre, and he sanctioned it?"

"They all knew, miss." The man's voice had regained its force and urgency, as if to say there could be no excuse and no mercy shown to those responsible, no matter who they might be. "The town council met secretly to discuss the 'disposition' of the asylum, as they termed their murderous scheme. The judges called the meeting, along with the guild heads, and everybody in any official position had a vote. They all voted to shut it down and bury the inmates alive. They tried to keep it a secret, but court clerks talked. Word got out. Names were named. Perridin was exposed as one of the main ones who wanted it done."

Devin pushed back her hat and ran her hands down her face. With new-kindled rage smoldering inside, barely controlled, she looked up at Sutter.

"He's got to die." Her voice shook with anger. "They've all got to die, but not the children they're holding."

She turned back to the boatman. "When we break down the door, will the deputies fight? Now that the sheriff is dead?"

The boatman tilted his head, pondering. Then he nodded.

"I believe they'll fight to the death, because they know they're dead anyway if we reach them in there." He gestured at the courthouse, which was now fully surrounded by shouting townspeople and ranch folk. People were touching the Beskil bubble, striking sparks as they fingered its surface, marveling at the invisible barrier that kept the guilty confined and the vengeance-seekers at a distance. But not for much longer.

"Oh, we'll reach the bastards," Devin swore.

She looked around the plaza at the teeming, vocal throng in which ranch folk now mingled freely with their town counterparts. Afternoon was beginning to move toward dusk, but Devin, Sutter, and the other Sykes would not need much time to breach the courthouse and snap the neck of anyone hiding in there who was not a child.

"Every one of those murderers will be dead before it's dark," she promised, shifting her gaze back to the boatman, and then to Sutter ... and then over Sutter's shoulder, to lock eyes with Jack. "That's what we came here to do."

☙ 19 ❧

THE BESKIL BUBBLE WAS all the protection Devin and the others needed when she syked the courthouse door open, and the deputies inside fired blindly out. Their rifle rounds hit the bubble's unbreakable surface and ricocheted. Some bullets struck the stone of the courthouse walls, producing sprays of dust that remained trapped, clouding the air inside the bubble. But many rounds rebounded straight back to the shooters. Cries of pain and screams of shock echoed from within the grand law court.

The shooting stopped, and Devin dropped the barrier directly in front of the open door. Around the rest of the building, she kept the bubble intact to ensure that no member of officialdom could escape out a window.

Side by side with Sutter, and backed by every Syke who could crowd in behind them, Devin rushed through the door, prepared to sweep aside all opposition. But every deputy they encountered in the front lobby lay dead already, victims of their own bullets. The survivors had scattered, the sounds of their footsteps ringing distantly off the lobby's marble walls as the panicked deputies raced upstairs, futilely seeking safety on the building's upper floors.

They found none. Every runner was caught and killed by the teams of Sykes who roved through the courthouse, breaking into every office, vestibule, courtroom, lounge, and janitorial closet on each of the three floors. Shouts rang from all directions, most of the cries breaking off sharply as those who emitted them died with their spines snapped in two.

Sutter rampaged from room to room, a cruel grin on his face. He was having the time of his life, pulling terrified judges, council members, and other erstwhile officials out of their hiding places, killing the town's authorities left and right.

Devin stuck close, her teeth set, inwardly appalled by the delight Sutter took in slamming his quarry against walls or flinging cowering functionaries down stairwells, breaking not only their necks, but every bone in their bodies. She did not wish to be witnessing this, seeing his maniacal savagery, but she had to be with him, watching to ensure he did not slaughter innocent children in his frenzy.

To her vast relief, Jack did not lose her in the mobs of vengeful Sykes who swarmed the building. He was at her side when they discovered the children huddled in the private chambers of the now-dead high judge. Most of the young hostages were wailing in abject terror, while others appeared too scared to make a sound. Many of the children had soiled their clothes.

Devin directed Sutter away from them, free now to let the man continue his killing spree without her supervision. She comforted the hysterical children as best she could, and with Jack helping to herd the kids from their hiding place, she got them all downstairs and outside. There, distraught parents gathered their offspring to their bosoms, shed tears of relief and gratitude, and bundled the traumatized youngsters off to hot baths and the reassuring safety of their own beds.

Standing in the courthouse door, watching the tearful reunions of children and families, Devin observed that the crowd in the plaza had greatly thinned. Many townspeople had followed the Sykes inside, but it appeared that most others had called it a day and gone home. With the children rescued, and the visiting Sykes delivering swift justice to every murderous villain who quailed within the courthouse walls, the "rioters" had no reason to remain. They had achieved their purposes.

"But I'm not done," Devin muttered under her breath, speaking only to herself. "I've got to find my father." Or at least see his dead body, and know for certain that he would never send another Syke to be tortured in a pit of horrors, the way he had sent her to a living hell.

Her search did not take long. The avenging army had swept through the courthouse from lobby to rafters to basement, and there now remained only a few dank cellars in which any vermin could hide.

In the lowest and mustiest of these, she found her father still alive. Guildmaster Perridin cowered in a filthy, long-disused cranny half-curtained with dusty cobwebs. The man had tattered the webs in his attempts to cram himself and his companion into a space that was too narrow for two people. Devin let out an involuntary gasp as she caught sight of his face peering from the cranny. But it was not her father who most startled her. Rather, the woman who clung to him made her breath come short.

"You!" Devin snarled.

She could form no other word, could say nothing, could think nothing in that moment. All was instinct now. And her instinct for self-preservation demanded the immediate eradication of her father's clingy companion. It took only a twitch of a mental reflex, faster than any thought, and the woman slumped lifeless in Perridin's arms. Without laying a finger on her, Devin had not only snapped every bone in the woman's body, she'd liquified each internal organ. Bodily fluids of various colors and consistencies dripped from the woman's sagging mouth, from her dead eyes, from her ears and nostrils, and down her legs. Master Perridin stood in an ever-deepening puddle of effluent that stank of vomit, blood, and shit.

"What have you *done,* you witch!" the man screamed at Devin.

He tried to release the woman's ruined body, but the two of them were packed together so tightly within the cranny, he could put no space between himself and the oozing corpse. Not without stepping out of the gap and meeting his daughter face-to-face, something he clearly did not wish to do.

"How long?" Devin demanded, finding her voice now that her instincts had slackened their grip upon her. She edged a little closer, still more than an arm's length away, and pinned the man with the power of her raw fury. "How long have you been cheating on my mother with that demon from hell?" Devin pointed at the corpse, certain of the truth of her accusation, for Perridin had had his arms around the woman in the way that a man protectively embraces his lover. "That monster *tortured* me at Peaceful Hills," Devin shouted.

She was panting from the horror that had filled her at sight of her old nemesis. "Did you know? That's my so-called 'therapist.' A sadist, more like. She got off on killing people's minds and destroying their souls, bit by excruciating bit."

Devin pushed up her shirtsleeve to reveal the scars from her trial by fire, her agonizing final test at Peaceful Hills. "Did that monster tell you what she *did* to me? And you made her your mistress? Can you deny it?"

The shock on Perridin's face gave way to a sneer.

"You're an evil little witch who should have been drowned at birth, and your mother is a cold bitch that I never should have married," he rasped. "She's frigid as ice. She forced me out of her bed and into the arms of a real woman. A woman with heat in her veins."

"Yeah, right," Devin scoffed. "Like I said: demon from hell. And now that she-devil is back in her home fires, roasting like a snake on a spit. You want 'heat,' *dad?* You'll get plenty. If there really is a hell, the two of you will burn in its eternal fires, and no one will hear you scream. Same as you didn't hear me scream after you shipped me off to that house of horrors."

So intent had Devin been on this confrontation with the man she had once called "father," she'd paid little heed to the pair of Sykes who had quietly joined her in the cramped, foul-smelling cellar. But now, one of the pair spoke. The voice was Estelle's no-nonsense drawl.

"That one don't deserve a quick death," her friend said. Devin had indeed come to regard Estelle as a friend, and she smiled when she looked over her shoulder at the woman standing behind her. "I'm not as strong as you are, up here." Estelle tapped her forehead. "I can't kill a man with just a passing thought. I sort of have to work at it. Today's been good practice. I'm getting better—more efficient, like. Even so, when I set my mind to crush the life out of a fella, it takes a bit before the hombre breathes his last. Let me at this one, girlie." With a jerk of her chin, Estelle indicated Master Perridin. "I can string it out real slow, so this varmint gets the death he deserves."

And so I don't commit patricide, Devin thought. She was entirely willing and able to kill her father, but Estelle seemed to think it might burden Devin's conscience, afterward. Devin seriously doubted it would. But the woman had the right idea about inflicting a slow and painful death, commensurate with the pain the Sykes had suffered in their treatment at Peaceful Hills, and then the slow starvation deaths that had released them from torment.

"Thank you, Estelle," Devin said. "Come up closer." She turned sideways to allow the bulkier woman to move forward while she slipped back behind her.

While they were engaged in this maneuver of swapping places in the tight space, Perridin lunged out of the cobwebby nook where he'd been crammed with his now-flaccid lover. He tried to shove the woman's still-dripping corpse at Estelle, as though to block her or knock her into Devin.

"No you don't!" exclaimed the other Syke who had entered the cellar with Estelle, and who had said no word until now. It was Jack, Devin's loyal knight, and he was having none of Perridin's final desperate evasions. Before either Estelle or Devin could react to the clumsily flung corpse, Jack syked the thing straight back to Perridin.

The body hit the man with the sound that a freshly slaughtered beef carcass makes when it's chucked onto a butcher's table and blood splatters everywhere. Perridin went down, landing on his ass, the corpse sprawled across his legs and lap, and one arm slapping him limply across the face.

Estelle laughed so hard, she could barely concentrate on the task at hand. As a consequence, the demise of Guildmaster Perridin took a good half hour, during which the man screamed, cried, and begged for mercy. Estelle showed him all the mercy that had been extended to the murdered Sykes of Peaceful Hills.

Before he entirely lost the power of speech, Perridin gasped out a few final, taunting words:

"Run home to your mama, witch!" he snarled at Devin. "See how you like what you find."

Shortly afterward, he breathed his last, and Estelle released his ruined body from her mental fist. The woman inhaled deeply, a sound that communicated her satisfaction with the work she'd done in that place. But the foul air in the cellar made Estelle choke and cough.

"Lawzy mercy! This skunk hole stinks to high heaven." She gestured at the paired corpses, both of which now oozed bodily effluents. Their blood, vomit, and urine mixed and mingled with the old filth on the floor of the abandoned cellar, raising such a stench as would make skunk-musk smell sweet. "That mess will have to be shoveled out of here pretty quick," Estelle observed, "or it'll stink up the whole building, high as the rafters."

"Somebody can take care of it tomorrow." With a tired, shuddering sigh, Devin turned to the exit, alongside Jack. "It's been a long day. We need to figure out where we'll sleep tonight."

She checked to be sure Estelle was following, out of the cellar and upstairs to fresh air. The courthouse basement didn't smell quite as bad as the bowels of the asylum had, after the corpses there had rotted for who knew how long. But still, asphyxiation seemed a definite threat, as Devin couldn't draw a proper breath until they were back in the lobby and heading out through the open front door.

By this hour, dusk had given way fully to night, and they found the lamplit plaza completely deserted. Every rioter had gone, and the ranch hands had also disappeared—looking for grassy lawns where their horses could graze, Devin imagined, and where the riders might be allowed or invited to spread their bedrolls for the night. To that end, Estelle went off in search of her own horse, her supper, and a place to bed down, leaving Devin and Jack alone in front of the courthouse.

"Let me just be sure ..."

Devin trailed off as she concentrated on the two Beskil bubbles she had earlier flung around the building. She removed the shield that wrapped the courthouse exterior. There was no need now to seal the building against the escape of any malefactor, but the place very much needed airing out. A fresh night breeze sprang up as if on cue, and went sighing through the open door.

She turned her mental energies next to the other bubble, the syketic glue that held the roof together. Estelle's mention of rafters had reminded her that the roof had been on the verge of collapse, prior to Devin's intervention. The bubble was doing its job, however, keeping the broken bits in place, preventing a cave-in. She could safely leave the roof's restoration until tomorrow. With the adrenaline leaving her blood, Devin discovered just how tired she was.

"I'm about done in," she admitted, reaching automatically for Jack's hand. "All I want is a blanket and a reasonably soft place to spread it."

"That'll do for me too, my lady." Jack turned toward the plaza verge where they had last seen their horses. "Let's see what we can find."

Their steps dragged as they headed off in that direction, and then down an equally deserted and horseless side street. Neither said anything more for several minutes. But Jack obviously had something on his mind. He'd squeeze Devin's hand, as though preparing to speak, but then he'd relax his grip like he had reconsidered the need to do so.

"Out with it," Devin finally said. "Tell me what you're thinking. Am I a monster because I let Estelle kill my father? And because I'm not a bit sorry that the man is dead?"

Jack stopped in his tracks, jolting Devin as he pulled her to a halt with him.

"That's not it at all!" he exclaimed, peering at her in the dim light of a lone streetlamp. "If ever a bastard deserved his death, it was that fellow." He took both of her hands in his, holding them tightly. "What I'm thinking, Devin, is that Master Perridin wasn't your father. Not your real father."

"Huh?" She was so tired, she wasn't sure she'd heard correctly, or understood. "Of course he was my father. My mother's husband. The man I called 'father' all my life, until he put me on the train out of Purity."

"But you're nothing like him," Jack insisted. "I stood there in the cellar right behind you, watching and listening, the whole time you had that bastard in front of you. I never saw a trace of a family resemblance between that guy and you. Not a hint of him in the way you look, or the way you talk, or how you stand, move, or carry yourself. Uh-uh." Jack shook his head. "I don't believe you're in any way related to that swine. Think about it. If your mother wouldn't let the creep touch her, then maybe she had a better man on the side. Maybe there was some other fellow she loved, and that other fellow is your real father."

"Huh," Devin said again, not in a questioning tone this time, but simply to acknowledge that Jack might have hit on something. "I guess my mother would be the one to ask about that. If I can find her."

Devin looked vaguely around, as lost in this place—her "hometown"—as any wayfaring stranger would be. She'd lived here for sixteen years but had never been out of the house, as far as she could recall.

"I've just realized that I have no clue where the great big Perridin mansion is. My mother never told me the address. But come on now." Devin tugged Jack back into motion. "I need food, and then sleep. We can go looking for answers tomorrow."

☙ 20 ❧

ANSWERS CAME FOR THEM the next day, some arriving earlier in the morning than Devin would have liked. She was rousted out of her bedroll by a loudly apologetic boatman, who gave his name as Pete.

"Peter Acosta, in full, but everyone calls me Pete," the man said as he thrust a plate at her, a fine porcelain plate piled high with hot biscuits and cream gravy. "My manners deserted me yesterday. In all the excitement, I forgot to introduce myself."

He stuck out his other hand, the one empty of biscuits.

Bleary from sleep, Devin accepted the offered handshake. "My name—" She got no further, for Pete cut her off.

"I surely know who you are, Miss Devin. The whole town knows who you are, which makes me all the more embarrassed that you were left to sleep in this park last night, like some homeless drifter."

Like a saddle tramp wandering the Old West, Devin thought. During her many days of riding to reach this place, she'd accumulated a coat of dust over a layer of sweat. Compared to the sun-blasted, treeless prairielands she had lately traversed, her present surroundings were luxurious.

Last night upon quitting the plaza, she and Jack had wandered through town until the scent and sight of campfires led them to a city park harboring a handful of their fellow ranch riders. The riders' horses grazed the grass and drank from an ornamental fishpond under stately trees, and from that same source the unfussy ranch folk filled their cookpots. They'd built fires in the sooty metal grates and grills that dotted the park, amenities which normally served picnicking townsfolk, but which suited the range riders just as well. Estelle had had supper waiting when Devin and Jack dragged into the park, and as soon as she ate, Devin collapsed into an exhausted sleep, wrapped in her blankets beside a flickering fire.

Now that campfire was cold, but the breakfast delivered by Pete the boatman was piping hot. Devin ate the gravy-drenched biscuits while the man jabbered apologies and explanations.

"We searched for you, Miss Devin, after we got those scared tots home and tucked up safe. What you did in the middle of all the killing, bringing the kids out without a scratch, had half the town looking to extend their hospitality, to put you up in their best rooms and feed you a supper fit for royalty. But nobody could find you."

"In the cellars," Devin mumbled around a mouthful of biscuit. "I was in the cellars till after dark." She gestured vaguely at the scattering of ranch hands who were cooking their own breakfasts on the park grills. Swallowing so she could speak without dribbling gravy down her chin, she added, "Is that where the rest of my folk are? Bunking with people in town, I mean?"

Pete nodded. "It's a joy to a great many families, having their loved ones home again. And with no one having to worry, now, that they'll be shot because they've got the gift."

"Gift?" Devin studied him. "You mean Syke power? 'Psychokinetic,' the way it's written in the books."

"Exactly that. Now we don't have to hide. None of us."

"You, nor Sutter's other spies, here in town?" Fearing she'd given offense, Devin hurried to add, "Pardon me if I shouldn't call you 'spies.' That's the word Sutter uses, and I don't know one that's better. Where is Mike, by the way?" She looked around at the handful of unhoused riders in the park, the ones who evidently hadn't enjoyed a reunion or been invited into the homes of family and friends. "Have you seen Sutter this morning?"

Pete waved her inquiry aside, seemingly indifferent about Sutter's doings.

"He's around somewhere. Attending to private business, I believe. But to your other question," the boatman moved on, sounding eager to pursue the subject, "my friends and I have surely been spies, and that's what we call ourselves. When I say, however, that 'none of us' will have to hide our gifts, I don't mean just the spies who slink around in the dark and listen at keyholes. I mean the greater part of the population of Purity—the common folk." Pete smacked his lips, a sound of satisfaction. "It's recently come to my attention, Miss Devin, that the gift of Syke power is considerably more common in Purity than I ever would have guessed. *Considerably* more common," he emphasized, "than the authorities—them as had that title, anyway—would ever have admitted."

Intrigued, Devin was about to encourage the man to say more of what he'd recently learned about his fellow citizens. But from the direction of the town square, Jack rode up in a rush, bringing Devin's saddled horse with him.

"Come quick, my lady." He tossed Devin's reins to her. "They're getting too ambitious at the law court. Some of the local lads have put that busted cupola back together. Now they want to hoist it up on the roof to close that hole."

"Not yet!" Devin vaulted into her saddle, swearing. "It won't take the weight. Damn! They're likely to bring the whole roof down on their heads."

* * *

The remainder of Devin's morning was devoted to repairing the damage Sutter had done to the courthouse roof. The crew of local carpenters who had set about a fix of their own backed off quickly, the blood draining from their faces when Devin explained about the cracked rafters and the beams that stayed up only because her mental construction wrapped the wreckage, invisibly preventing the roof's catastrophic collapse.

To effect her repairs, Devin had to climb into the building's attic to see clearly what was broken and where the pieces must go to be whole again. As Estelle had predicted, the stench from the befouled cellar did indeed rise to the rafters. But the hole Sutter had made in the roof when he tore the cupola off provided enough ventilation that Devin could breathe.

When she had the roof structure sound again, everything lifted and shifted back to where it should be and solidly re-supported, she climbed high enough to poke her head out of the hole. The view from atop the three-story courthouse made her breath catch. Her previous experience of surveying the town from on high—that day in her childhood when she'd syked her way through the roof of the Perridin mansion to look out upon the neighborhood streets she'd never been allowed to explore—Devin had seen little more than the tops of the lower, surrounding houses.

But now, the whole town was laid out before her, revealing what a compact place Purity really was. The entire town nestled within a narrow bend of the Contagion River. Most of the homes and residences were on the splayed-out east side, with small factories and other such places of manufacture confined to the tight western riverfront. There, the workshops and boatyards were surrounded on three sides by the river that swept around the town in a hairpin bend. Along that bend, built closer to the riverbank than Devin would have thought prudent, railroad tracks gleamed in the morning sun.

She followed the tracks with her eyes, seeing them part from the river as they curved around the south side of town. Out past the city limits, past the outermost farms and smallholdings, the tracks arrowed due east across the plains for nearly as far as she could see. But at the most distant point of vision, she could make out a gradual curving of the tracks to run more to the northeast.

Continuing on that line, the tracks would eventually enter the mountains, where they would zigzag up and then down the slopes, and drop over a low ridge, at last, into the pit of an old strip-mine. The tracks' easternmost terminus was the sheer rockface behind the concrete bunker that had once, presumably, sheltered refugees from the Great Sickness. Now that bunker was no more, reduced to dust by the intensity of Devin's loathing for the evil which had later metastasized within the bunker's walls.

Shuddering, she swung her gaze back the other way, all the way back west to the tracks' starting point at the riverbend. There, on the rails or close beside them, something had burned. Devin made out a scorched, black, rectangular shape.

Had it been a factory of some kind? A workshop? Was that what had made the smoke she and Jack had seen over the river when they rode through the residential parts of town yesterday? And was the fire accidental, or had it been set during the huge riot that stopped the Sykes from advancing on past the central, courthouse square?

A shout from the square recalled her to the present, reminding Devin that she hadn't climbed into the rafters to rubberneck and speculate. The carpenters, having successfully rebuilt the broken cupola—and topped it with a new weathervane in the shape of a torch flame—were eager to get the structure raised into place.

Devin obliged them. She motioned the carpenters to stand clear, and then levitated the cupola off the sturdy sawhorses upon which their completed work rested. As the structure floated into the air over the plaza, Devin expected exclamations of astonishment or even fear from the carpenters and a good-sized crowd of onlookers. She was giving them a demonstration of syketic power that could not have been seen in Purity in living memory. Before last night, anyone who dared to do as she now did—assuming they'd have the necessary mental strength for such a feat—would have faced a hail of bullets from the sheriff and his deputies.

But the onlookers did not cry out in shock. Rather, they cheered and applauded. The roar of approval that rose from the plaza almost disturbed Devin's focus as she floated the cupola up to the roof. Keeping it level and straight, she dropped the structure neatly into place, capping the hole at the highest point of the steep-sloped roof.

At some point during this maneuver, Devin's hands had come up, as though to physically wrestle the cupola into place. Seldom did she accompany her mental exertions with any such gesture. The muscles of her body did not come into play when she translated thought into action: syketic energies operated independently of a practitioner's physical being.

But with her hands raised in front of her, Devin's fingers were only inches from the latch mechanism that fastened the cupola's windowlike door, holding it shut from the inside. She lifted the latch, pushed open the small door, and leaned far out over the sill, much as the ill-fated sheriff had done yesterday, calling Sutter's wrath down upon him.

"It's all yours now, fellas," she yelled at the carpenters, shouting to be heard over the applause that still resounded from the plaza. "Come on up, and bring nails."

Devin climbed down through the rafters, descended the attic stairs, and was met on the second floor by carpenters who had entered through the still-gaping front door. The men were on their way up, nail aprons around their waists, ready with the final fasteners to secure the restored cupola in its place. The carpenters thanked Devin profusely, then continued their climb while she headed for the lobby.

All around her, as she descended the wide marble steps of the main staircase, the courthouse buzzed with activity. Townspeople were removing the corpses of officialdom, all the functionaries who had died in yesterday's purge. From the building's upper floors, determined-looking citizens pitched bodies unceremoniously out of windows. The stiffened corpses landed in wagons that had been parked under the windows in back of the law court.

Devin's attention was drawn to a gray-haired woman in a flowery dress who looked too frail to lift so much as a heavy handbag. Even so, the old lady showed herself adept at carcass-clearing. She stood at an open window, and barely twitched a muscle as she methodically floated one corpse after another over the sill and down to the waiting wagons.

That must be one of Sutter's spies, Devin concluded, watching the woman. The beldam took obvious pleasure in exercising her syketic talents, probably for the first time she had ever dared, in her long years, to be open with her abilities. The woman gave Devin a friendly wave, which Devin returned, but neither of them veered from their separate purposes to speak together. The old lady remained intent on her task, and Devin continued down to the lobby and out the front door, determined to find some place with hot water and a bathtub. She was tired of being filthy.

"Marvelous work!" exclaimed Pete the boatman, who had made his way to the plaza in the wake of Devin's abrupt abandonment of him at the park. "This town is ever more indebted to you, Miss Devin." Pete gestured up at the restored cupola, from which the sounds of hammering emanated as the carpenters finished nailing the structure to the roof-peak. "But now, please allow me to introduce my sisters." The man brought forward two frumpy women. "These are Gertie and Becky, and they'd be proud to offer you the hospitality of their homes."

"Have you a bathroom?" Devin inquired, more bluntly than courtesy would countenance. Under her layers of grime, she blushed at her poor manners, but pressed on. "I'd give the world right now for a bath."

* * *

She got it, and more: laundered clothes, a private suite of rooms on the second floor of Gertie's grand house, and a lavish luncheon to which Jack was also invited, served in Gertie's back garden.

The sisters lived next door to one another, each residing alone in houses that seemed too big for single women without dependents, but which worked out splendidly for the women's guests. Becky—a veritable mother-hen of a woman—took Jack under her wing and installed him in a spare bedroom of her house, directly across from a window of Devin's suite at Gertie's. The riders' horses were accommodated in the women's shared backyard, it being a single joined expanse of grassy, tree-shaded lawn around a large fishpond, providing the animals with water and grazing. Had Devin possessed a magic wand and the necessary powers to work sorcery, she could not have conjured a more comfortable arrangement.

As she took her seat next to Jack to eat the bountiful lunch their hostesses served under the trees, Devin mentally ran through a list of questions to pose to Pete. The boatman had been, so far, her only real source of information about the unexpected scene that had greeted yesterday's arrival of the ranch Sykes.

But Pete did not attend the luncheon, and his two sisters overflowed with so much chatter, Devin couldn't squeeze a question in. She resolved, therefore, to spend the hour gorging on the best meal she'd had since leaving Angelina's ranch-house kitchen, while listening for any nuggets of useful intelligence the sisters might drop. Would they shed any light, in their nonstop prattle, on what Pete had said that morning about a wider-than-suspected prevalence of syketic talent in Purity's general population?

Gertie and Becky, however, seemed indisposed to move beyond the trivial. They spoke of grocery shopping, favorite recipes, and where in town they could buy bolts of cloth and sewing notions. The "girls"—as they called each other—appeared oblivious to yesterday's momentous events. Listening to them, one might have thought that riots in the town square were commonplace ... that the citizens of Purity often thronged the plaza, armed with kitchen knives and garden tools, to vent their fury on malefactors holed up in the courthouse ... and that a mounted army of Sykes thundering into town and proceeding to eradicate Purity's entire sitting government was an affair not worthy of comment. Over their plates, Devin and Jack exchanged glances, he with an eyebrow raised, but neither of them attempted to break into the sisters' unending flow of minutiae.

Devin gave up listening and let her mind wander, her thoughts turning to her mother as they had last night, when she'd admitted to Jack that she did not know where her mother lived—did not even know what the house looked like from the outside. Mistress Perridin had not been among those assailing the courthouse yesterday, as far as Devin had seen, and the woman made no appearance on the plaza this morning. The crowd of onlookers who cheered the cupola's restoration had been small enough that Devin could search every face. She'd seen none that was familiar.

An icy hand crept around her heart. She would go in search of her mother—on that much, she was resolved—but what would a reunion hold for the pair of them? How could she possibly reconcile with a mother who had been so ashamed of her that she'd locked her up at home and never let her out into the world? ... a mother who had allegedly renounced her after she'd broken free from the asylum's torments.

Devin's study of the old Syke history in Sutter's library, a history in which the Beskil family's powers and accomplishments were celebrated, had sent her scrambling down the mountain on a soon-obstructed quest to carry that knowledge to her mother—a woman who was a confessed descendant of that clan. But Mariah Beskil Perridin had admitted to the kinship only once, and only in private. If she was ashamed to be Devin's mother, most likely she was also ashamed of her heritage as the daughter of a Syke clan.

Devin found herself questioning her childhood memories of the wistful tenderness with which her mother had seemed to treat the family scrapbook. Maybe she had only imagined the woman telling her to be proud of their ancestry. Maybe Devin had invented those memories out of a desperate desire to feel pride instead of guilt, to replace her ingrained self-loathing with some shred of self-respect.

Drifting into her thoughts, as Devin polished off the last of her large lunch, were the final words from the pain-contorted mouth of

Guildmaster Perridin. *"Run home to your mama,"* he'd snarled. *"See how you like what you find."*

How had Mistress Perridin reacted to the news that her husband was dead? Those tidings must certainly have been delivered, by now, to the newly made widow. How would the woman reckon Devin's role in the Guildmaster's death? A good lawyer might make the case that Devin was not, in fact of law, guilty of patricide. It had not been her own mental cudgel, after all, that had bashed the man into a soggy heap of shattered bone and minced flesh.

But Devin would not so argue. Just as Master Perridin was culpable in the deaths of the imprisoned, abandoned Sykes, she bore the responsibility for his murder. It did not matter that each of them had worked through intermediaries to do the killing.

"Excuse me, ladies." Devin almost shouted to be heard over the hubbub of the sisters' chatter. She pushed back from the table and stood, ignoring the icy feeling in her heart. "Lunch was wonderful," she said sincerely but firmly, cutting across the women's babble. "But now, I really must go see my mother."

☙ 21 ❧

"CAN YOU TELL ME where Mistress Perridin lives?" Devin asked of the two women who had risen from the table when she did.

"Why, certainly, we can," the sisters chimed together. "She's practically our neighbor. Which street is it, Becky? Two over?" said the one to the other. Came the reply: "More like three, I'd guess, Gertie. Perhaps even four."

Devin's patience frayed. "Which direction?" she demanded.

"We'll take you, miss!" the sisters exclaimed, again in unison. "How long since you last visited the Perridin house, Gertie?" asked the one. "I don't recall, Becky," answered the other. "It's been a good while, I believe."

This continued as the women led the way from the garden through a side gate, and thence to the street that fronted their nearly matching houses. Devin and Jack fell in behind, following the sisters three streets over and into a neighborhood of stately homes on a tree-lined lane ending in a cul-de-sac. Gertie and Becky marched up the steps of the biggest house of all, a dual-winged, three-story mansion set back on a large lot at the street's closed end.

"Mariah!" shouted Becky, as Gertie pounded on the front door. "Someone here to see you. A regular cowgirl, by the look of her."

Devin gave a start, hearing herself so described. But as she looked down at her boots and denims, the leather belt at her waist, and the snap buttons on her clean shirt—the last clean garment her dusty saddlebags had yielded—she broke into a grin.

A glance at Jack, who stood at her side, found him smiling also.

"Townie no more," he murmured. "Won't your mom be surprised."

But Gertie's insistent pounding brought no one to the door. "I'm sure she's here," the woman said, frowning. "Mistress Perridin is the biggest homebody in town. No one's seen her leave the house in ages."

"Girl," said Becky to her sister, "you take Miss Devin and go around that way." She pointed at the lefthand wing. "Mister Jack and I will spy out this side of the house." She indicated the other, the righthand wing. "Look for an open door or window. It's not sitting easy with me, that we can't raise Mariah." Becky shot her sister a look that, to Devin's eyes, seemed laden with meaning. "You know what that husband of hers is like."

"Humph," Gertie grunted. "Men like him are exactly why I never married."

The woman took Devin's arm and steered her leftward, away from the front door and along that wing of the house, while Becky and Jack went the opposite way.

As they walked, pushing through flowerbeds, bushes, and ornamental plantings under the windows on this side of the house, Devin asked, "What did you mean, Gertie, about my mother's husband? Is there some kind of ..." She paused, searching for the right word, and landed on *disrepute*: "... some kind of disrepute that attaches to the name of Guildmaster Perridin?"

Gertie gave a snort. "I'm no gossip, Miss Devin"—a statement that was patently untrue, since the two sisters had spent the better part of their lunch hour gossiping about everyone and everything under the sun—"but I've heard that Master Perridin is nothing short of a brute. They say he actually *strikes* his wife." She made a sound of disgust. "Him a town leader and all, and that's how he behaves in private, when he's home where no one sees. But there's a housekeeper who comes from time to time these days, and she brings a maid or two when the place needs a buff-up. They see what goes on."

Devin's sense of disquiet increased with every word out of Gertie's mouth. *See how you like what you find,* the dying Perridin had taunted her. What would she find in this house?

She shoved at every window they passed in their circuit of the lefthand wing, and was trying to force open an iron-barred door they'd discovered at the back of the house, when Jack gave a yell. He and Becky had also come around back, approaching from the opposite direction as they finished their go-round of the other wing.

"Here!" he shouted. "This door's unlocked."

Jack shoved it open, then stepped back. He had to physically restrain Becky, who seemed intent on barging ahead of everyone. But Jack was giving Devin first entry.

From her position at the barred accessway, a little along the back of the house, she came at a run, needing only a few steps to close the distance. She bounded through the open door, but was immediately brought up short. She had entered a kitchen, a vast space when compared with the cozy *cocina* that Angelina ruled at the ranch. Four doors opened off the space in three directions: one to the left, one to the right, and a pair of doors directly in front of Devin, set into the wall facing the threshold from outside. This was in fact a double kitchen, equipped to serve the mansion's two separate wings from a central hearth.

As Devin stood paralyzed, unserved by any memory of this space, Becky barreled in through the open backdoor. The woman pushed past her, to wrench open the righthand exit and scurry into a sort of butler's pantry from which stairs climbed steeply.

"This way," Becky panted. She was exerting herself beyond her usual habit, Devin surmised, grateful for the woman's determined show of initiative and her disinclination to dawdle. "Mariah brought me this way one time. Quiet and sneaky, like," Becky gasped as she climbed a back staircase, a flight of steps such as servants would use to unobtrusively access the upper stories of this wing. "Her sitting room's up here."

As Devin leapt up the steps behind the woman, the clatter of Jack's hard-soled boots sounded behind her, as did the thump of Gertie's no-nonsense brogues. The three were on Becky's heels as they burst together into a dark, stuffy lounge.

Gertie rushed to draw back the heavy drapes and throw open the windows to let air and sunlight into a space that felt as oppressive as a crypt. Becky, still in the lead, charged through a connecting doorway, took several steps into what proved to be a large bedroom, and then stopped so abruptly that Devin, following her at speed, almost knocked her down.

"Mariah!" Becky shrieked as Devin tottered off-balance, barely keeping her own feet as she wrapped her arms around the smaller woman to hold Becky upright. "Go look, please, miss," the woman urged, pushing Devin in front of her when both had found their footing. "I'm afraid to see. Is she dead?"

"Where?" Devin looked around in anxious confusion. The bedroom was as dark as the sitting room had been, and she couldn't immediately make out what had stirred Becky's alarm. But with Gertie yanking back the drapes next door, the slanting rays of the afternoon sun stabbed into the bedroom through the connecting doorway. The light fell full upon a richly upholstered couch, and picked out the figure who sprawled there.

"Mother!" Devin shouted.

She sprinted to the couch and knelt beside the figure. Her fingers sought for a pulse in the woman's neck, and for several instants, silence reigned in the two rooms. No one moved or spoke.

"She's alive!" Devin gasped, throwing the words over her shoulder. "Fetch a doctor! Please, somebody, bring a doctor."

"I'll go," Becky said. "Doc Falcón lives not far."

"Right you are, girl," her sister called from the sitting room. "Bring that nurse, too, the old gal who lives at the corner. She's got training that's beyond me, but I'll do what I can until the medicos get here. Mister Jack," Gertie added as Becky went pounding down the stairs, the small woman putting on such a burst of speed as would set a stitch in her side by the time she reached the physician's door, "fetch water from the kitchen—a big pitcher with a washbowl and a drinking glass. No telling how long Mariah has ailed in this hot room without a drop to drink."

* * *

Doctor Falcón found that Mistress Perridin was dehydrated to a dangerous degree. The woman also had a badly dislocated shoulder, a cracked rib, and numerous deep bruises. Falcón and his nurse, gray-haired Lupe, got fluids down their patient, bound Mariah's ribcage, gently moved her shoulder back into its socket, and supported the injury with a sling.

A crew of men was called to the house then, to undertake the delicate task of carrying Mistress Perridin downstairs on a stretcher—using the wide central staircase and exiting through the grand front entrance this time, instead of negotiating the narrow back stairs.

Through all of this, Devin kept out of the way, but she never took her eyes from her mother's semiconscious form. Before Falcón's arrival, Mariah had responded with a barely audible groan when Gertie dabbed her face with a wet cloth. Never did the woman open her eyes, but she moaned again as Falcón and his nurse worked to stabilize her enough that she could be moved. The doctor said it was a good sign, that Mistress Perridin was not entirely insensible to her condition.

Now the lady was resting in another of Gertie's spare bedrooms—resting comfortably, to all appearances, for she had fallen silent and slipped into an easy-seeming sleep. The doctor was gone, leaving Lupe to watch over the patient. The nurse gave Devin a sympathetic smile and moved off to sit beside the guestroom's open window, catching the late-afternoon breeze.

Devin pulled a chair up to the bed, as close as she could get, and sat hunched at her mother's bandaged shoulder. She didn't dare try holding either of the woman's hands for fear of causing pain, given the extent of Mariah's injuries. Devin contented herself with studying the face that she knew well, but now seemed to see for the first time.

Mistress Perridin had once been a beautiful woman, with fine features and high cheekbones. But her face was deeply lined now, and her closed eyes sunk into her head. The woman's hair—once as brown as autumn leaves, brown with an undertone of red, the same earthy shades as Devin's hair—was faded now, dull and dry, streaked with gray. The years that had passed since Devin's removal from the family home—

Had it indeed been years, or only months? Devin could not say with certainty, because time had lost all meaning while she was trapped at the asylum.

But however long it had been, Mariah Perridin had aged dramatically. A surge of pity constricted Devin's throat as she gazed at her mother's drawn face and traced the outline, through the bedclothes, of the woman's bruised body.

Sometime late in the night, long after Lupe had fallen asleep on a cot that had been rolled in for the nurse's use, Mistress Perridin stirred. She gave a faint moan, and before the sound had died away, Devin was ready with water for the woman's cracked lips.

Mariah took only a sip, but enough to wet her tongue. The woman opened her eyes, gazed up at Devin in the light of a single lamp that burned beside the bed, and managed to whisper, "It's you?"

Devin couldn't stop herself taking her mother's hand then.

"I've come home," she murmured. "I had to see you, and I have to know." She fought back tears as she asked the question upon which everything between them rested. "When I was ... away ... did you ... did you disown me, Mother?"

"Never."

At that soft but emphatic word, a knot loosened inside Devin, a knot of resentment that she had carried since learning there was so much more to the Beskil story than Mariah had ever chosen to tell her. The Beskils weren't merely an Old Family of Purity—they were *Sykes*. Devin's so-called criminal insanity was in fact her great legacy from them: a legacy of power. She had been taught to feel shame, when she should have been acclaimed as a worthy Beskil heir.

But looking upon her mother's battered form, Devin could not sustain the feeling of betrayal that had weighed her down for so long. Guildmaster Perridin would have publicly and vocally renounced her, just as Orlando had said. Of that, Devin was certain. How could she doubt it, after hearing the bastard's hate-filled denunciation of her when she'd cornered him like a rat in the courthouse cellar?

But Mariah? No. This woman had been rendered mute—voiceless, powerless, and worse.

"Did your husband do this to you?" Devin asked, her voice quiet, but shaking with anger. "Did he beat you?"

Mariah grimaced, closing her eyes. When she reopened them, her gaze was cloudy, haunted. She answered in a barely audible whisper:

"Yes."

"That scum!" Devin spat. Lupe stirred on her cot. But when the nurse did not awaken, Devin continued in a lower voice, "You're safe now, Mother. Believe me when I tell you he'll never hurt you again.

He won't hurt either of us, because he's dead." She hesitated only a moment before adding, "I killed him."

Mariah's gaze cleared. A smile touched the woman's dry lips. Devin offered another sip of water, which the woman swallowed a little more easily this time. She managed only three more whispered words before sleep reclaimed her, but they were words that brought ease to both their hearts.

"Bless you, daughter."

❧ 22 ☙

AT GERTIE'S HOUSE over the next several days, the doctor came and went regularly, checking on his patient. Becky visited often from next door, sometimes with her lodger, Jack, in tow. But Devin urged the ranch-born young man to go out into the town, exploring. Jack had never seen a city, and even if Purity didn't precisely fit the definition of "city," the town held wonders for a boy from a mountain stock-farm.

Devin suspected it held lingering unrest, too. What Pete had said, that morning in the park, about the town's formerly hidden Sykes no longer needing to keep their abilities concealed, had piqued her interest but also raised troubling questions.

In what ways had the dynamic changed between the mentally gifted townsfolk and the ordinaries? Was there a risk of new violence between the two? With the entire city government wiped out, who was in charge? Who would keep the peace? —without anyone getting shot, the way the ordinaries had cruelly terrorized the Sykes who filled them with unreasoning fear.

Also gnawing at Devin's peace of mind was the question of Sutter. What had that man been up to since she'd last clapped eyes on him, when he moved through the courthouse killing every authority-figure in sight? What was the "private business" that Pete had mentioned? Where was Sutter now?

Devin quietly conveyed her concerns to Jack as she sent him off on his explorations.

"As you wish, my lady," he murmured, and with a gentlemanly tip of his hat, he slipped away to nose around, leaving Devin to return to her mother's bedside.

That Mariah was eager to speak with her daughter, the convalescing woman made clear. It was some time, however, before she had the strength to utter more than short phrases. It cost her an effort, early in her recovery, to demand that her nurses—Lupe now shared the duty with other caregivers—must no longer address her as "Mistress Perridin." She was Mariah Beskil, and the name of *Perridin* must never be mentioned in her hearing again.

Pleased beyond measure, Devin immediately adopted Beskil as her own surname. She filled many hours thereafter, as she sat at her mother's bedside, reading aloud from the book she'd taken from Mike Sutter's library, the old volume with the gilt-stamped title: *Mind Over Malady—The True Story of the Psychokinetic Pioneers of Early-Day Purity and Their Triumph Over the Great Contagion.*

Devin hardly needed to look at the pages as she read out the chapter on the Beskil clan. She could recite it almost word-for-word from memory, so closely had she studied that account before slipping the book into her saddlebags when she rode with the army from the ranch. Now she told Mariah of the matriarch, the woman named Indomitable, who had raised a syketic shield to protect the young town of Purity from the pestilence, and with her kinsfolk had held the barrier in place for all the years that it took for the disease to die out.

As she shared the story of their illustrious ancestors, Devin spoke also of her own mastery of the Beskil bubble, how she could fling a protective shell around anything she wanted to defend, confine, or wrap up so tight it could not move. She described Sutter's attempt to pull down the courthouse roof, and how she had held the rafters together with the unremitting strength of her mind and her unyielding bubble.

Mariah's eyes widened as she listened to all of this, and for a moment Devin feared she had frightened the woman. But then came a low chuckle, and Mariah's lined face split into a grin.

"A Beskil, indeed," she murmured.

Gradually, the woman gained the strength to sit up in bed, and then to sit for brief periods in a chair at the open window. The sunshine and fresh air helped restore her. She began to speak at more length. Her short phrases became sentences sufficient to recount what had happened, in their recent family history, to condemn Devin to the asylum.

"I have much to tell you, daughter," Mariah rasped, "and much for which to seek your forgiveness."

Devin started to shake her head, to protest that Mariah did not need to be forgiven for anything, that it had all been Guildmaster Perridin, the man Devin had called 'father' but had never loved. The woman, however, cut her off.

"That monster was not your father!" Mariah exclaimed as if she'd heard the question Devin had forborne to ask outright, although the matter had been on her mind since Jack suggested it. "Your father," Mariah declared, "was a man named Rodrigo. I believe Rodrigo to be dead, but I do not know for certain. I loved him."

With notes of yearning in her voice, Mariah recounted a tale of passion and heartbreak: clandestine trysts with a handsome, dark-haired man who drifted into town and into Mariah's arms, and then disappeared, leaving his young lover unwed and pregnant. A forced marriage followed. Mariah's family had standing in Purity, and a reputation to protect. They bribed Hanus Perridin to marry the girl to avoid a scandal. It was a loveless marriage from the start, and the relationship soured drastically when Rodrigo's child was born—a girl who, from an early age, showed signs of being a strongly persistent Syke. Perridin would have smothered Devin in her crib, had Mariah's family not held such a high position in Purity. He feared the family's wrath.

But he was wily, cunning, and entirely without scruples. Perridin chipped away at the family's power and enlarged his own. When Mariah's parents grew old, he tricked his in-laws out of their double-winged mansion, and took the house for himself. Once ensconced, he locked his detested wife and her bastard child in one wing, refusing to let either of them out of the mansion, or any visitors in. To explain his actions in hiding his family away, and to conceal Devin's growing syketic powers, he spread the story that his "daughter" was a brain-damaged invalid, and his wife was so devoted to the poor, darling idiot, she would not leave Devin's side.

"You had to have been the worst-kept secret in Purity," Mariah said, gripping Devin's hand as she told this tale. "I'm willing to bet every cent I still have to my name—whatever crumbs of the family fortune are left to me—that everybody from this side of town, and clear to the river, guessed the truth. They all knew you were a Syke. But as long as the Guildmaster kept his 'darling daughter' locked up at home, they looked the other way. No one would cross the Master, he was vindictive and ruthless. And they might even have believed the rumors that you were being 'treated' at home, getting the same therapy you would have gotten at Peaceful Hills." Mariah made a sound of disgust. "Such an arrangement would have been highly irregular, of course, and strictly forbidden to anyone else. But the Guildmaster scorned the law, and the cowed dogs of the law allowed it. Our captivity—yours, and mine—continued for years."

"Until I blew out a wall," Devin said, taking up the part of the story that she knew firsthand. "I was so frustrated, so desperate to break out of prison, I couldn't stop the impulse. It wasn't a deliberate act of destruction—I just lashed out."

She tilted her head, recalling the narrow staircase she'd recently climbed at the rear of the Perridin mansion to find her mother unconscious in the second-floor bedroom. The exterior wall of that back staircase was the wall Devin had smashed with her Syke battering ram.

"I suppose the Guildmaster called in the bricklayers to patch up the big hole I made, but that would have been after he got rid of me," she reflected. "I don't remember much after the wall exploded, except that something stung my arm. It hurt."

"A dart," Mariah supplied. "He shot you with a knockout dart. Else, he could never have subdued you and put you on the train, not without you killing him. You would have snapped the fiend's neck, had you been conscious." Mariah sucked her teeth, a sound of unreserved disgust. "I swore and screamed at the brute, but he threw me across the room—not the first time he'd done that, either. While he had me down, he drugged me, too. I was out for at least two days. By the time I came to, Devin, you were far away on those tracks, probably in the mountains by then."

"I do remember some of that," Devin muttered. Of her final hour in the family mansion, she had only hazy, doped-up impressions, but she remembered raised voices ... a sound like glass shattering ... and a scream. "I'm sure I remember your scream," she told her mother. "After that ... just silence. Silence and darkness ..."

... and pain, Devin added silently, but she kept that memory to herself. Her mother had suffered enough. No need to deepen her hurt.

The woman sighed bitterly. "While I was unconscious, that brute locked me into rooms even smaller—fewer—than the prison you and I had shared. At least we had a library when you were little." Mariah's tone was wistful. "We had space for your reading and schoolwork, and for those wonderful little plays we staged for just ourselves. But I lost those rooms when I lost you, daughter." She hung her head. "I failed you, my dearest one. Years before that monster took you from me, I should have busted out a window and called for help."

"Who would have given it?" Devin demanded. Quick she was now, to absolve her mother of all blame. "The law would have been set against you, with all the town. Purity's official policy, after all, was 'Death to Sykes'." Devin grimaced as she added, "But mercy could be shown, I guess, if the Syke in the rifle's crosshairs happened to be from a family with money and status. Then, the lunatic only got condemned to be tortured."

She shuddered, remembering the "therapies" to which she had been subjected. As it turned out, she would have welcomed long-term residence in an actual sanatorium for the mentally ill. Even if the doctors there had engaged in such medieval practices as blistering, purging, and bloodletting, she would not have suffered the agonizing damage to mind and spirit that she had sustained inside the Peaceful Hills pit of horrors.

No, her mother was not to blame. Mariah Beskil had fought for her daughter, fought to keep Devin out of the loony bin, as the Peaceful Hills orderlies cynically and inaccurately called the place when their superiors could not hear.

Devin rose from her seat, and bent to put her hand under her mother's chin. Gently, she lifted Mariah's face to look into the woman's eyes.

"I am so very grateful to you, Mom," she said, holding her mother's gaze, "for keeping me hidden until I was old enough, and strong enough, to have a chance of surviving the asylum. If I'd gone to that hellhole as a child, lacking full possession of my powers, I would have died. But I went there as a nearly grown Beskil"—Devin smiled, savoring the sound of her clan name—"and I came out stronger than any of those Peaceful Hills devils could have imagined."

Devin paused, then added softly, "When I was a child at home, I know I frightened you sometimes. I broke things because that was my instinct: to break, in hopes of breaking out of my prison, I suppose. Instinct was all I had. But these days I have *intention*, not just a mindless reflex. Now, I can mend as well as break. I swear I'll never do anything to frighten you again."

Mariah closed her fingers around Devin's. "It's true that you startled me sometimes, my darling one. You displayed such extraordinary powers of the mind! But my real fear, my deepest fear was always that you'd be found out and taken from me. I was desperate to keep you from those who would harm you."

"What you did, Mother," Devin assured her, "keeping me safe at home for so long, has brought justice to our family, and to all of Purity. The people in charge—those who decreed that Sykes must die—are gone now. They're all gone to a mass grave, I'm told, out in the flats beyond the garbage pits. I'm further informed—though I still have questions for the boatman who told me this—that every Syke in this town can live openly now. Free of fear, free of persecution."

"Truly?" Mariah's voice trembled with hopeful wonderment.

Devin nodded reassurance. "No one from 'officialdom' will threaten us again, I promise. They all came to a bad end, as they deserved. But as for the bit about Sykes having nothing to fear, any longer, from their ordinary neighbors ..."

She trailed off, her free hand raised in a questioning gesture. "If you're feeling well enough to spare me for a few hours, I'll track down the boatman and hear the story he started to tell me."

* * *

Though Pete's sisters lived in houses that seemed oversized for single, middle-aged ladies, he did not room with either of them on the genteel side of town, but stuck to his boatyard in the bend of the river, over on the working-man's side of the city. Devin rode there, accompanied by Jack, early enough the next day that the sun cast their long shadows ahead of them as they bypassed the courthouse square and continued into the western precincts, into the heart of Purity's commercial and manufacturing areas.

They rode at a leisurely pace, but alert for any disgruntled ordinary or bereaved family member of a functionary who had suffered the deadly wrath of the Syke army. Devin had been so much with her mother these last days, she'd had no real chance to take the town's temperature, and now she couldn't help thinking of all the rifles that had fallen from the hands of the doomed deputies when she and the army invaded the courthouse. No rifles had been in sight, the next morning, when she returned to repair the roof. The weapons had been gathered up and carted off, Devin knew not where, nor to what purpose.

Consequently, she rode watchful at Jack's side, ready to fling a Beskil bubble around both of them, should any resentful citizens of Purity choose to take potshots at the visitors from the mountains. No one disturbed the peace of their crosstown ride, however, and they dismounted in Pete's boatyard while the fellow was having his morning coffee.

Invited to join him, they settled at a table near the river, shaded by one of the few trees to grow in this industrialized part of town. Devin swallowed a sip of astoundingly bitter coffee, then opened her mouth to begin her questions.

Pete got in the first word, however, and followed it with a great many more.

"I'm glad you've come, Miss Devin," he declared. "I need your help with Sutter." He drummed his fingers on his knee, a nervous gesture.

What's the man done? Devin started to say. But with a sense of inevitability, she amended that to, "Who's he killed?"

Pete left off drumming, and scratched his ear.

"I like that about you, Miss Devin. You get right to the point. But before I answer you on Sutter's latest doings, maybe I'd best finish telling you what I started to tell you in the park, t'other morning."

"Please do. I've been wondering ever since."

"Well," the boatman carried on, leaning back and getting comfortable in his chair, "it'll come as no surprise to you, I'm sure, to hear me admit that I wasn't on the river by chance when Sutter came along that day, leading you ranch folk down from the north."

"We know you were waiting for us," Devin said, aiming to speed up the tale by acquainting Pete with what information she and Jack already possessed. "You brought Sutter the news that Purity was not yet aware of the army's approach. Sutter sent you back down the river to deliver a message to your—his—spies. You were to tell them to clear out, to get to safety because Sutter meant to sweep into town bringing ruin and destruction." Devin cocked her head. "But the army got quite the surprise, didn't we, when we thundered in like a storm on hooves and found the townsfolk up in arms, but with hardly anyone giving our troops more than a passing glance. There we were, a regiment of mounted strangers invading the town, and it's like we were expected, and not at all feared."

"That's exactly the way of it," Pete exclaimed. "Things didn't go as planned when I advised my spy-folk to take to cover. Sutter had told me, there on the river, the whole despicable story of the Peaceful Hills massacre." The boatman frowned, and his knuckles whitened where he gripped his coffee cup. "Rumors about it had already been flying around Purity. One of the 'doctors' who came in on the last train actually bragged about locking up the loonies and leaving them to die. She was half drunk and talking trash, but plenty of people who were drinking in the bar that night heard every word she said. Then, too, we had their kitchen help and cleaning staff, and the mechanics who kept the asylum running. They'd been whispering about dark deeds and dead Sykes."

"But would anybody in Purity care?" Devin challenged the man. "Any of the ordinaries, I mean. I'd expect most people to thoroughly approve of what went down at the asylum."

"That's just it, Miss Devin." A smile touched Pete's lips. "When I put out the word to my spy-folk that Mike Sutter was coming with an army of Sykes to give the ordinaries their comeuppance, we discovered that 'most people' in Purity aren't *ordinary*. Well over half the population, we now estimate, have Syke powers to some degree."

"Huh?" Devin stared at the boatman, struggling to make sense of what he was saying. "Sykes are a minority. A persecuted minority since ... well, pretty much forever, the way I understand it. The gift—the talent—is rare."

Pete tilted his head. "That's what we thought, Miss Devin. What we'd always thought. But we found out different, and we learned it pretty quick after Sutter's message spread through the spy web."

"How?"

"Well, the thing is," Pete explained, "I'd never known just how many of us were in the network. No one had a complete list, not even Sutter. It was too dangerous for any spy to have contact with more than one or two others. Information was 'compartmentalized,' I believe is the proper word for it. Never before this past week, that being the case, had a single message been sent or received by the entire network. But the news of Sutter's army spread like wildfire from spy to spy, and word of it couldn't help but leak out of the 'compartments' and reach the ears of other Sykes. Folks who weren't spies, you know, but who had friends and family secretly in the network. As it turned out," Pete concluded, his grin widening, "that wider circle of friends and family was pretty damned huge."

"Isolation is powerful," Devin murmured, catching at a glimmer of understanding. "It can incapacitate a person ... or a whole bunch of people. A whole community. They—the ordinaries—used isolation to control Sykes at the asylum. They never let any inmate know there were other Sykes in the building. They were afraid of an uprising."

"Which is exactly what they got, here!" Pete exclaimed, almost crowing now. He released his coffee cup and reached across the table to squeeze Devin's hand. "When our gifted folk started coming out of the woodwork, and we realized—to the astonishment of us all—how many Sykes there *really* are in this town, we decided not to wait for Sutter's avenging army. We grabbed our pitchforks and went after the killers."

"That's why the army's arrival caused so little fuss." Devin nodded, comprehending now that the rioters at the courthouse square, whom she'd deemed to be Purity's "ordinary" citizens, were in fact the town's insurgent Sykes. "We really were expected. I guess you-all looked upon us as little more than reinforcements." She laughed. "How you stole Sutter's thunder! He'd been so looking forward to playing the role of conquering warlord."

Pete's expression sobered, and as he freed her hand, the smile also ebbed from Devin's face when she thought of how Sutter's cherished plan had fallen by the wayside. She knew from personal experience that he did not like having his thunder stolen.

"There's something about all of this that I still don't understand, Pete." Devin contemplated the boatman and his description of a persecuted people who had found new strength in numbers. "What ordinary could ever fight a Syke and win? I've heard the stories about the sheriff standing Sykes up against a wall and riddling them with bullets." She shook her head and raised one hand questioningly. "How could that happen? Why didn't the Sykes yank the rifles out of the deputies' hands? Or break the officers' necks, for that matter?"

Pete sighed. There was pain in his eyes as he answered.

"It all comes down to isolation, Miss Devin. The ordinaries have long known how to cut their victims out of the herd, to use an expression I'll borrow from you ranch folk. When they single out their quarry—any poor soul who falls under the shadow of suspicion—they never confront the suspect directly. A sharpshooter kills from a distance, without warning, unless there's to be an example made. Then the Syke gets hit with a tranquilizer dart. As I believe you've discovered for yourself, Miss Devin, a drugged-up Syke can't fight back. The powers of the mind fail when the brain is in a fog."

"Oh, hell. I learned that only too well," Devin muttered, remembering the poisonous haze of apathy and indifference that had immobilized her in the asylum, and for long weeks after her release.

"So that was one trick the sheriff used," Pete went on. "Him, and all the sheriffs before him, going back as far as anyone can remember. They shoot a Syke from a distance, dropping them with a bullet or a sedative before the victim can even begin to fight back. They take no chances with the drugged ones, either, when they line the poor souls up in front of a firing squad. The executioners always number at least ten, so if the Syke rouses enough to turn one rifle aside—or snap a shooter's neck, as you say—plenty of others are left on their feet to put the Syke in the ground."

"A reign of terror," Devin murmured.

She glanced at Jack. The color had drained from the young man's face. All through his childhood at the ranch, he'd heard stories about what happened to Sykes in Purity if they came to the notice of "the authorities." But Pete's account added a new and shocking dimension to what had been the harsh reality in the town, during all the years—generations, in fact—in which a ruthless, tyrannical minority ran a government that oppressed the citizenry through fear, isolation, and state-sanctioned violence.

"That's what Mike Sutter knew and experienced." Devin looked from Jack, back to Pete. "Sutter grew up on this side of Purity, as I understand it"—she gestured at the modest abodes that attached to the nearby workplaces—"and he spent his youth knowing that a bullet could come from anywhere and take him out at any moment, and he wouldn't see his death coming."

"That brings us to the present problem with Sutter." Pete sat back in his chair again, and his fingers resumed drumming on his knee. "Mike's best friend from boyhood died exactly that way. They were good buddies. They'd known each other since they were tots."

"Tony, right?" Devin guessed. "I heard him shout that name when he dragged the sheriff off the courthouse roof."

Pete nodded. "He got his revenge on the sheriff, sure enough, and every Syke in town is grateful that he split the fellow's skull. But now, Sutter's set himself to kill everybody who he thinks is even a tiny bit to blame for Tony's death. From the doings at the courthouse, he rode straight to the boy's family home and broke Tony's old dad in half." Pete, his fingers restless, picked up a dry twig that had fallen on his boatyard table, and he snapped the twig in two to emphasize his words. "The neighbors saw the whole thing. They say Sutter was screaming at the old man, accusing him of being a coward for not protecting his son, not standing up for him. But Tony's dad wouldn't have lasted a minute against the sheriff and all his riflemen. Sure, the fellow was a Syke, but his gift was on a par with what most of us have. Which isn't much."

Pete paused, toying with the pieces of broken twig.

"I'm not sure if you quite realize, Miss Devin," he went on then, glancing up to briefly meet her eyes, "just how special you are. You and Mike Sutter, both. The pair of you have powers of the mind that far surpass what a typical Syke can conjure up."

The boatman dropped the snapped twig on the table, then lifted his hands to put his fingers on his shoulders. "Watch this."

He screwed up his face, an expression of deep concentration ... and the two pieces of dry twig leapt from the table to land in his nearly empty coffee cup. The cup skittered about three inches along the tabletop, then came to rest.

"That's it." Pete's face relaxed into a slightly embarrassed smile as he looked across at Devin. "That's pretty much the extent of it, for any Syke in Purity."

"Really?" Devin marveled at this piece of information. "That's ... all?"

"That's all."

Pete dropped his hands from his shoulders and splayed his fingers on the table. "Which makes the whole thing kind of tragic, don't you think? All these years, the ordinaries have been terrified of Sykes, afraid of what we'd do to them if they didn't keep us beat down and under their thumbs. When really, we couldn't have hurt them hardly at all, even if we'd wanted to. And most of us would never have wanted to. Ungifted folk are our neighbors and our customers, and 'most all of us have got ordinaries in our own families. It would be rare, in fact, to find a family without an ordinary in it." An edge came into his voice as he added, "We never needed to deny those kinfolk like they had to deny us."

"But Sutter regards all ordinaries with contempt, and he's got a pretty low opinion of weak Sykes, too," Devin muttered, remembering the fate that had befallen her predecessor, the damaged man who had failed to save himself when Sutter threw him off the mountain. "I don't pretend to know Mike Sutter's demons—what he's got inside, that drives him. But I know he can be cruel. There's a part of him that enjoys hurting people."

"A big part, and his demons are riding him hard right now." Pete shot her a worried glance. "He's off on a rampage, down south of town. After he killed Tony's old dad, most everyone who'd ever known Tony, his family, or even Sutter and *his* family, back in the day, took to their heels. My spies—some of 'em are still at it, keeping me up on what's afoot in the town and out on the fringes—my spies tell me that Sutter has tracked Tony's people to a sort of refugee camp on the river a few miles south of town. There's Sykes there, as well as ordinaries, but there ain't none of them can stand against him. He's too strong."

"We'll go." Devin pushed back from the table. "This town has seen enough killing. Sutter's had his revenge, and now he needs to leave."

"You'll send him back to the ranch?" Pete looked both hopeful and dubious.

"That'll be the best thing for him."

Devin left it at that. But as she walked alongside Jack, to where they'd left their horses grazing a grassy patch on the riverbank, she remembered another question she had meant to ask the boatman.

"About that fire." Devin pivoted on her heel to call back to Pete, and without her realizing it, her fingers found the welts on her arm. "When I was up on the courthouse roof, fixing what Sutter broke, I saw where something had burned, close to the river not far from here. I suppose we'll ride right past it if we follow the river south. But what was it? These are good horses"—Devin's fingers moved from her scarred arm to stroke her mount Diego's neck—"and I don't want to ride them into a burn scar where there's broken glass or twisted metal, or something like that to cut their hooves."

Pete shook his head and pointed at the riverbank. "Take the path along the water, below the railroad tracks, and you'll be fine. The only thing that burned was sitting right on the tracks, and it's still there. It's just a burned-out shell now, but it used to be the sleeping car in the train that ran back and forth to Peaceful Hills." Pete gave her the sort of conspiratorial look that Devin imagined came naturally to a spy. "I believe you rode in the comfort of that car a couple of times, Miss Devin."

"Not that I could tell you anything about either trip. Neither going nor coming. But how'd the car catch fire?" she pressed him, taking a few steps back toward him. "Did it happen during the uprising when all you Sykes marched on the courthouse?"

"It was early that same day, yeah." Pete gave an offhand shrug. "I believe I told you that we had the names of the medicos who'd ridden the train back to town after deserting the asylum and the inmates. Our first order of business, even before we chased the top-dog authorities into the courthouse, was to round up the so-called therapists and the mind-doctors. We threw them into the sleeping car, locked the doors like they'd sealed the Sykes into a tomb at Peaceful Hills, and set the car on fire."

"They ... burned to death?"

"They did. Justice served."

Devin nodded. "That's what I'd call poetic justice."

As she turned away and headed again for her horse, her fingers resumed rubbing the scars on her forearm. When Devin became aware of it, she made herself stop, and silently swore off the habit.

☙ 23 ❧

THE SOUND OF A WOMAN'S scream guided Devin and Jack through the tents and other crude shelters that dotted the riverbank a few miles south of town. They rode in upon a scene of desperation. People cowered, covering their heads with their hands. Others kneeled, shoulders hunched, while some prostrated themselves, begging for mercy.

Mike Sutter was not in a merciful mood. Two bodies lay together in a tangled, bloody heap, as limp and lifeless as rag dolls, their broken limbs bent at unnatural angles. Sutter held a third man suspended high off the ground, and that man was still alive, but choking to death. Without laying a finger on him, Mike was squeezing the life from the fellow, his mental grip like an iron hand around the man's throat.

"Stop it!" Devin yelled.

She flung a Beskil bubble, and before Sutter knew she was there, he was trapped. He spun around and cursed, but his shouts came muffled from inside the particularly thick-walled shell she had wrapped around him.

"See to your wounded," Devin encouraged the frightened, wailing knot of refugees. "Please help that man." She pointed at the fellow who had plummeted to the ground when her bubble broke Sutter's mental hold on the man's neck. "Check for broken bones, and for a crushed voice box. Make sure he can breathe."

The previously kneeling and prostrated people sprang up from the ground, rocketing to their feet. Most of them took off running, leaving only one woman and one elderly man to tend to the badly bruised fellow who had dropped out of the sky. He was drawing ragged, rasping breaths. The sounds, though painful, offered hope that his throat hadn't been crushed. He might recover.

For the two bodies in the tangled heap, nothing could now be done except a decent burial. Devin looked past the invisible mental bubble that encased and penned Sutter. Two of the women who had initially fled with the others had come creeping back to the scene of the murders. The women's tears mingled with the blood of their loved ones as they crouched over the mangled bodies, mourning their dead.

"Let's give them their space," she muttered to Jack as she swung out of the saddle.

With a jerk of her head, she compelled Sutter's imprisoning sphere to float along behind her as she walked down to the riverbank. Her head-jerk had not been necessary to bring the bubble along while Sutter wobbled inside it, shouting epithets she could barely hear. But Devin wanted the man to see as well as feel the power she held over him.

"Here's how it's going to be, Mike," she said when she had positioned the bubble on the riverbank and moved to face him, her eyes inches from his. They glared at each other through the transparent shield of her syketic construction. "You've had your revenge, and it's time for you to go home to your ranch. There's nothing more for you here. You've avenged your friend Tony. And now, Purity belongs to its own Sykes. You stirred them to action, but they freed themselves, and they're not yours to control or boss around. Or brutalize," she added, glancing again at the bodies.

Sutter had quit shouting. A silence filled the bubble and the air around it, a heavy, brooding kind of calm.

"You *owe* me, *partner,*" Sutter finally snarled, making Devin's former title into a cussword. "If I hadn't pulled you off that train, you'd be dead now. Or a vegetable for life."

"I know what I owe you, Mike." Devin's voice was steady, and her gaze direct. "That's why I won't kill you ... unless you force me to."

Sutter laughed. His old sardonic grin settled into place upon his features. "Sure of yourself, aren't you, friend? You really believe you're a match for me?"

"I'm *more* than a match for you. I've known it since that day in the meadow on the mountainside. That's when you realized it too, Mike. What you saw me do, that day, panicked you so bad, you threw me off the cliff with no intention of saving me, that time, if I couldn't save myself. But I managed my own rescue far better than you could have foreseen, climbing a ladder I made of this." Devin tapped the rigid mind-projection in which she'd wrapped Sutter, and he winced as though a gong had sounded inside his skull. "That's when I knew I had a power greater than anything you could throw at me."

She smiled, recalling a silly notion that had flashed through her head that day, when she'd been caught up in the excitement of self-discovery and a new-blooming self-confidence that bordered on conceit. *He's king of this particular mountain,* she had thought then, *but I could knock him off his throne if I wanted to.*

Any such ambition, however, had been transitory. If that mountain belonged to anybody, it and the ranch it shadowed belonged to Sutter. That was where he should go.

"Let's finish this before the day gets older." Devin refocused on her captive. "You have two choices. The first, and the best, is to get on your horse." She gestured at Sutter's mount, which Jack had found grazing among the scattered tents and brought to the riverbank along with their own two animals. "Mount up and ride out of here. Swear you'll never return. Don't pass through Purity, but swing east through the outskirts before you pick up the river again and follow it back to your mountain."

Sutter smirked. "And if I don't choose to be ordered around by you, friend?"

"In that case, you'll stay in the bubble. But not here on dry land. I'll push it into the river and you'll float downstream inside it, until you run out of air." Devin still wasn't sure whether her Beskil bubbles were airtight, but she chose to let Sutter believe his prison had that property. "I wonder what you'll see, down south of here?"

She cocked her head as though contemplating the grand—or quite probably desolate—vistas that might appear on a journey down the length of the river. "Is it mostly desert, like people say? That would get boring. And hot. No shade in here." Again she tapped the bubble lightly, with a fingernail; again, Sutter winced.

"I think I remember reading, though," she continued, "that some explorer long ago discovered a mighty waterfall with a spectacularly long drop. What would happen if you went tumbling over it?" This time, Devin tapped her chin, musing on the consequences of such a fall. "I suppose that *might* be enough to crack open this bubble." She rapped its surface with the knuckles of her other hand, hard, and Sutter's hands flew to his ears. "But a fall like that would almost certainly kill you ... if you hadn't already suffocated by then, from want of air."

"You won't do it. You're not cold-blooded enough."

Sutter tried to project supreme confidence. But as he lowered his hands from his ears, his face wore a strained and uneven grin. He was rattled.

Rightly so.

"You think I'm not in earnest?"

Devin gave the bubble a stiff mental shove, accompanied by a sweep of her hand for theatrical effect.

Sutter's enclosing sphere barreled down the riverbank. With a great splash, it hit the water, him flailing inside.

She allowed the current to carry him down the river a fair distance. Walking the grassy bank alongside, she kept pace until the bubble got hung up on a sandbar. There, Devin observed Sutter's attempts to right himself, his movements awkwardly comic. He was not standing erect inside his invisible prison, as he had been when she'd first encased him. The rolling and bobbing of the sphere had put him on his side, and at an angle. Now he lay with his feet over the sandbar but his upper body extended barely above the water.

Devin chose that moment to pop the bubble, doing it with a suddenness that dumped Sutter headfirst into the river. The water was not deep at the sandbar's edge, but he fell from the vanished bubble with his feet higher than his head, making for many graceless moments as he got his hands under him and raised his face into the air.

He came up spluttering and raging. With the first good lungfuls of air he could gulp, Sutter flung profanities at Devin in a voice like a bull's bellow. But overtopping the force of his swearing was the syketic blast he also hurled at her—a discharge of mental energy so intense, it seared the air and would have gutted her, if the blow had landed.

But she was ready. The moment Devin dismissed the bubble around Sutter, she enclosed herself and Jack in a protective shield opposite him. And while Sutter still remained off balance, floundering in the river shallows, she opened a tiny aperture in the otherwise impenetrable wall of her shield. Through the little hole, she worked her will upon him, directing a thought so precisely cast and finely focused, she broke a single bone in the pinky finger of his left hand. It was the bone nearest the palm.

Sutter howled. He'd finally regained his footing and waded out of the water. He stood now on the riverbank, sopping wet, and only a few feet from Devin and Jack. His right hand clutched his left, and as he glared at Devin, his expression blended fury with shock.

"How many bones can you stand for me to break?" Devin yelled at him through the aperture; she'd left it open to ensure her threats were in no way muffled. She wanted him to hear each word. "I can break every bone in your hand, one at a time." To illustrate, she sent another fine-tuned intention, a thought that cracked the next bone in his little finger. He howled again.

"After I've snapped every finger of your left hand, I can do your right," she continued after he'd quieted a bit. "Or I can crack your collarbone. I've read that a broken collarbone is quite painful and debilitating. You won't be able to lift your arm, and that'll make saddling a horse a chore. Like I told you before, Mike," she reiterated, "your best option is to get on your horse and ride out of here right now. I don't want to kill you, but there's many ways I can do it ... like leaving you so broken in your body, you'll never be able to ride a horse again."

This threat seemed to move him more profoundly than the menace of suffocation inside an airless bubble had. Sutter scowled, and for long moments he made no reply. Then he gave Devin a crooked, mirthless smile, and raised his undamaged hand to tip his hat to her.

"You win, partner," he called across the slight distance that separated them. "Let it never be said that I don't know when I'm beat. Give me my horse, and I'll leave you two lovebirds"—his sneer encompassed Jack and Devin together—"to enjoy the humdrum of town life. I predict that this one"—he indicated Jack—"will have a bellyful of boredom before the month's out. But don't be thinking, son, that you'll be welcome back at the ranch. I don't ever want to see your face again."

"That's fine," Jack replied, a deep calm suffusing both his tone and his expression. It was the first time since early morning that he had uttered a word. But his voice was clear, in no way rusty from the day's disuse of it. "Truth be told," he continued, "I got bored years ago with riding herd on a bunch of mean-tempered cows."

To Devin, he added softly, "Let me out from behind this thing." He tapped the bubble wall, and both of them winced at the low percussive resonance his action produced.

Devin dropped the shield, freeing both of them. But she remained on guard, alert to any syketic energies that might emanate anew from Sutter. While focused on her opponent, she saw from the corner of one eye that Jack stooped to pick up a short stick, on his way to fetch Sutter's horse. Devin moved to maintain her clear view of both men as Jack led the animal to Sutter, put the reins into Mike's undamaged right hand, and set about splinting Sutter's broken finger.

Jack first attempted to use the short stick to hold the two cracked bones straight and unmoving. But so close to the knuckle was the finger broken, that arrangement proved unworkable.

"Just lash it to my ring finger," Devin heard Sutter mumble as he held his hand out, his unbroken fingers as straight as tent pegs. "Use a string off my saddle. Wrap it tight like a piggin' string. That'll help the pain."

"Does it hurt bad? Can you make it back to the ranch okay?" Jack's questions barely reached Devin's ears, but his concern was evident.

Sutter scoffed. "You won't remember this—you were in diapers at the time—but I once rode back to the ranch with my leg broke. Damfool horse spooked at a rattler and threw me." He grinned, looking like the devil-may-care rogue Devin remembered from her first sight of him, when he took her from the prison train. "If I can ride with a broken leg, son, I can sure as hell make it back with a busted finger." He nodded satisfaction as Jack finished tying off the thin leather string he had taken from Sutter's saddle. "That'll do me fine until I can get Angelina to take a look at it."

"Well, then," Jack muttered, and found nothing more to say. He simply stood and looked at Sutter ...

... and that was when Devin *saw:* really saw them both, in the profiles the two men presented to her.

Her hand flew to her mouth as she took in their similar brows and chins, their identical noses, the way their heads met their necks, and the set of their shoulders. She saw the way both men carried themselves: easily, almost loose-jointed, but with their sinews and muscles ready to snap into action.

Family resemblance.

Jack's words came back to Devin, what he'd said when he'd declared—correctly, as it turned out—that Guildmaster Perridin could not possibly be Devin's real father. *"Not a hint of him in the way you look, or the way you talk, or how you stand or move,"* he had said.

How had Devin missed it, all this time? All the obvious hints? The evidence stood right in front of her, as plain to see as the river that rolled on, unnoticing and uncaring, at Sutter's back. When Mike called Jack "son," he didn't mean the word as a familiar term of address, older man to younger, or mentor to protégé. Though he'd never been sincere when addressing Devin as his "friend," Sutter was perfectly honest when he called Jack his son.

* * *

"He didn't mean it," Devin said to Jack as they rode side by side, trailing Sutter through the sparse eastern outskirts to be sure he departed as agreed, avoiding the more populated parts of Purity.

"What?" Jack looked at her. "You think he'll come back and make more trouble? Kill more people?"

Devin shook her head. "I doubt he will. Now that his blood's cooled, he can see that his revenge is complete. He got the sheriff, and more in the courthouse than I could count, taking out the officially responsible parties. Then he killed his friend's father, and whoever else that was, back there." She gestured vaguely in the direction of the refugee camp where Sutter had slaughtered his final victims. "There's nothing to bring him back here."

As she said this, Devin slid a sidelong glance at Jack, wondering if he would agree with that. A son, whether acknowledged or not, was not "nothing." But she hurried on, offering only clarification of her original statement.

"I'm sure Sutter didn't mean what he said about never wanting to see you again. You know you'd be welcome at the ranch, Jack, anytime you wanted to join him there."

Jack gave her a measuring look. "You want rid of me?"

He asked it so seriously, Devin reined up, prompting Jack to do likewise.

"I don't want *rid* of you, mister. I want to marry you."

Jack's seriousness evaporated. A gleeful whoop escaped him.

"I want to marry you too, my lady, as soon as may be." His head tilted pensively then. "I reckon, though, that your mother could have some thoughts on that. On the 'soon' part, anyway."

Devin bit her lip, and nodded. "She'll ask us to wait a couple of years, and I won't fight her on it. That'll give you time to be sure of what you really want." She lifted her reins and started her horse moving again, unwilling to let Sutter get too far ahead of his escort. "You may decide, like Mike said, that town life isn't for you."

Jack, matching his horse's pace to hers, looked solemn again.

"And maybe *you'll* decide that a rough-edged cowhand isn't the husband for you. I've seen that family home of yours, that grand pile. You're out of my league in more ways than one, Devin." A shadow clouded his face, but he brightened when she rode close and leaned from her saddle to grip the hand he stretched toward her, holding it like she meant to never let go. "Whatever happens, my lady," he added then, "I can make you this promise: I will always be your devoted knight."

If they hadn't been keeping an eye on Sutter, they might both have come off their horses at that moment, for they were passing an enticingly plump haystack. It would have provided all the privacy a young couple would want, for the proverbial roll in the hay.

But duty first. Devin had an obligation to see Sutter safely back to the river—that source of the water he must have on his return journey to the mountains. They were nearing the river now, rejoining it where it bent around the north side of Purity and straightened in its wide course, affording an easily rideable riverbank all the way to the mammoth triple waterfall that dropped from the mountains and made a turquoise lake in the foothills.

Easily rideable, that is, except for one stretch of private property.

"I ought to warn you, Mike," she called to the figure who rode ahead of them at an unhurried pace. For his return journey, he had but the one horse, and he would not push the animal, risking a footsore mount that could not carry him the two hundred lonely miles that lay ahead.

"Remember the woman with the sheep farm?" she called louder when Sutter showed no sign that he'd heard her. "You'd best show that shepherdess the proper respect when you reach her land. She wasn't happy with what you did to her walls. Go around them this time. Drop down the riverbank and wade the shallows if you have to, to get past without touching anything. That's safest."

For a long moment, Sutter gave her no response. Then his shoulders began visibly to shake. The man was laughing. Guffawing.

His hand came up—his left hand, with the two wrapped and tied fingers—and he gave Devin a dismissive, flippant sort of wave. He had heard, but he wasn't taking her advice to heart.

"Don't be a fool, Mike," she muttered under her breath. "Don't be a hotheaded fool."

"There's no helping that." Jack had heard despite Devin's low voice. "You've done what you can for him, and I've said my goodbyes. When I shook his hand back there"—Jack gestured as Devin had earlier, in the direction of the downriver camp Sutter had attacked—"I meant it for the last time. My gut tells me we won't see him again. Not in this life."

☙ 24 ❧

ONE PERSON THEY DID see again, defying expectations, was Orlando.

The former vanguardian turned up in Purity not long after Devin and Jack returned to the more populated precincts, after seeing Sutter off on his solitary journey. Orlando had been missing since the Syke army's arrival in town. When he resurfaced, he presented himself at the head of a substantial herd of the horses Sutter's troops had ridden to Purity. The animals were now surplus to requirements.

Many of the once-fugitive ranch folk had been welcomed home with open arms and unrestrained joy, their families and friends rejoicing at the safe return of the Sykes they had thought lost to them forever. Those range-riders would not be going back to the ranch. Some kept their horses, but many were given over to Orlando's care. He now sought Jack's help to ensure the horses were properly shod and in fit condition to retrace their steps to the ranch, a journey that Orlando was adamant must be undertaken.

He headed out early one morning, accompanied by a handful of riders who had no ties in Purity and no desire to make a life in the city. With them rode Estelle. Though sorry to see the woman go, Devin was glad the pragmatic Estelle would be in the company when they approached the riverside farm that belonged to the woman with the turquoise eyes.

"Make sure Orlando doesn't damage that lady's fences—those mud-brick walls she uses for sheep fences," Devin urged Estelle. "Tell him he must ask politely if he can cross her property. I believe she'll say yes if he keeps the horses on the riverbank and stops them damaging her pastures. She might even open the way wide for all of you. I saw her do surprising things to one of her walls, so I'm pretty sure she can move them out of the way to let you through, if she chooses to. But not if anyone offends her. It's important that you show her every courtesy."

After Sutter's reckless dismissal of her warning, Devin was intent on driving the point home with this next band of returning riders.

Estelle promised, and word came later that she, Orlando, and the others had successfully negotiated their safe passage across the land of the shepherdess. They'd made it back to the foothills, and thence into the mountains and up the knife-narrow valley to the ranch. Sutter, however, despite his fortnight's head start, was not at the compound to greet the returning riders, and he had not shown up by the time Estelle found the means of sending Devin a message to that effect.

"Damn," Devin muttered, out of Jack's earshot. "The shepherdess said Sutter would regret it, if he ever busted down her fences again. I wonder what she did to him."

But maybe, she consoled herself, Sutter had gotten safely past and had gone on north even farther than the ranch. Maybe he'd found his way to the headwaters of the Contagion River, something he'd wanted to do since he was a teenager on the run from the Syke-killers of Purity.

Devin carried that hope in her heart for a long time.

"I know what I owe you, Mike," she whispered, and she wished him well.

* * *

Pete the boatman was elected mayor of Purity, and a new town council formed. The majority of council seats went to Sykes, but three were reserved for the representatives of the town's ordinary citizens. Judges took the bench in a like ratio: mostly Sykes, but with enough magistrates from the ranks of the ordinaries to ensure respect for minority rights.

One of the new mayor's first actions was to arrange a tour of the courthouse for the children who had been held hostage there by the previous administration. Those children had been on a field trip from school, learning about the town government and the workings of its law, when the fugitives from justice holed up in the building and used the kids as shields, attempting to escape the wrath of the insurgent Sykes.

"I believe it's a rule among you ranch folk," Pete remarked to Devin and Jack, "to get back on the horse that throws you. We can't have a generation of schoolkids running scared from their town's leaders. Undoing the damage will take time, but it's a first step, getting those youngsters back in the courthouse and showing them they don't need to be afraid of the folks in charge, now."

Devin and Jack joined the children in returning to what had been a scene of terror, but was now a seat of benign governance. The day went far to calming the children's lingering fears, though some of the younglings clung to Jack and Devin all during the courthouse tour, for they remembered how the pair had brought them out of danger and delivered them into their parents' arms, that evening when officialdom died.

* * *

Pete's sisters continued rattling around in their too-big houses and never, ever gossiped about the goings-on of the townsfolk. Gertie and Becky were grand examples to the ordinaries of the town, for in most respects they were supremely ordinary. Gradually, the common folk emerged from hiding. Many had gone no deeper than their root cellars when the local rioting started, and all had kept their heads down when Sutter's ranch Sykes galloped into town. Those everyday citizens trickled back into view, first at their homes, and then at their shops and businesses ... nervous, many of them, but increasingly reassured when they discovered their gifted neighbors bore the innocent among them no ill will, and were in many cases their previously undisclosed blood relatives.

A string of community fairs, dances, and street parties brought the two groups together, and over time there was much intermarrying, no longer unwitting, but now done knowingly. With each new generation, the gift of syketic power increased in the population.

* * *

Devin and Jack added to the increase. Eighteen months after they plighted their troth, they were married in the courthouse. The newlyweds made their home in one wing of Mariah Beskil's grand family mansion.

It was the wing Guildmaster Perridin had occupied, and Devin and her mother were at pains to purge the place of his every trace. They sold all the furniture and bought new, and Devin called in an herbalist from the outskirts of town to purify the rooms Perridin had once walked through. The woman, Carmelita, burned sage and spoke her sacred words in a chanting, mystical voice, cleansing the space. All who entered afterward could feel the lightness and a sense of benevolence in the air.

Carmelita so strongly reminded Devin of Angelina that she asked if the woman could make persimmon *mermelada,* and maybe sprinkle in a little *magia antigua?*

The woman smiled and said, "*Sí, señora.* For you? Of course."

The marmalade proved such a hit with the Sykes of Purity, the herbalist got rich selling it. She built herself a fine house—still in the remotest outskirts east of the city—and opened part of the adobe structure as a school in which she taught herb lore, canning and preserving, and the making of *mermelada.*

The Sykes of Purity ate magic marmalade on their toast every morning, and swore that their powers of the mind increased daily.

* * *

Jack continued to wrangle horses. Despite the numbers that had gone back to the ranch with Orlando, the horse population of Purity had increased considerably with the homecoming of the formerly exiled, range-riding Sykes. To house those animals, Jack built stables on land in the outskirts, not far from Carmelita's home and school. His and Devin's children learned to ride as soon as they were out of diapers, and the oldest of the Beskil brood studied with Carmelita when they were not being schooled at home by their well-read mother.

It was by mutual consent, that Jack and his wife had taken for their family surname the name of Devin's illustrious clan. Jack, after all, had no surname of his own.

Devin had left it to her husband—her knight in shining armor, steadfast as the mountains—to say if he knew who his father was. In all the many happy years of their marriage, he never did.

Devin was secretly pleased that Jack did not wish his children to carry their grandfather's name. In all the lands on and near the Contagion River, there could only ever be one Sutter.

☙ Epilogue ❧

THE PHYSICAL AND EMOTIONAL abuse Mariah Beskil endured for years at the hands of her hated husband took a heavy toll. She never fully recovered in either body or mind. A Syke she was, but an abstainer lifelong, so thoroughly conditioned to hide her abilities that her husband never guessed. Devin wouldn't have known either, had the woman not eventually divulged her secret.

After that, Mariah had a few good years in which she saw her daughter happily married and could dote on the children the marriage produced. But she remained frail, and in her middle years—much earlier than it should have happened—her mind began to wander. She was no longer aware she had grandchildren, she could not remember their names, and she ceased to recognize Jack.

Always, though, Mariah knew her daughter. The sight of Devin and the sound of Devin's voice would bring the woman out of the deep mental bewilderment to which Mariah increasingly succumbed.

The woman took to wandering the rooms of the one wing of the family house that she had shared with Devin for so long, the two of them relying solely on each other for company and emotional sustenance in those years. Mariah spent hours in the library, not reading, simply staring into space. She abandoned her own bedroom to sleep in the sky-painted room that had been Devin's. Though it seemed she slept little. In the middle of the night, she would wander, and often she ended up in the top-floor sunroom that, during Devin's childhood, had been their special place for games and fresh-air exercise.

That was where Devin found her one morning. Mariah lay curled on the floor under an open window. The house was so situated that the room caught the afternoon sun but remained in shadow for much of each morning. Even so, there was no chill in the room. High summer had come again, the ninth summer since Devin's return to Purity, and the final summer of Mariah's life.

In the shadows under the window, Mariah's face appeared peaceful in death. As Devin cradled the woman's body and cried tears of sorrow and of love, she took comfort from the smile that lay softly on Mariah's pale lips. Perhaps the woman had been reliving, in memory, one of the fanciful, elaborately staged plays that had provoked gales of laughter from herself and Devin in this very room ... where they could forget, for a time, that they were in prison.

After the funeral, Devin and Jack needed little discussion to set their future course. Their minds turned the same. They would return to the ranch, and there they'd raise their children to know the freedoms that Jack had known in his boyhood: exploring the forested mountain slopes and the bare, windswept ridges ... racing horseback across high meadows … camping under stars that glittered so near, they seemed close enough to touch.

Their return journey took them, by necessity, through the riverside property of the shepherdess. The woman with the turquoise eyes greeted them warmly, and she nodded approval when Devin told her she was no longer "Miss Perridin."

"Beskil is a fine old family name," the shepherdess said. "It is good and rightful that you fully claim it."

She smiled at Jack and Devin's three children, and laid her hand on the brow of each child as she intoned their names … seeming, with the act, to bestow a benediction upon each:

Angel Beskil, the youngest, she they called Angie, barely out of the crib but already at home on the back of a horse …

Mariah Beskil, in the middle, a loving sister to both her siblings and a happy little girl, always laughing when she didn't have her head in a book …

… and Michael Beskil, Devin and Jack's headstrong firstborn, who showed signs already of prodigious syketic powers.

"Thank you," Devin whispered to the shepherdess when the benedictions were concluded. And then, although she dreaded to hear the answer, she asked the question she must:

"The man—Sutter—who broke your walls that summer … did you see him again?"

The woman's friendly smile turned enigmatic, impossible to read.

"He came here, displaying no improvement in his manners."

What did you do to him? The words were on the tip of Devin's tongue. But something in the flash of the woman's gem-colored eyes warned her to demand no accounting. This shepherdess did as she would.

However: "He isn't dead," the woman said then, surprising Devin with her bluntness and her ability, evidently, to read the question that must have been on Devin's face. "He got what he asked for."

"Umm ..."

Devin faltered. What had Mike Sutter ever asked for, except a chance to revenge himself on Purity ... and ...

"The headwaters?" she ventured tentatively. "He told me once that he'd tried every which way to reach the headwaters of the Contagion River. Is he ... could he be ...?"

She didn't finish the question, for the silver-and-gold-haired woman had laid one of her surprisingly youthful-looking fingers alongside her nose. Devin wasn't sure whether the gesture meant *"It's a secret,"* or, *"You've guessed correctly."* Either way, she decided to be satisfied and press no further.

"Thank you," she said again. "I'm glad to know he's not dead."

"Oh, don't thank me." The woman's inscrutable smile deepened. "Not if the man has your sympathies. It's very cold up there."

"Oh!"

Beyond that single sharp utterance, Devin could say nothing for a long moment. She rubbed her lower lip, staring at the woman while considering—imagining—the predicament Sutter might have landed himself in. Then she returned the woman's smile.

"Well, it's a cliché, I suppose ... but as Sutter told me a time or two: What doesn't kill you makes you stronger."

Note on the Origins of the Town of Purity

MIKE SUTTER'S DESCRIPTION of the founding of Purity (chapter five) was correct, as far as it went. He neglected to mention, however, that Purity was a reclaimed ghost town.

The millions—billions—who died in the Great Contagion left behind many an empty and abandoned settlement. But though abandoned, the buildings of a formerly bustling town, on a navigable river west of the mountains, were not decrepit. Under the protection of the Syke shield that was raised by Indomitable Beskil and the others of her kind and her clan, those fortunate few individuals who survived the pestilence settled into the remote prairie town and made it their own. There were empty houses aplenty to move into, and government buildings; and on the riverside, shops and factories awaited refitting and reopening.

Thus it was that the town once known as Riverbend became Purity, a place that was free of the Great Contagion. After its founding, however, the town knew many dark years as neighbor turned against neighbor, and the gifted descendants of the original Syke protectors became ostracized, hunted, and persecuted.

When those descendants rebelled at last against their oppressors, they reclaimed their proud heritage. From hidden libraries locked away in secret closets and sealed chests, the Sykes of Purity drew forth their own copies of *Mind Over Malady*—the original history of Purity's founding and its Syke pioneers. The book in Sutter's collection was not the only copy in existence, but it was the only copy to be displayed openly upon a shelf before the Sykes revolted and reformed their city.

Much paper was made then, printing presses inked, and new copies of the book churned out by the boxful. The history became a textbook in every school, prescribed reading. Never again would the people of Purity—whether exceptional or ordinary—delude themselves into believing that psychokinetic ability was a condemnable mental disease instead of a civilization-saving gift.

Note on the Lineage of the Three Wise Women

ANGELINA—Daughter of Mountains, concerned with events in the heights

CARMELITA—Daughter of Plains and Prairies, concerned with events on the grasslands

THE SHEPHERDESS OF THE RIVERSIDE—Daughter of Turquoise Waters, those flowing or frozen

It is given to none to perceive these women as they really are, and none may know their ages. They are, perhaps, eternal.

But perhaps also, one might safely suppose them to be women of the Beskils, continuing their legacy of protection, set to guard and nurture an ancient legacy through the ages.

Note on the Origins of the Great Contagion

THOSE WHO HAVE READ the *Waterspell* fantasy series, penned by the same Deborah J. Lightfoot who took it upon herself to relate this history of events in a world different to that of Waterspell's Ladrehdin, may well find themselves wondering: Is this world's Great Contagion the same pestilence as the bleeding disease that threatened Ladrehdin?

Readers of the Waterspell books will remember that ...

(> SPOILER ALERT! Skip to page 318 if you don't want to know. <)

... the heroine of that saga, the lost traveler called Carin, arrived in the magical world of Ladrehdin from an island in Earth's Pacific Ocean. That island may have been one of the less built-up isles of the Hawaiian chain, or a place quite reminiscent of such a remote seamount. Furthermore, those connoisseurs of fantasy and paranormal literature who have gone on to read this present volume may perhaps postulate that the setting of this current book is the mountains-and-plains country of the American West.

Is it reasonable, therefore, to conclude that the plague which swept both worlds—Earth as well as Ladrehdin—had a common point of origin? We know from the events of Waterspell that the two worlds have long been connected through space and time. Or perhaps they are parallel worlds, intrinsically linked but having their existences in overlapping dimensions. Whatever the nature of their bond, a terrible disease spread from one to the other, and the outcome on Earth was utter devastation: billions dead, civilization all but destroyed, survivors clinging to life in remote pockets of settlement, and those survivors slowly rebuilding in their isolated outposts and territories.

Gentle Reader, you must decide for yourself whether the Waterspell universe does indeed encompass this present volume, which has no subtitle to declare such a connection, and makes no explicit claim to any such association. Alas, neither Carin nor Devin can shed light on the matter, for the two women are not destined to meet. Some four or five thousand miles—much of that distance being impassable desert and open ocean—lie between their Earthly homes. Which is perhaps a loss to them both, for if they were to meet, they might be friends. Certainly, they would have tales to share around their evening campfires and their homely hearths.

(END OF THE SPOILER)

If you're reading this note but you have not yet read (or listened to) the Waterspell fantasy series, the six books of the saga await your discovery. Readers have called *Waterspell* "marvelously complex and captivating," "fascinating, riveting, unforgettable," and "a unique blend of fantasy and soul-searching." One NetGalley reviewer declared it "a must-read for fantasy enthusiasts who enjoy immersive world-building, well-developed characters, and a storyline that seamlessly blends magic and human emotion."

The books are:

Waterspell Book 1: The Warlock
Waterspell Book 2: The Wysard
Waterspell Book 3: The Wisewoman
Waterspell Book 4: The Witch
The Karenina Chronicles: A Waterspell Novel
The Fires of Farsinchia: A Waterspell Novel

Available in print, ebook, and audio, anywhere books or audiobooks are sold.

Thank you for reading. If you have enjoyed this book or any of the titles listed above, please leave a review.
Reviews are gold to a writer.

THE END

About the Author

DEBORAH J. LIGHTFOOT, a native of West Texas, got her love of history from her grandfather, a High Plains cowboy. From her mother, an artist and avid reader, came her love of books and all things mysterious and magical. Dark horsemen entered her imagination through such early influences as the television show *Have Gun Will Travel,* in which Richard Boone's Paladin was "a knight without armor in a savage land." Small matter that the sophisticated Paladin wielded a six-shooter instead of a sword.

Six-shooters figure in Lightfoot's award-winning books of Western history and biography, *The LH7 Ranch* and *Trail Fever.* Swords and sorcery provide the action in her epic fantasy series, *Waterspell,* a six-book saga with medieval overtones and historical background. *Adverse Reactions,* a Western/paranormal/fantasy blend, brings together her various interests in a cross-genre work of speculative historical fiction. With a journalism degree *summa cum laude* from Texas A&M University, Lightfoot has worked on both sides of the editorial desk for periodical and book publishers. She has taught creative writing at the college level and won numerous writing awards.

Waterspell.net

www.ingramcontent.com/pod-product-compliance
Lightning Source LLC
LaVergne TN
LVHW020531100826
845148LV00010B/1416

* 9 7 8 1 7 3 7 7 1 7 3 9 3 *